ALSO BY DAVID SAZLAY

London and the South-East
The Innocent

DAVID SZALAY

Spring

VINTAGE BOOKS
London

Published by Vintage 2012

6 8 10 9 7 5

First published in Great Britain in 2011 by
Jonathan Cape

Vintage
Random House, 20 Vauxhall Bridge Road,
London SW1V 2SA

www.vintage-books.co.uk

Addresses for companies within The Random House Group Limited
can be found at: www.randomhouse.co.uk/offices.htm

The Random House Group Limited Reg. No. 954009

A CIP catalogue record for this book
is available from the British Library

ISBN 9780099552772

Penguin Random House is committed to a sustainable future for
our business, our readers and our planet. This book is made from
Forest Stewardship Council® certified paper.

Printed and bound in Great Britain by Clays Ltd, St Ives plc

Typeset by Palimpsest Book Production Limited,
Falkirk, Stirlingshire

Spring

I

London light in the scuffed, keyed windows of a Piccadilly-line train from Heathrow. London light on the open spaces it hurries past, on the passing spokes of perpendicular suburban streets, on playing fields seen through a perimeter line of faint-shadowed trees. The train stops in outlying stations. Then it enters the howl of the tunnel and there is no more London light until he finds it later on the hotels and plane trees of Russell Square.

He is worried that things are not okay. When he phones her, standing in the stale silence of the flat, it is only because he wants to know that things are okay. On that question he is insatiable. Frustratingly, she does not answer her phone. Probably she is still on the tube.

They finally speak later, in the early evening.

Initially she sounds fine. And when he asks her how she is, she says, 'I'm fine.'

'What are you doing tonight?' he says.

'Staying in, I think.'

There is a silence, the very quiet hissing of the line, the pittering of the rain on the skylight. She says, 'I've got things to do. I've got to unpack, I've got to do some washing . . .'

'Okay,' he says. 'That's fine.'

'I just need some time on my own . . .'

'Okay,' he says. 'It's fine. What are you doing at the weekend?'

'The weekend?' she says. 'I don't know.'

This was what he feared. Something like this mysterious evasiveness. Something is not okay, has not been okay since Monday, when he missed the minibus that was supposed to take them to the snowline. At twenty to eleven on Monday morning he was in the Internet place in the medina – they were in Marrakech – in the hiss of frying, the whirring of the juicer, and the histrionic sorrow of a woman wailing an Arabic love song from the old stereo, trying to find out what had happened at Fakenham. It turned out that nothing had happened at Fakenham – the meeting had been abandoned due to waterlogging. Leaving the shop, he had five minutes to get to the Djemaa el Fna. Which would have been fine, if there hadn't been an accident in one of the narrow lanes of the medina – a moped had smashed into some scaffolding – forcing him to find another way, which in that labyrinth was easier said than done.

He was ten minutes late, and there was no sign of the minibus where she had said it would be. Nor was there any sign of her. He waited for a while, and then made his way through the alleyways of the medina to the hotel, where he went upstairs. She was not there. Nor was she at the pool. Nor on the terrace. When he tried her mobile there was no answer. It seemed she must have left without him and feeling forsaken, feeling *forlorn*, he went for a lonely walk in the souk. She was still not answering her phone.

To his surprise, he then found her at the pool, on a sun lounger, in the quiet of the sparrow song.

'I thought you went to the mountains,' he said.

And surprisingly, she laughed. 'No, of course not.'

He sat down on the neighbouring lounger, taking his feet out of his flip-flops and trying to get a sense of her mood. This was not easy – they had not known each other long, less than two months. The fact that she was wearing huge inscrutable sunglasses which hid not only her eyes but most of the upper half of her face did not make it any easier. Her nose was pale with factor forty, her Anglo-Swedish skin sensitive even to this spring sun. He stared at her through his own sunglasses, prescription Aviators, the dry wind fiddling with his thinning sandy hair. 'Where were you?' he said. 'I've been looking for you for the last two hours.'

'I went for a walk.'

'Where?'

'In the medina.'

'See anything interesting?'

She just stuck out her lower lip and shook her head. Then she picked up her book.

'I'm sorry I was late. There was this thing. I . . .'

'It's okay,' she said, without looking up.

'Well . . . I'm sorry.'

It was the siesta hour. The palm trees that stood in a line on one side of the terrace were whispering in the warm wind, their shadows mere stumps. 'Do you want to go tomorrow?' he said. 'To the mountains.'

'No.'

'Are you sure?'

'M-hm.'

A few minutes later she went for a swim and in the small shade of his newspaper he tried to work out what it was about her mood that was so strange. There *was* something strange about it. She was lying in the pool with her arms stretched out on the side, her shape wavery in the water, her face tilted to the sun. (Her slick wet hair had an almost metallic sheen.) Her eyes were shut. He had expected her to be more upset. There was something strange about it.

He was still wondering what it was later, in the eucalyptus whisper of the steam room.

And he is still wondering now, tonight, in his flat in Mecklenburgh Street. He tries to picture that hour at the poolside, as the hotel's shadow moved slowly over the water, tries to picture everything that happened.

'I thought you went to the mountains,' he says.

Surprisingly, she laughs. 'No, of course not.'

The strangeness of that moment has been there ever since. It started on Monday at the poolside, and has just not stopped.

2

Once he wanted more than he does now. Once, his idea of his own life, of what it was meant to be, was something magnificent. It seems a sort of insanity now. A sort of megalomania. An impediment to a proper view of the world. That idea of himself was formed when he still knew nothing about life, when he was still at school – and it has taken life twenty years, the last twenty years, to purge him of it. Probably that is an unusually long time.

He is shaving. The mirror is haloed with feeble steam. He isn't the same as he was even a few years ago. Even a year ago. Is it just tiredness? Is he just *tireder* than he was?

For quite a few years the space in which he lives has been shrinking. He has never seen the metaphorical force of this until now. Only half a dozen years ago he lived with Thomasina – sweet Thomasina! – in the house on Victoria Road. It was never even properly finished. For tax reasons, it was technically the property of Interspex, his Internet start-up, and Interspex was worth some eye-popping figure at the peak, in the millennial year. Many millions, tens, hundreds of millions. And then nothing, and the liquidators seized the house on Victoria Road while the Milanese artisans were still tiling the single-lane swimming pool . . .

He stirs the razor in the scummy water. The next spring – *après le déluge* – found him washed up in Fulham. Then there were other places, each smaller than the last, and finally, Mecklenburgh Street. The ex-local-authority flat is in an unfaced terrace of London brick. The front doors of the houses are painted black – dust-bleared fanlights, massed doorbells. The basement flats have their own entrances. Metal steps, textured like a fire escape, tack down via a square landing. The area is littered with dead brown leaves. The bedroom curtains are permanently closed.

He pulls the plug and the shaving-water noisily sinks away. No more magnificence. Now he just wants things to be okay. He wants somewhere okay to live. An okay job. One or two holidays a year. Perhaps a few modest luxuries. A middle-class life in other words. And a woman. Of course a woman. She is the indispensable ingredient for such a life. Without her it would have quite a sad, lonely look. Yes, without her, there would be something sad, something futile, about those few small luxuries. He towels his face in the forty-watt light of the bathroom – it is an odd stooping space, under someone else's stairs, the frigid London morning sliding in through a lint-furred vent. There is this Katherine King. This woman he has been seeing for the last month or two. Indeed, it is possible that she is the inspiration for this whole train of thought – that the idea of a middle-class life in London, forever, has its sudden look of enticing plausibility now that it is framed in terms of a middle-class life in London, forever, *with her*. These days, to imagine other things – new things – leaves him feeling exhausted. (And, he thinks, splashing the sink's limescaled surface, surely *that* has as much to do with its sudden look of enticing plausibility as she does.) She is still married to someone else, of course. Not an insurmountable problem. They met at a wedding, a winter wedding in London. Her father was some sort of Swedish financier, and it showed – her straight, sharply parted hair was sawdust. She had her English mother's voice. They exchanged phone numbers. Met up the following week ... (He turns off the tap and tugs the sprung string of the light, snapping on the darkness.) The start was unpromising, to say the least. In fact, things started with a total fiasco. On their first night together he was unable to have sex with her. That wasn't the fiasco, of course. That was essentially fine. They fell asleep in a loose spoon with the light still on in the hall. No, that was not the fiasco.

The next Tuesday they had supper at the old trattoria near his flat – a place that still offered a prawn-cocktail starter served in a little stainless-steel dish and flaunted the stale-looking desserts in a transparent fridge. There, they were unable to keep their hands off each other and having made a spectacle of themselves for an hour they walked back to Mecklenburgh Street. As soon as the door was shut he started to kiss her. Still standing in the hall, still urgently kissing her, he lifted her short skirt and pulled everything down as far as her mid-thighs. Still kissing him, she seemed to make a weak effort to stop him. Instead he pulled everything further down, past her wavering knees, until she lifted first one foot and then the other to let him tug the things off. They stumbled into the bedroom and ended up on the floor. It seems to him that what happened next has introduced a permanent flaw into everything that followed. He was moving in a fog of fear there on the floor as he started hurriedly to unfasten his trousers. His view of the situation was mechanistic – it seems strange to him now how straightforwardly mechanistic it was. For what had happened last time to happen once, he thought, was okay. If it happened twice it might start to seem like a problem.

'Please don't come inside me,' she said.

Suddenly still, they lay there in silence for a few seconds. Then she said, 'Did you come inside me?'

He was not even sure. He had been so preoccupied with other things . . . 'I don't know,' he said.

She laughed and sat up straight, pulling her skirt into place. 'What do you mean you don't know?'

'I don't know. Maybe . . .'

'You don't know whether you came?'

'No.'

She laughed again and said, 'I can't believe this.'

'What?'

'Is that just *normal* for you?'

'No . . .'

She was shaking her head. 'I . . . I never let anyone come inside me. I've only ever let one person do that. Someone I was totally in love with.'

For a moment he wondered who this man was. Then he stood up, stumbling in his lowered trousers. 'Look, I'm sorry,' he said.

'You don't know whether you *came?*' She sounded shocked, on the verge of tears.

'I'm not sure. I think so.'

'That's just weird.'

'I'm sorry . . .'

'What if I get pregnant?'

'You're not likely to get pregnant . . .'

'Why not?' she said. 'What do you mean?'

'I mean you're not likely to get pregnant. It's not likely. From one . . . you know . . .'

She seemed to be looking at something on the floor, though outside the shape of light that spilled in from the hall it was too dark to see anything. 'This isn't what I expected,' she said. He put out his hand and touched her. When he tried to hug her she stood stiffly in his embrace. He sighed and sat down on the edge of the bed. Leaving him there, she went to the bathroom, evidently to settle the question of whether or not he had ejaculated inside her. He heard the toilet flush, fistfuls of water splash in the sink. When she unlocked the door, she picked up her things from the floor in the hall and went into the living room.

The standard lamp was on and she was standing next to his desk, inspecting her tights. She did not look at him.

'I'm sorry . . .' he said.

Still without looking at him, and in a more quivering-lipped tone than the first time, she said, 'This isn't what I expected.'

The wind howled in the dark shaft over the skylight.

He stood there, wondering what to do.

'I think I'm going to go,' she said quietly.

However, she did not put on her tights. She was still standing there next to the desk. She seemed to be waiting for him to say something. 'Don't go. Please don't go,' he said, shocked into total sincerity. 'Please. That would be terrible.'

*

In the morning she had a shower and, when she was dressed, he said he would walk her to Russell Square station.

'No,' she said. 'It's okay.'

'Are you sure?'

She nodded quickly. 'M-hm.'

He followed her out into the frigid shade of the area, where the dead leaves were veined with ice, and watched her walk up the metal steps. On the pavement, in a flare of sunlight, she waved to him, but when they spoke on the phone the next day, she sounded strange, and vague, and as if her heart was not in what she was saying. He persuaded her to see him on Sunday – she wasn't free, she said, until then – and then when they spoke on Sunday afternoon, she said she was tired, that she had been working since eight in the morning, and how about meeting some other time?

There was a longish silence.

He said, 'Look, I want to see you. Today. Please.'

She sighed. 'I'm tired, that's all. I look shit. And I won't be much fun to be with. I've got to do some ironing . . .'

'Why don't we meet at your place then?'

'Well . . .' she laughed. 'If you don't mind watching me iron.'

'I don't mind watching you iron,' he said.

On the tube he started to wonder whether he should have forced it like that. She very obviously did not want to see him. For a few minutes he loitered in the foyer of Angel station, wondering what to do. Then he set off up Essex Road in the sleet, and when she opened the door he was soaking wet.

Her flat was on the upper floor of a modest terraced house on Packington Street. The downstairs entrance hall was a narrow moth-eaten space full of unloved objects, from where severely straitened steps went up to a landing under a light bulb and the plain front door of the flat.

'Do you want a towel?' was the first thing she said.

He said he did, and while she went for one he waited in the hall, and then followed her into the living room.

'How are you?' she asked.

'I'm okay. Wet.'

'Do you want some wine?'

She had already started on the wine. He took off his jacket and towelled his soaking hair. He had a sense, handing her the towel, exchanging it for wine, that things were not quite as hopeless as he had thought. It had started with the way she looked at him when she opened the door, the way she took a moment to let him fill her eyes. And she was not ironing; there was no sign of the ironing board. Still, when the wine was finished he expected to be encouraged to leave – so he was surprised when instead she said, 'Do you want to get something to eat?'

'Sure.'

'There's this Indian,' she said. 'It's okay.'

'Fine.'

Leaving the house he wondered whether this was the moment to touch her, whether even to try and kiss her. Something about her posture – hands shoved in pockets, shoulders hunched – prevented him. The pavements shone wetly as they walked. They stopped in front of the Taste of India on Essex Road, under the sopping green awning, and he touched her for the first time as they went in. It was not much of a touch – letting her precede him through the plate-glass door, he placed his hand lightly on her back for a moment. She might not even have felt it through the substantial white puffa jacket she was wearing. Inside, in the tired velvet shadows and quiet, seemingly formless sitar music, they studied takeaway menus. There was a palpable Sunday-night atmosphere. Standing there, poised to take their order, the waiter yawned.

While they were waiting, he touched her a second time. Sitting side by side at a table near the entrance – a stained tablecloth, plastic flowers – they had lapsed into silence and he put his hand on her thin jeaned thigh and stroked the fabric a few times with his thumb. She did not seem surprised. She did not tense up or move her leg. She just lifted her eyes from the Taste of India carpet and looked at him steadily for a minute with no particular expression on her face – or an expression, at most, of tolerant indulgence. Then the smiling waiter approached with their supper.

They ate it with the television on. Her flatmate, Summer, was there – she had been away for the weekend with some man; her suitcase was still in the hall. He had not even known of her existence until they found her sitting on the sofa with her small stockinged feet on the old leather pouf, watching TV. Her presence had the effect of taking most of the interesting tension from the situation – things seemed flat now that she was there – and when Katherine went to do the washing-up, leaving them to talk amongst themselves, he felt that it was probably time for him to leave.

He found her standing at the sink in the kitchen. She may not have noticed he was there until, stepping up to her, he put his hands on her waist. When she did not move even then, he went a step further and, tucking down the tag of her sweater, kissed her exposed neck.

'Do you want to stay the night?' she said, still sloshing things in the sink.

'Do you want me to?'

'It's up to you.'

He seemed to think for a moment. 'Yes, I'd like to.'

'Okay.'

'Are you sure?' he said.

'Am I sure?'

'Are you sure it's okay? I don't want to stay if you don't want me to.'

'It's okay,' she said, freeing herself from his hands, which had stolen onto her stomach, and taking a dishcloth.

Her pale hair was tied up severely, showing the high pallor of her forehead, and her face had a freshly scrubbed look. She was wearing a loose T-shirt and old-fashioned pyjama trousers. 'I've still got my period,' she announced, turning down the duvet.

'Okay.'

Sitting there, he found it slightly difficult to see what the point of his presence was – she was under the duvet now, and did not seem to pay him any attention as he slowly undressed and joined her. She was lying on her side, facing away from him, and she did not move when he put out his hand and sent it down the shallow slope of her side and up the steeper hill of her hip, feeling under his fingertips the filled, homely fabric of the pyjama trousers.

'Are you sure you want me to stay?' he said.

A sudden susurration of the sheets – she turned. In such proximity her face looked different. His perusal of it, and his silence, seemed to unnerve her and shaking her head on the pillow, she said, 'What?'

'Nothing . . . I like looking at you.'

She smiled very slightly and he kissed her. She let him. She let him kiss her unparted lips, once, twice, and even then it seemed no more than a sort of tolerant indulgence, until her mouth melted open and for a few seconds seemed to be searching urgently for something inside his. His hands were inside her T-shirt. 'I don't want to have sex,' she said. 'I told you, I have my period. And even if I didn't, I wouldn't want to have sex.'

They lay still for a while.

She put her hand on his face and said, 'I'm sorry. I'm pleased you insisted on staying.'

'Insisted? I didn't insist . . .'

She smiled. 'Okay, you didn't insist . . .'

Taking it from his face, he kissed the palm of her hand – plump and mild and slightly damp – and that was the start of a tortuously slow exploration, an exploration *sub specie aeternitatis*, of the sense of touch.

Towards morning – they were naked on the mattress, their senses painfully peeled in the warmth of the storage heater – she muttered, 'I don't think I can not have an orgasm,' and letting her knees fall open, quietly started to play with herself.

*

Suddenly, unexpectedly, no longer even seriously hoped for, there were a few lovely days. Sun-fire on frozen ponds. Everything seemed okay then.

Then on Saturday afternoon, towards the end of the afternoon, when the winter daylight was starting to fail, he met her at Angel tube station, and there was something wrong. He had sensed it earlier in the day when they had spoken on the phone, and when he met her at the station and tried to kiss her she just turned and started to walk away.

They had walked some way up Essex Road – past Packington Street, were in front of the open facade of Steve Hatt the fishmonger, standing on the stained pavement in a faint sea smell – when she stopped and said, 'What are we doing? Where are we going?'

'I don't know,' he said. 'Where *are* we going?'

'I thought you wanted to get a drink,' she said.

'Is that what you want to do?'

'Isn't that what you want to do?' . . . 'Do you want to get a drink?' she said.

'I don't mind. What do you want to do?'

If it was a drink he wanted, she insisted on returning to Angel, and they were nearing Islington Green, still in silence, when he stopped and said, 'Look, if you're not going to say anything, maybe I should just go.'

She went very still.

'You're not saying anything either,' she said half-heartedly. Then she said, 'I'm sorry. I don't know . . .'

'What?'

'I'm sorry.' She put a hand on his arm. 'I feel a bit weird.'

'What do you mean you feel a bit weird?'

'I've been feeling a bit weird this afternoon, since earlier.'

'I don't know what you mean when you say *a bit weird*.'

'Let's just get a drink,' she said. 'Let's just get a drink and see how it goes.'

'See how it *goes?*'

'Yes,' she said.

He followed her into the nearest pub. Not a particularly nice pub. The Nag's Head. And she still seemed to be feeling quite weird. While they stood at the bar waiting to be served, surrounded by screens shouting about sport, she started to laugh. Perhaps it was just the fact that they had ended up *there*, in the Nag's Head, a straightforward pub with a passion for sport, and a sour smell of lager soaked into wood. They sat down at a long table which they had to share with some other people. She seemed strangely exhilarated. There was a strong flush in her pale skin.

He was wary. He pressed her on what she had meant outside when she said she was feeling a bit weird.

She stopped smiling. 'I just . . . didn't . . . feel anything,' she said.

'You didn't feel anything?'

'No.'

'What do you mean? When?'

'This afternoon.' Seeing the expression on his face, she took his hands in hers and said, 'It was just something weird. I don't know what happened. I'm sorry.'

'This isn't just what you're like, is it?' he suggested, smiling sceptically.

She laughed and shook her head. 'No.'

'You're sure?'

'I'm sure.'

Over the second pint they started to talk about other things – he told her how he had once owned a pizza-delivery franchise nearby, and how he had mortgaged it to produce a film (directed by Julian Shoe – the name made her laugh, he swore he wasn't making it up), which had never found a distributor, forcing him to sell the pizza franchise and work instead as an estate agent at one of the snootier Upper Street outfits – Windlesham Fielding, pinstriped suits moving in the shop window. Though she knew by then that he had old links with the postcode, this was the first time they had been mapped out for her. He told her how – after a stint in the City which ended in minor scandal – he had set up on his own as an Islington estate agent. For a while he was successful. He owned up to having owned a Porsche – to having been a Porsche-owning estate agent. (She laughed at that.) He said he had lived in several thousand square feet of warehouse flat overlooking the canal. He had not seen the place for years and he suggested they walk over there tomorrow.

'Okay,' she said.

It was dark when they left the Nag's Head. Under towering streetlights, the junction at Angel pumped people and vehicles like an exposed heart.

He was sufficiently upset by what had happened to seek a meeting on Monday with Toby, at whose wedding they had met. Toby had known her since university; they had been at Cambridge together, had shared history tutorials as undergraduates at Trinity. And Toby had something to tell him. She was married. Separated for a year or so, but still, so far as he knew, married. Her husband – *he* had left *her*, was Toby's feeling – was some sort of photographer. Fraser King.

'He's some sort of pap. She hasn't told you this?' he said, surprised.

'No.'

'She's not mentioned him?'

'No.'

James thought, and then said that the only hint he had had

of it was that nestling in the mess on the little night-table next to her bed – among the tumblers of stale water and screwed-up tissues – he had noticed a watch. A man's watch. It looked like a pilot's watch or something. A very macho watch. He had of course wondered who its owner was.

'Probably Fraser's,' Toby offered. An overweight City lawyer, tanned from his Indian Ocean honeymoon and still in the suit he wore to the office, he was jiggling his portly knees and looking wistfully towards the door. They were in a pub and he wanted to smoke. 'Sounds like the sort of watch he would have.'

'Did you ever meet him?'

'A few times.'

'What was he like?'

Toby shrugged. 'He was okay,' he said, putting the emphasis on *okay* so as to make it vaguely praiseful.

'She's said some things . . .' James said, thinking aloud.

'What?'

'Things about the past. I don't know. That she still has ties to the past or something. Nothing specific. That must be what she meant . . .'

'Probably. Mind if I step outside for a minute?'

They went and stood in front of the pub. It was on a quiet, pristine Chelsea street – Toby's local. In summer it looked like it was made of flowers, and even now it was festooned with elegant wintergreens. Toby sucked hungrily on a duty-free Marlboro Light in the sharp, smoke-blue evening air. 'So how's it going, generally?' he said.

James told him it was going fine.

What he did not tell him was how on Saturday night after supper, though she had with some solemnity invited his hand into her unbuttoned jeans to feel how wet she was – very wet – she would not let him fuck her. He was left pleading there, literally kneeling on her living-room floor (Summer was away for the weekend again) while he unknowingly paraphrased Marvell.

Had we but World enough, and Time,
This Coyness, Lady, were no Crime...

He had not in fact actually fucked her since the night of the fiasco. She had not let him. In that sense the fiasco was very much ongoing – the latest thing was that she had started to talk of wanting to get him looked over by a doctor. 'I don't know where you've been,' she said. 'I don't know what you've been doing.' He promised her that he had no diseases. They were at that point in bed and he finally turned over and sulked.

No, he did not tell Toby these things.

'Are you married?' he said.

What followed – they were having a late supper in the trattoria with the plastic plants next to Russell Square tube – was surprisingly short and simple.

'Yes,' she said. 'Separated.'

She was obviously prepared for this.

'Were you planning to tell me?'

'I'm sorry,' she said. 'I know I should have told you already. It doesn't make any difference, though. I haven't seen him for more than a year.'

He was full of questions he wanted to ask her. He had imagined that they would spend the whole evening on the subject. In the end, however – it was obvious that she did not want to talk about it – he just said, 'Is that his watch by your bed?'

And she said – 'Yes.'

(And the next time he looked, the watch was no longer there.)

So that was that. Except that that night, for the first time since the fiasco, she took the erection which was pressing fervently into the small of her back and pulled it into her. She immediately started to sob. In the very faint light that leaked in from the street he saw her scrumpled face, the shine in the tiny valleys to the sides of her eyes. 'It's okay,' she whispered, worried that he might not understand her tears. 'It's okay.' She smiled tearfully. 'It's okay.'

*

Things must have been okay then, in mid-February – there was a minibreak. In the monochrome interior of the Eurostar as it flew through the Kentish twilight, she laid out the key facts – a medieval port, the largest in northern Europe, a sort of doublet-and-hose Hong Kong or Singapore. Then the Scheldt silted up and stopped the opening to the sea (a poor fate for a port), leaving it, for the last four hundred years, an exquisite fossil.

She had a list of things she wanted to see, and he tried to keep her warm – they would have needed a polar explorer's microfibres to do the job properly – as she led them to grey-skinned emaciated Christs, and many quiet vistas of narrow little houses with their feet in the water. It was the water that made the strongest impression on him. The very sight of it, its black viscosity, made him shudder. In the morning, seen from the hotel window, steam stood thickly on its still, house-edged surface. At the end of each afternoon the sun shone on it, a strange cold yellow. It was heavy and heatless. He pitied the fish in it, and wondered why it wasn't frozen. The streets were frost-scoured, and the tourist-trade horses – he pitied them too – steamed with their dung in the stone squares.

There was something almost hallucinatory about the place.

The tangle of streets, squares and waterways. Everything was extremely small in the Middle Ages – that was very evident. For instance, the tavern they stooped into one twilight. It occupied the lower floor of a tiny house which teetered forward into its alley. There were only two tables, space for no more than a dozen people. The whole interior was made of wood, and smelled of warm smoke from the fireplace. They stayed there for an hour or two, the evening thickening in the quarrels of the windows, while she told him about John of Gaunt – that is, John of *Ghent* – son of Edward III and Chaucer's friend and patron, who was born in the Flemish city in 1340 while his parents attended a summit meeting that went on for more than a year. Time, she thought, was different then. Partly for technological reasons. Partly because of the presence of a living idea of eternity. Look at Jan van Eyck's *The Madonna and Joris van der Paele*. (They did look at it, in the Groeninge Museum.) The living presence of eternity – a painter striving to paint it. Who would try to paint such a thing now? And why?

Later they hurried through silent streets laughing at the sheer shocking lowness of the temperature, every last joule having seemingly evaporated into the yawning interstellar spaces overhead. For a moment she stopped and looked up at the mess of stars and thought tipsily – *The living presence of eternity . . .* Tight-jawed, he hurried her on through the stinging air, towards the lobby of the hotel.

He has often wondered how small birds, stuck outside in them, survive nights like that. Walking Hugo on winter mornings when the puddles are ice and hearing, in the leafless park, their pathetically subdued tweeting always touches him with pity, and a sort of wonder that they are able to survive the subzero night, to make it through to the morning to whistle with such touching fortitude – though weakly – as he walks by swaddled and scarfed up to the eyeballs, and *still* shivering, still stamping his feet in a struggle to keep the numbness from them. How do they survive?

She shrugged. 'Don't know,' she said.

The question did not seem to interest her.

'You've never thought about it?'

She shook her head. 'No,' she said.

They were on the train to Ghent. Outside the windows the Netherlandish banality of the landscape was mitigated by a frost so thick it looked like snow and sparkled in the flooding sunlight.

He said, 'Am I just being sentimental?'

'I don't know. Maybe anthropo . . . whatever.'

'What?'

'Anthropocentric? Is that the word?'

There was something about the way she said, *Is that the word?* Without the slightest fear of seeming stupid or ignorant. She just *knew* she wasn't stupid or ignorant. It was something that secretly impressed and intimidated him, which took him uneasily back to the times he used to sit with Miriam and her friends on his Islington terrace. In the presence of those men – and they were invariably men – James the estate agent would tend not to have much to say for himself, especially when the talk turned intellectual. And the talk was often oppressively intellectual when Miriam's visitors were there, sitting on his terrace, with the faint odour of vegetation floating up from the water, supping his champagne. Magnus. Karlheinz. And Linhardt. Linhardt. He was the worst. That French twat, with his high forehead and serial killer's blue eyes . . .

'The famous are part of us,' he is saying, when James steps onto the terrace with the second bottle of Veuve Clicquot, 'of our identity. That is why they are so fascinating to us, why we feel strange when we see them, why we have even a sense of awe. You can say they are half-abstract beings, ideas, belonging to the world of the mind . . .'

'Who's your favourite celebrity?' Miriam says.

Linhardt ignores her. 'I make visible these ideas,' he says, looking at James, 'which I think is completely consistent with the definition of art . . .'

James nods, pours . . .

Linhardt. The thought of him still makes James want to kick something. Then, he took it out on the towpath – pounding it all the way to Victoria Park, under the low bridges, through the spaces laced with moving light when the sun was shining on the water.

Katherine's lack of interest in the travails of little birds should not have surprised him. A week or so earlier, he had told her the story of the hatchling thrush – another one set on the terrace of his old Islington flat. One spring morning he had looked out through the French windows and seen a dead hatchling thrush on the decking. It must have fallen from a nest somewhere higher up. That in itself was sad, but what made it so memorably so – what in fact pierced him with a sorrow he has never been able to forget – was the way its parents spent the whole morning offering it worms. With worms in their beaks, its mother and father would frequently land next to it, where it lay lifelessly still on the decking, and wait there for a few moments, turning their heads in the way birds do, unable to understand why it wasn't taking them.

She said, 'Aaww.'

Though she was trying to sound sad, she didn't. It was obvious, anyway, that she was not being pierced by a sorrow she would never be able to forget.

He was irritated that the story had flopped. He wondered, in his irritation. if this meant that she was just not a very nice person. Was she *just not a very nice person*? Was that it?

No, she was just not as sentimental as he was. He was sentimental. She made him feel sentimental.

The train pulled into Ghent station at noon. They had lunch, then walked to Sint Baaf's cathedral to see van Eyck's altarpiece. That was why they were in Ghent. That was what she wanted to see. One of the Masterpieces of Western Art. It was a strange image. In the middle, an important-looking sheep stood on a table with blood flowing in a neat stream from a hole in its front into a metal cup. The sheep did not seem to be in pain, or even to have noticed what was happening. There was a subtly painted suggestion, too, that it was shining with light. In the field around it were lots of expensively dressed people, mostly men, some with wings . . . Yes, it was very strange. He knew that the sheep was a symbol of Jesus Christ – he knew about the angels and saints. He was familiar with the iconography. What made it *seem* strange, and this was what she was explaining to him as they perambulated around the altarpiece in its perspex house, was the way it was painted. The familiar symbols of medieval art had been painted as if they were real things. *That* was what made them seem strange. The sheep looked like a real sheep, like a photo of a sheep. That was what was strange. And she drew his attention to the swallows or swifts flitting about in the luminous evening sky near some palm trees – very small, to indicate their distance from the spectator – and not one of them the same as the others, each painted in a specific position in flight, obviously observed from nature – one swooping, another soaring, another spiralling – escapees from a world of symbolic and stylised art.

When they had seen the masterpiece she said, 'Should we get

totally pissed?' They were leaving Sint Baaf's. It was not something he normally did. Pensively, he stroked his jaw. Then he said, 'Yeah, okay,' and they went and drank a lot of Duvel, and Westmalle Tripel, and Piraat, and Sint Bernardus Abt 12, with its laughing monk on the label. It was still just about light when they stumbled out into the Grote Markt several hours later, and presumably freezing though they were insensible to it now. Looking for the station, they quickly found themselves lost in the streets of a disappointingly twenty-first-century town – plastic trams, ATMs . . . A taxi . . . A stiflingly overheated Merc. When James addressed the driver in slurred French, the man answered in unfriendly English. The fare for the two-minute drive was €6. At the station, they struggled with the question of which platform to wait on. A well-insulated local told them to take the next train to Zeebrugge.

And Zeebrugge, very tediously, was where they woke up. They spent two whole minutes on the platform there in a knifelike wind that whipped in off the North Sea, then took another taxi – another overheated Merc – all the way to their hotel (the fare was €80), where they went straight upstairs and fell asleep.

The next morning, their final morning in Flanders, hungover and eating hot *frites* from a paper cone, she snuggled into him as they walked under the frozen copper-sulphate sky and said, 'I feel nice with you.' Things seemed okay then.

*

On Friday, towards the end of the afternoon, he takes Hugo for a walk. The St Bernard dislikes the subterranean flat. He usually spends the day lethargically filling the sofa, or when James is sitting on the sofa, the whole vestibule – a huge, sad-eyed harlequin.

Under the sky-scraping London planes of Russell Square,

which are just starting to venture forth their leaves, James throws a tennis ball for him; and if he is throwing it with more than usual vigour it may be an effect of what she said to him on the phone as he walked to the square from Mecklenburgh Street. She said she was tired. She did not want to meet tonight. Someone was off sick, she said, and she had to work an extra-long shift. Then, perhaps hearing the disappointment in his voice, she said, 'Let's do something tomorrow.'

He perked up slightly, said he'd try to think of something special . . .

'No,' she said, 'nothing special. Let's just go to the cinema or something.'

He asked her what she wanted to see.

'I don't know. What is there?'

He said he'd have a look.

And then, just when that seemed settled, he said, 'Are you sure you don't want to do something tonight?'

And she sighed and said, 'I'm tired. Let's do something tomorrow.'

He slings the tennis ball in the twilight under the trees, slings it with all his strength, twisting his torso and whipping into the throw, trying to find the trajectory that will send Hugo furthest over the still-wintery lawns. His excitable voice as he pursues it punctures the low moan of the traffic endlessly orbiting the square. Something is not okay. He is thinking again of that strange moment on Monday afternoon at the poolside. Something happened in Marrakech, something he does not know about. When they leave the square it is evening and the signs on the hotel fronts are illuminated.

3

On Sunday there is this lunch at Isabel and Steve's. 'No Katherine?' is the first thing Isabel says, opening the door to see her brother standing there on his own. He wishes she hadn't mentioned her. Everything is pretty fucking far from okay.

He spent Saturday morning under the skylight in the living room, seeing what films were on, interrogating the Internet in his seldom-used spectacles. Surveying the listings he felt lost, ill-equipped to find something that she would like. He does not yet have any sort of instinct for her taste. It is not easily predictable. Miriam, for instance, only touched unimpeachably art-house films, made him sit through the plotless offerings of French and Russian men, whose names still affect him the way memories of lessons at school do – a trapped mind-numbing feeling, a surly sense of personal insufficiency, and a quiet thankfulness that he is not in the experience now. Though Katherine sometimes shows an interest in such films too – he has noticed some DVDs lying around her flat with titles like *Andrei Rublev* and *Tokyo Story* – she is more omnivorous, more promiscuous in what she enjoys. This does not make working out what she will enjoy any easier. Quite the opposite. .

He had just finished making an eclectic shortlist when she phoned. Almost as soon as he started talking about what films were on and where, she interrupted him. 'James . . .'

'Yes?'

'Um.' She seemed stuck. She said, 'I don't . . .' then stopped again.

'What?'

'You're not going to like this,' she said.

'What?'

'I don't want to see you today.' Silence. 'I just . . . I need to spend some time on my own. Is that alright?'

'If that's what you want,' he heard himself say.

'Phew,' she said. She sounded less nervous. 'I was worried you'd be angry.'

'I'm not *angry*. I'm . . .'

'Disappointed?'

'I wanted to see you.'

'I know. I'm sorry.'

'Why . . .?' he said. 'Why don't you want . . .?'

'I just need some time on my own,' she said. 'I need a weekend on my own. I need to get my head together. I haven't stopped moving since we got back from Marrakech. I haven't had any time to myself. I still haven't finished unpacking . . . I'm sorry.' Then she said, 'Thanks for understanding. Thanks for making it easy for me.'

Later he wondered whether he had made it *too* easy for her. What should he have done though? Made a scene? Tried to force her to see him? Even if he had wanted to do that, he just didn't seem to *feel* enough at the moments when it might have been a possibility. He felt only a kind of numbness, and the infantile frustration of not getting what he wanted. And then the moment had passed and she was saying, 'What are you going to do tonight?'

'Well . . . There's this party. You know – the one I told you about.'

Yes, there was this party.

And now, on Sunday, he is hungover. There is a painful-looking sty, Isabel notices – a vivid purple, like a Beaujolais nouveau – just under the lip of his left eye.

'No,' he says, in answer to her question about Katherine. 'She couldn't make it.'

'That's a shame,' Isabel says. 'When are we going to meet her?'

'I don't know. Hi.'

She kisses him. 'Hi.'

He hands her a bottle of wine wrapped in tissue paper and follows her in. She and Steve have the lower half of the house, with their own entrance at the side – 97A – and what is by London standards a huge garden with (they are widely envied for this) a wooden door leading directly onto Hampstead Heath.

'How are you?' she says.

'I'm fine.'

He takes off his jacket in the pale grey entrance hall next to the pair of Banksy prints in white maple frames which match the white maple floor. It sounds like there are quite a few people in the living room – more than he expected. The whole event is on a larger scale than he expected. He knows the sort of people they will be. Some lawyers from Isabel's firm – Quarles, Lingus – and their spouses. A selection of her university friends, mostly media types now. A few friends of Steve's perhaps, smoking in the garden in jeans and trainers. Probably that vegetarian architect who always seems to be at things like this. There will be some pregnant women. A smattering of noisy toddlers. A shocked-looking, marble-eyed baby.

Entering the living room – long and high-ceilinged, with a

large sash window at each end – he wishes he had stayed at home. He feels like he has only just woken up and, in spite of the Nurofen, he has a nagging headache. He has not even surveyed the room to see who is there when he finds himself face to face with Steve.

'Alright, mate,' Steve says. 'How's things?' Though he is smiling, Steve seems nervous. He is wearing a brown T-shirt with a technical-looking drawing of an open-reel tape player on it and holding a glass of prosecco. Without waiting for James to answer his question, he says, 'I hear you got a new lady-friend.'

'Yeah . . .'

'That's fantastic. How's it going? I hear you took her to Morocco.'

'Yeah . . .'

'That must have been brilliant. I love Morocco. Do you want a drink? What do you want? Prosecco?'

'Uh, just a glass of water actually . . .'

'Sure.'

James follows him through the talking people towards a table on the other side of the room. Halfway there, he squeezes past the vegetarian architect, whose name he has forgotten, and who is earnestly listening while a middle-aged woman lectures him about something. 'Oh alright, mate,' the architect says, with a sudden smile.

'Alright, mate,' James says, also momentarily smiling.

Steve is pouring him a glass of Perrier. When he has poured it he looks up and hands it to him. James thanks him. Steve smiles. He is a head shorter than James and wears glasses with heavy oblong frames. 'So,' he says. 'You took the lucky lady to Morocco.'

'That's right.'

'Where . . . where was that exactly?'

James is about to tell him when Steve, whose eyes immediately wandered, sees his four-year-old son, Omar, looking lost in the forest of legs. 'Sorry mate, just a sec,' he says, and leaves James standing there while he sweeps Omar up and takes him out of the room.

While he waits, James turns to the sash window overlooking the street and has a sip of prickling Perrier. It is a quiet, tree-lined street, on a steep slope – and he sees, walking up the slope, looking slightly lost, just as Omar had a few moments earlier, a smartly dressed man, probably in his seventies. At the sight of this man, James wishes, even more than before, that he had stayed at home. The man is obviously looking for a specific house. Finding number ninety-seven, he first walks up the steps at the front. The door there, however, is only for the two flats on the upper floors, and after peering puzzledly at the name-plates for a few moments, he looks around – as if hoping to see someone who will be able to help him – and then returns to the pavement. He looks up at the house. Then he notices the sign saying 97A, and pointing to the path at the side.

Though the sharp trill of the doorbell is hardly audible over the hubbub of voices, James's pulse quickens at the sound of it and he looks for someone to talk to. There, standing near the fireplace, is Miranda, an old friend of Isabel's. Isabel once tried to set them up in fact. They went out once or twice. Without hesitation he walks over to her, interrupting the man she is talking to. Though he tries not to show it, this man – Mark, a singleton from Quarles, Lingus – is obviously put out by the way Miranda seems positively to welcome James's interruption. He was just telling her about his planned skiing holiday to Norway with 'some mates', hoping to work around to suggesting that she might like to join them, when she turns away from him while he is in mid-sentence – 'Most people don't know how fantastic the skiing is up . . .' – and says, 'James! Izzy promised me you'd be here.' She puts her hand on James's shoulder and kisses him. She has to stand on tiptoe. He leans forward to help her. 'Did she?'

'Yes.'

'And how are you?'

'I'm okay. You?'

'Fine,' James says. He is about to say something else when Mark stops looking impatiently off to the side and thrusts out a hand. 'Mark!'

'Hello.'

'I was just telling Miranda about . . .' He starts on Norway and skiing again, and James's eyes move to the door, where, smiling nervously, the smartly dressed older man has just entered with Isabel. She is entirely focused on him. From the way she is treating him, he seems to be some sort of VIP. With his eyes on them, James is not listening to what Mark is saying – 'And they all speak English, which is –'

Following James's stare, Miranda says, 'Who's that?'

'Oh, he's –'

'They all speak English,' Mark insists, 'which is –'

'He's my uncle.'

Isabel has ushered him to the drinks table, and is pouring him a glass of prosecco – with his thumb and forefinger he indicates that he does not want much. Then, with a slightly worried look, she scans the room. James knows she is scanning it for him. She sees him, and says something to their uncle, and they start to move towards him.

Miranda has just turned distractedly back to Mark, who says, 'So, yes, they all speak English, which is –'

'Sorry to interrupt,' says Isabel. 'I need to steal James for a minute. Is that okay? James, look who's here,' she says, with her hand on the old man's shoulder.

'Hello, Ted,' James says, smiling pleasantly. 'It's been a long time. A very long time. How are you?' As they step towards an empty patch of white maple, he hears Mark say, with a sort of wearinesss now, 'So, yes, um, they all speak English, which is . . .'

Ted is tall – the same height as James, more or less – and has the same high forehead, the same long face and squarish jaw. These are all things that flow to James from Ted's side of the family, his mother's side. Ted, though, is losing his white hair. The tightening skin is turning transparent on the prominences of his skull, while the skin of his neck has lost its hold entirely. Isabel has left the two of them to talk, and the first thing Ted says is, 'The last time I saw you, you were doing very well.'

James smiles. 'Was I?' This was one of the things he had feared having to talk about when he saw Ted in the street.

'You had some sort of Internet firm.'

'Yes.'

'What happened to that?'

When James tells him, Ted seems sincerely surprised. 'Oh?' he says. 'Did it? That's a shame. Um . . . I'm sorry to hear that.'

'Don't worry. It wasn't the only one.'

'No. No, I suppose not. There were lots of them, weren't there? What happened with all that? I never really understood what that was all about.'

'I don't know,' James says. 'I'm probably the wrong person to ask.' Then, seeing that his uncle is hoping for a proper answer, he stops smiling and says, 'There was massive over-investment, essentially. I suppose there was this idea that whole sections of the economy were about to move en masse onto the Internet. I thought so at the time myself. Lots of people did. That's why there was so much over-investment, which pushed up share prices so much. Then there was the herd mentality too. That took over.

These things have their own momentum. Nobody wants to be left out.'

'Of course not!' Ted says emphatically.

'Even if you think it's all nonsense, if you see people doubling and tripling their money in a few months, even if you think they're total fools – maybe *especially* if you think they're total fools – you might be tempted to get involved. Ideas of value go out the window. Then it's not even speculation. It's just . . . a sort of pyramid scheme. Alan Greenspan called it "irrational exuberance", I think.'

'Alan Greenspan? Wasn't he . . .'

'The Federal Reserve.'

Ted nods. '*That's* right.'

'In a sense I didn't lose anything,' James says with a smile. 'I had nothing at the start, and nothing at the end.'

Ted does not smile at this. He just peers at his nephew thoughtfully, and mainly to forestall any follow-up questions, James says, 'You still live in Wimbledon?'

'Yes. Yes, I do.'

'The same . . .?'

'The same house, yes.'

On that, they simultaneously turn their heads and look out into the living room, at one end of which they are standing. For a moment, as clouds manoeuvre somewhere out of sight in the sky, pale sunlight pours in from the street end, then fades. Not entirely. Though the shadows lose their sharpness, they stay. They know they are thinking of the same thing – the Victorian vicarage in Wimbledon, the weeks that James and Isabel spent there in 1974. James remembers surprisingly little about those weeks. Not even how many weeks it was. How many was it? Though it seemed like a long time then – and seems like a long time now – it might only have been two, or even one. One or two weeks at the very end. That would make sense. He remembers the thick ivory shagpile in the vestibule and on the stairs. It was unlike any carpet he had ever seen.

Ted does not seem aware of the fact that his hand is fiddling nervously with one of the buttons of his suit jacket.

'How's Jean?' James says.

'She's fine. Well . . .' Ted's voice takes on a more serious tone. 'She's okay. She's having trouble with her hip. That's why she's not here today.'

'It would have been nice to see her.'

'She very much wanted to be here.'

'Do send her my love,' James says.

'I will. And she sends you hers.'

They smile sadly at each other.

'And how's your father?' Ted says.

'He's fine. He lives in France now. You probably know.'

'Yes, he's lived there for a while, hasn't he? In Paris, or . . .?'

'No, in the south. He used to live in Paris. He lives in the south now.'

'Lovely,' Ted says. 'Do you visit him much?'

'Sometimes. Not for a while actually.'

'No?'

'I was there last spring. I may go next month.'

'It must be lovely down there.'

It was a damp spring in the south of France. The light was milky, the sky a passionless mother-of-pearl. The palm trees looked flustered in the wind. From Nice, he took the train along the sea – watched the white manes tossing far out on the water – and then a taxi inland from Antibes. He arrived at the house in time for lunch. The question was whether to eat outside, where the awning was flapping fitfully. There was a feeling that

36

James, fresh from the fumes and interiors of London, would want to, and they set up on the terrace. Four places. Isabel was there. Unexpectedly. On her own. She had been there, it seemed, for a few days. The light was hard and grey. Under the awning it was quite dark.

No explanation of Isabel's presence was immediately forthcoming. Over lunch there was at first small talk. How was James's flight? (Fine – flights are always fine.) How was London? What was happening in the village? How much longer would the local shops hold out against the new Carrefour . . .

They were talking in a superficial way about Alexander's work, something he was writing, when he and Isabel slipped into one of the intellectual play-fights they enjoyed so much. From then on Esmeralda said little, and James less. The question of the day was – Is the world changing more or less quickly than it was? Alexander said LESS quickly. The world was changing *less* quickly now than at any point in the twentieth century. Think, he said, of the fact that in 1900 there was no powered flight at all. The Wright brothers and their experiment on the sands at Kitty Hawk were still some years in the future. And not much more than half a century after that, there were supersonic airliners, spy planes photographing from the edge of space and men on the moon – while in the almost half a century *since* then we have essentially not moved past that point. We are still using, he exclaimed, as if it were an outrage, except that he was smiling, essentially the same equipment to fly around in as we were in 1970!

James smiled too, palely, when his father's excited eyes met his own.

Then Isabel threw the Internet at him. Alexander waved that away. It was, he said, merely the latest step in the development of a technology that started with the telegraph (invented 1837), and then flowered into the telephone (1876). Electronic computers, the other necessary ingredient, were invented in the 1940s. What's more, their period of exponential increase in speed and power seemed to be plateauing. This was his point, he said. Following an historically extraordinary period of invention from the mid-nineteenth century to the mid-twentieth, a sort of technological Russian spring, there was then a further period of working through the practical applications of many of these inventions, a period which in the last few decades had produced things like the Internet and the mobile phone. *This* period, he said, was now ending – that was his point. Fluently, initially marking them off on his fingers, he listed some of the inventions that had made the hundred years from 1850 to 1950 so extraordinary – the sewing machine, the fridge, the washing machine, the internal combustion engine, the typewriter (1867), the phonograph, the microphone, electric light, the pneumatic tyre, the zipper (1893), wireless communications, the submarine, the electron (1897 – i.e. during the reign of Queen Victoria), the tape recorder (also a Victorian invention), television (1925), the jet engine, penicillin, nuclear weapons, the helicopter, the now ubiquitous electronic computer (1946), the transistor, the contraceptive pill – even, more than half a century ago now, the structure of DNA, which was obviously the fundamental step that has made all subsequent efforts in the life sciences possible. And that was hardly something new, it was hardly of *our* time. 'Hardly,' he said to James and Isabel, 'of *your* time.' (And then to Esmeralda, with a smile, 'Or yours, my love.') It was a discovery made the year that Stalin died. That was its era. His own era just about. (He was a man of the mid-century, a political journalist of Cold War years, witness of *événements* in Paris and anti-Vietnam protests in Grosvenor

Square.) And since then, he stated provocatively, since the 1950s, there had not been a *single* invention on a par with the major items on his list.

In spite of the provocative tone in which he said this, Isabel seemed to have lost interest. She seemed to lack the energy to keep up her end of the debate. She just said, 'Well, maybe,' and – as if tidying it up – trimmed a sliver from the Pont l'Evêque with a silver knife. The awning flapped. Underneath the vigour of his speech underneath the sense of excited engagement, his father seemed tired, James thought. His keen, mobile eyes were moist on the exposed terrace. His hair, still thick in his mid-seventies, was slightly unkempt. His hand, however, was steady as he poured the last of the wine, a Provençal rosé. He was making an effort not to *seem* put out by their presence – that was perhaps what all this energetic talk was about. This did not necessarily mean that he *was* put out, only that he was worried that he might *seem* to be. This sort of thing James was used to. His father was not an easy man to interpret, in spite of the wary expressiveness of his hazel eyes.

Now he was saying that scientific, technological and social change had for a long time in themselves provided us with a sense of purpose, of progress – 'and this sense was definitive, in its way'. It was an important part of our self-definition as a society. It was what we were *about*. It was what we *did*. We progressed. (Think of avant-gardism in art, how seriously – on the model of scientific progress – that was once taken! All those 'experiments'. Think of Marxism. Think of our fixation with the 'modern', with 'modernity'.) All of which in turn profoundly shaped our sense of what time was – we thought of time as a vector of progress. The slow erosion of that idea would have all sorts of implications – political, social, 'even spiritual'.

*

When they had finished lunch, Alexander said that he had to work for a few hours, and went down to his study, and for the first time since his arrival James found himself alone with his sister, in the long *salon*. The old house was not designed for those thunderheads sagging over the valley. There was something almost Romanesque about its spaces. It had a vaguely ecclesiastical atmosphere. The furniture, the *objets*, the knickknacks, the paintings, the small windows punched through the formidable walls, with their seatlike wooden ledges . . . These were things so familiar that they did not normally notice them. Their father had owned the house – it was in one of those troubadour villages – since the Sixties. It had always been there.

Isabel was sitting very low on a sofa, looking through a wide, flat book.

'How long are you staying?' James said.

'I don't know, a few days.'

He did not ask her why she was there. There were, he had heard from Esmeralda when they were alone in the kitchen for a minute, 'problems'. That is, problems with Steve. He was not sure what sort of problems exactly. Perching in one of the window nooks, he looked out at the wet olive trees, the miserable blue shape of the swimming pool. 'How're things?' he said.

'They're okay.'

'Yeah?'

They sat in silence for a minute. The pages of the book creaked as she turned them. Looking out the window, he heard the whisper of her hand smoothing the tissue paper that screened the plates.

'Oh I like that one,' she said.

'Which?' He stood up to look.

It was the sort of day, he thought, still standing there as she turned the page, when it would be nice to have a fire. Only a fire would be able to deal with the sad damp that, in this sort of weather, permeated the whole house.

Isabel looked up questioningly – he was still just standing there. 'What?' she said.

'What's up?'

'What's up?' she echoed, as if she didn't understand the question. 'Nothing.' And then, perhaps feeling that that wasn't plausible – 'I don't want to talk about it.'

'Okay . . .'

'I'm going downstairs for a bit,' she said. It was a peculiarity of the old hillside house that the street entrance was on the top floor, so that what you would normally expect to find upstairs, you found downstairs.

On his own, he wondered why he was there. Only out of habit, it seemed. He had spent so much time in that house. The memories merged together. Memories of school holidays. People from different epochs of his life mingled there as they never had in time. He listened to the sound of the rain intensifying on the olive trees, of thunder fraying like acoustic distortion down the valley. The house itself had little or no sense of memory. It was always the same. This dim ecclesiastical light in the stillness of the *salon*. No photographs on public display, except, as if they had been forgotten there, a few in an unlit whitewashed alcove where the hall turned, including one of his mother. It was a snapshot from the early Seventies in which she was flanked by Isabel and himself. Somehow the setting does not seem to be London. Paris? He does not think he properly understood, at the time, what was happening. She was ill. However, even that he did not understand – it was just an explanation – some words that he himself would offer in his husky voice to explain the situation – he did not understand what they meant. He has no memories of the hospital, nothing like that. All there is is the thick ivory shagpile in the vestibule of the Wimbledon vicarage. In his own flat there are several framed photographs of her, this person of whom he has no actual memories, this utterly mysterious, utterly numinous person. What he finds painful now is imagining it all – that is, those months in 1974 – from *her* point of view. Imagining *himself* from her point of view. Thus he sees himself as if from the outside, through her eyes. Thus he fumbles towards some estimate of what he might have lost. Well.

The temper he had in the years that followed . . . They lived in a four-storey house in Kensington. Today it would be a multi-millionaire's house. Kensington was not the same in the late Seventies. Except for the light. The light was the same then – the London light, flat and plain on London streets. The green electric typewriter muttering in the study on Sunday afternoons.

In the seating plan, Isabel has put Ted between herself and Kevin Staedtler's wife. Kevin is the senior partner at Quarles, Lingus, and he and his wife, being in their fifties, are nearest to Ted in age – that was presumably the thinking there. James is down the other end, Steve's end, where topics in the early part of the meal include the films of Pier Paolo Pasolini – someone whose name James associates with Miriam. Yes, she once made him sit through *The Canterbury Tales* . . . Even so, he knows little or nothing about his films and does not feel able to participate. Nor does he particularly want to, though Miranda, who is sitting on his left, keeps making efforts to include him. He is touched by these efforts but he finds it hard to live up to them – every time she asks him what *he* thinks, he just shrugs and says some variant of *I don't know*.

Eventually she tries a new line of approach. She turns to him and says, 'So what are you up to these days?'

The main course is just being served – two waitresses are doing the serving. Isabel has pulled out all the stops for this one, he thinks. Probably to impress Ted, to show him how well she's doing . . .

'The last time I saw you,' Miranda says, 'you had a magazine. I even remember the name. *Plush*.'

'That's right . . .'

'Do you remember the last time I saw you?'

He thinks. 'No,' he says finally, laughing. 'No, I don't. I'm sorry.'

She hits him. 'It was at the magazine launch party!'

'At least I invited you to the launch party . . .'

'No, you didn't. I went with Izzy. I told you I thought *Plush* was a ludicrous name. You didn't think that was very funny. Sorry if it upset you.'

He has no memory of the incident. Not even of speaking to her, not even of seeing her at the launch party. 'That's okay,' he says. 'And anyway, you were right. It was a ludicrous name.'

'Of course it was. The magazine failed, I hear.'

'It did.'

'So what are you up to now? Izzy says you're always up to something. When she told me the magazine had failed I said, "Poor James, is he okay?" And she laughed . . .'

'She laughed?'

'She *laughed*,' Miranda says, smiling, with a secretive inclination of her head, 'and said, "Oh don't worry about James. He always finds something new."'

'She said that?'

'And now she says you own a horse. You know my parents are members at Newbury racecourse?'

'No, I didn't know that . . .'

'I've been there loads of times. You should come one day.'

'I'd love to.'

'What's his name? Your horse.'

'Her name. Absent Oelemberg.'

When he says the name, she says, 'Sorry?'

'Absent Oelemberg.'

'What sort of name is that?'

He shrugs. 'A horse's name.'

'What does it mean?'

'I asked the trainer – he said he had no idea.'

'Has she won?'

'Not yet.'

'I suppose it's all totally fixed like you hear. How come you have a horse anyway? You didn't used to be interested in horses, did you?'

'No.'

'So?'

'Last year,' he says, pouring them both some wine, 'I had a sort of tipping service.'

'What do you mean?'

'I mean I sold tips on the Internet.'

'What, horse-racing tips?'

'Yes.'

She stares at him for a few seconds. Her eyes narrow nicely. 'I can't believe you were involved in something like that,' she says. 'And you look so nice and honest.'

'Of course I do. I *am* nice. I am honest . . .'

'*Ha!*'

'It's not dishonest,' he protests.

'Where did these tips come from? You?'

'No. I employed someone.'

'Who?'

'A pro,' he says innocently.

'A pro? And did his tips make a profit? If his tips made a

profit, why did he have to be employed by you? Did they make a profit?'

'Sometimes.'

She laughs. 'Sometimes? So much for being nice and honest!' she says. Her eyes narrow smilingly again. 'You really are quite louche, aren't you?'

'Not at all,' he says, smiling also.

'And then what happened?'

'To the tipping service?'

'Yes. Was it shut down?'

'Not exactly. My tipster was arrested . . .'

Her loud laugh turns Mark's head. For the last twenty minutes, he has struggled to seem interested in what some pregnant woman is saying to him while his peripheral vision was teasingly filled with Miranda talking and laughing and hitting James playfully on the other side of the table . . . What *they* were saying – though he wasn't sure what it was – seemed infinitely more interesting than what was being said to him, though he wasn't sure what that was either. Though he is still smiling fixedly in her direction, he has no idea what the pregnant woman is talking about, and when she finally stops – she may have asked him a question – he just says, 'Yes, yes,' and then turns to James and says, 'Did I hear you say you're a horseman?'

'No,' James says.

'Oh. I thought I heard you say you were a horseman.'

'I do own a horse. Or part-own it.'

'Oh, I see.' Mark turns to Miranda. 'Your parents live in Newbury then?'

'No,' she says, 'they don't.'

'Oh they don't? I know Newbury quite well.'

She laughs. 'Well they don't live there.'

'Where do they live?'

James leaves him to it and looks down the long table. At intervals there are vases of white flowers, and at the far end French windows into the garden. Most of the suits are up that end, and he sees Ted being introduced to Omar, while Mrs Staedtler looks on through an uninterested smile. Suddenly he hears Steve saying vehemently, 'Now James was fucking loaded. I mean seriously fucking loaded.'

He turns and Steve says, 'Do you remember the weekend we went to Sussex or wherever, and you were looking at those houses? Like manor houses and stuff. Me and Isabel and you and your girlfriend at the time – what was her name?'

'Thomasina.'

'Yeah, that's right. How much were you worth then?'

'I don't know,' James says. He is embarrassed to find people staring at him. 'Honestly.'

'It was hundreds of millions, wasn't it?'

'It was nothing in the end.'

'Yeah, but for a while it was hundreds of millions. You were in the *Sunday Times* Rich List, weren't you?'

'Was I?' James says. 'Maybe. I don't know.'

Steve nods. 'You were.'

Slowly the long table loses its hold on the party. The French windows are opened and some smokers step outside. Then other people start to wander upstairs. Eventually there are only a few left, too intensely into whatever it is they are talking about to notice that they are laggards. Finally they too stand up and leave, and the uniformed waitresses move in to finish their work, speaking Polish to each other over the silently smoking wicks.

James does not want to be the first to leave and for a while he waits outside on the oval lawn. It is a mild afternoon. Some friends of Steve's are there, smoking what seems to be a spliff next to a small magnclia tree, its sticky-looking buds just starting to break open. Soft-focused with wine, James watches them pass the spliff from hand to hand. They make him think of people he used to see on Brick Lane . . .

He hears a woman's voice shout his name.

It is Miranda, walking towards him from the French windows, tottering slightly in her heels on the soft turf of the lawn. She is, he thinks, a nice-looking woman. The white dress she is wearing honeys her skin and her smile is an orthodontist's masterpiece. 'James,' she says, 'you didn't finish telling me about . . . your horse. What's her name again?'

'Absent Oelemberg.'

'You said she would win this week. Where? When? I need the money!'

He says, 'I did tell you. It's next week, not this week. She won't win this week. A week tomorrow,' he says, 'at Huntingdon.'

'Which race?'

'I don't know yet. Whatever race she's in, she should win it.'

'A week tomorrow, Huntingdon.'

'Yes.'

She thinks for a moment. 'That's the thirteenth!'

'Yes.'

'Is that lucky or unlucky?'

'This isn't about luck.'

She laughs. 'Oh isn't it!'

James sees Mark wander into the garden. When he sees James talking to Miranda, he stops and with his hands in his trouser pockets looks up at the sky. A minute later he is followed by Isabel. 'Ted's just leaving,' she says.

James looks at his watch. 'I should be off too.'

And Miranda immediately says, 'Yes, me too.'

And Mark, suddenly at her shoulder, says, 'Yeah, I have to head as well.'

*

Hugo meets him in the shadowy vestibule, wagging his tail, and they do a slow lap of Mecklenburgh Square in the quiet, sinking light, stopping frequently for Hugo to sniff and officiously micturate. James lets him precede him into the flat, and from the kitchenette hears him lapping at his water bowl. James waits in the hall – the kitchenette is too small for them to be in there at the same time – until Hugo lifts his streaming muzzle and looks unhurriedly around. His weary eyes meet James's and he waves his tail once or twice. When he has left the kitchen, James has a draught of tepid London tap water himself.

Then he phones her.

She picks up instantly – he is practically startled – and says, 'Hello, honey. How are you? How was your sister's lunch?'

'Fine,' he says.'How are you? What's up? What are you doing?'

'Ironing.'

'Yeah?'

He is pleased that she is ironing – it seems so safe and stable. He hears that the TV is on, and imagines her half-watching the Sunday evening telly while the warm iron vaporously sighs. They talk for twenty minutes and suddenly everything seems okay. Even more so when he asks her when he will see her and she simply says, 'Tomorrow?'

'Tomorrow? Okay.'

'Okay?'

It is not until a few minutes later, when he has hung up and is feeding Hugo, that he starts to think about something that happened while they were speaking. He thought nothing of it at the time. He just heard what sounded like the front door of her flat slam shut, and Summer's voice saying something, and then a man's voice saying something which he didn't make out. He thought at the time that it must be something to do with Summer.

Now it occurs to him that what he half-heard Summer say was, 'Hi, I'm Summer.' In other words, she was talking to someone *she had never met before*. He starts to think through the implications of this.

It takes him a few minutes to face up to the obvious implication – the man was visiting Katherine. If so, who was he? Katherine has a brother in London. Unfortunately, he knows for a fact that Summer has met him. A male friend then? Possibly. Though it would seem strangely intimate for a male friend to be turning up at her flat on Sunday night. The fact that she was ironing when he arrived – there would be something strangely intimate about that too. He knows of no male friends, heterosexual or otherwise, whom she would see on those sort of intimately informal terms. Most of all, if this was nothing more than an innocent visit from a friend, why did she not mention it to him? That was specifically unlike her. It was her way to end phone calls by saying what it was that was making her end them, even if it was something totally spurious. So for there to be something so obvious – that someone she was waiting for had just arrived – and for her not to mention it . . .

Her voice tensed up at one point. It was such a tiny thing that he was not even sure, at the time, that it had happened. First, she lost the thread of what they were saying. He had just said something, and she did not seem to hear it. There was a silence on the line. Then she said, 'What? Sorry?' This was immediately after he had heard the door slam, and then the voices, Summer's voice and the wordless rumble of the man's voice. It seemed obvious that she had been distracted. That in itself was not surprising or suspicious. They then talked for several more minutes.

It is those minutes he is thinking of now. There was something tense about her voice, as if she was talking with someone else there, someone standing there, standing over her, waiting for her to finish.

4

The next afternoon, Monday, he meets Freddy. James and Freddy were at school together, twenty years ago, at a famous school on the fringes of London. On Monday they meet in Earls Court – one of those streets of trucks stampeding past exhaust-fouled terraces, of youth-hostels, and veiled, slummy houses full of subletting Australians, and other houses with tarnished nameplates in Arabic on the doors and the paint falling off in stiff pieces. There, under a two-star package-tour hotel, they meet. Freddy is piquey and jaundiced. In one of his down moods. His hair looks like it has slipped off his head – there is none on top, where the skin has the look of a low-quality waxwork, or the prosthetic scalp of a stage Fagin, but plenty further down, where it trails like the fringe of a filthy rug over his collar – the old collar, white-edged with age, of an otherwise blue Jermyn Street shirt stolen from his landlord.

They are meeting today to talk about the horse they part-own, and the 'touch' that is planned for next Monday. It is Freddy's fault, all the horse stuff. It was he who introduced James to Michael – the tipster, the 'pro' James mentioned at Sunday lunch. Freddy was 'seeing' Michael's sister, who was still at school at the time – this was nearly two years ago – and he quite often went to the house in Shooter's Hill when her parents weren't there. Sometimes, while Melissa was having a shower and Freddy was in the kitchen pilfering food from the fridge, Michael would emerge to pour himself some Coke, and Freddy would talk to him. He asked him, for instance, what he did all day. Michael was in his late twenties, still lived with his parents, and did not seem to have a job.

His answer was – 'Systems testing.'

'What sort of systems?' Freddy said.

When he heard what sort of systems, Freddy started to take more interest in Michael. He pressed him for more information about his systems – monosyllabic Michael was not very forthcoming – and finally managed to persuade him to send him their selections by email every morning. For a week, Freddy just monitored these selections. Michael himself had said he did not put money on them, in spite of the fact that he kept a tally of their performance, which showed them to have made a profit over several years. And they made a small profit in the first week that Freddy monitored them. In the second week they made a large profit and Freddy plunged in. Soon he was making several hundred pounds a week. It was then – very full of himself and his several hundred pounds a week – that he told James. It had obviously never occurred to Freddy, as it quickly occurred to James, that there was the potential here to make much more than that by selling the tips on the Internet or through a premium-rate phone line.

One afternoon, they took the train down to Shooter's Hill to see Michael. He was a large man, putty-pale. There was something odd about him. James explained that he wanted to pay him for his horse-racing tips. He had had in mind to pay him a percentage of subscription fees, or winnings, or something like that. However, it was obvious that Michael would prefer a flat fee, so James offered him £200 a week. He also wanted him to work in an office – he wanted the tips, the spreadsheets, whatever there was, on a hard drive he owned, in a space he paid for. Though this he was initially less keen on, Michael was soon spending an enormous amount of time in the office. Most of the time, in fact. The following scene was fairly typical.

Michael is sitting at his desk, working. The door opens. Michael does not look up or say a word. James shuts the door. 'Morning,' he says. 'How's it going?' Still Michael says nothing. 'How's it going?' James says again. This time Michael says, 'Have you got my Coke?' With a thud James puts the two-litre plastic flagon of Coke on Michael's desk. Michael does not thank him. Without taking his eyes off the monitor in front of him, he opens the Coke and pours some into a plastic cup. 'So how's it going?' James says again, sitting down at his own desk. When Michael still does not answer, James tries a more specific question. 'Lots of selections today?' Purposefully mousing, Michael does not seem to hear.

Michael's systems, of which there were many, were purely quantitative – for all James knew, Michael had never seen a horse in his life. He seemed to have no idea that horse racing is something that actually happens, that the names of the tracks are the names of actual places, that people and horses and money and mud are involved; to him it seemed to be nothing more than an endless supply of new numbers on a screen – numbers in which to search for patterns, a puzzle that was never finished. For the first few months these numbers – marketed by James under the name of 'Professional Equine Investments' – showed a nice profit, and the service soon had a few dozen subscribers. Unfortunately the first few months turned out to be unusual. More typical was a situation in which one week's profit was offset by the next week's loss, and the service just scraped along. Then started a monstrous sequence of losers, and James would sit at his desk while the rain fell outside, waiting for some antediluvian version of Windows to appear on the smouldering monitor and staring with something like hatred at

Michael's slack face, his sensuous mouth hanging open as he worked mechanically through the fiddly statistical analysis of his systems. He did not seem to notice that he was on a monster losing spree. That the subscribers were losing money while he still picked up his £200 a week. At such times, his wanting a flat fee seemed sly and even dishonest to James, who was unable to help feeling that this strange man, this hulking idiot in his nylon jacket and milk-white trainers, had somehow swindled him out of thousands of pounds.

Michael was spending less time in the office too. He was in later – sometimes quite late, and looking like he had not slept – and he left earlier. Indeed, he seemed to have something on his mind. For instance, he had started to stare out the window. That was not something he had ever done in the past, and now he would sit there for minutes at a time, while the Coke hissed in his cup, staring out the window at the East End sky.

'Michael,' James would say.

And Michael would not seem to hear.

'Michael!'

And finally he would turn his oversized, unkempt head – exactly the way that Hugo did – unhurriedly and with a vacant expression in his docile chocolate eyes.

None of this prepared James for the phone call he received one Monday morning in early November.

He was out with Hugo when Freddy phoned. This was surprising in itself – it was not even eight.

'I thought you might want to know,' Freddy said, with a smile in his voice, 'that Michael is in police custody.'

'What?'

'I thought you might want to know,' Freddy said, even more slowly than the first time, 'that Michael is in police custody. I'm not joking.' He started to laugh. 'He's in a cell in Thamesmead Police Station.'

'What are you talking about? Why?'

'You'll love this. Some sort of sexual assault.'

A long silence. Then James said, 'You're joking . . .'

'No I'm not! That's the point. I'm not joking! I just found out myself.'

'How did you find out?'

'Melissa. She sent me a text. I just spoke to her . . .'

'What did she say?'

'Just what I told you. Michael's in a police cell, and it's some sort of sex offence. I don't know what he did exactly,' Freddy said. 'I just thought it was quite amusing.' He seemed frustrated that James did nct share his amusement.

'You're noz joking?' James said.

'No.'

'What's Melissa's number?'

'Why?'

'I need to speak to her. I need to find out what the fuck is going on.'

Melissa was on her way to work.

'Yeah, that's right,' she said. She didn't sound particularly put out. 'Michael's in the nick.'

He was apparently arrested on Sunday morning at the house of a woman who lived a few streets away in Shooter's Hill.

The facts emerged at the trial the following summer. What seems to have happened is this – some time in September Michael was in a supermarket near his home. As he was paying, something startled him and he dropped his money onto the floor. The woman who was next in the queue had helped him pick it up. She smiled at him. Their hands momentarily touched. That was the first time he saw her.

Starting the next morning, he waited near the supermarket, hoping to see her again. When he did, he followed her home. It was a few days later that she first noticed him. She started seeing him in unexpected places, sometimes far from Shooter's Hill – on the tube, in shops in the West End – and it was obvious that he was following her. When he followed her home and stood waiting outside, she phoned the police.

The next day they stopped him in the street and issued an informal warning. They told the woman they expected he was 'scared out of his wits' by their intervention – he had looked scared out of his wits when they walked up to him – and that he would now leave her alone. And he seemed to, until a week or so later she spotted him outside her office and he followed her onto the Docklands Light Railway. It was typical of Michael that when the police told him he'd be in trouble if he kept hanging around outside her house, he started hanging around outside her office instead. The second warning was more formal than the first. This time they took him to the station and made him sit in an interview room for an hour while they said things like, 'You don't want to go to prison, do you, Michael?' They said that if they had to have him in again they would tell his 'mum and dad'. 'And what would they think, Michael, if they knew about this? Eh?'

For a few weeks there was no sign of him.

Slowly she stopped expecting to see him everywhere.

(This was the time of maximum listlessness in the office, of prolonged window-staring through sleepless eyes.)

Then one Sunday morning she was in the bath and thought she heard a noise downstairs. She stayed very still in the water, listening. There was a long, tingling silence. Then there was the sound of something smashing. To the hollow thump of footsteps on the stairs, her wet hands fumbled tremblingly with the lock. There was only one tiny window, which did not even open properly. Terrified, in tears, she was wrapping herself in a towel when someone tried the door. The pathetic flimsy lock had no hope of withstanding his weight. It surrendered at the first meaningful shove.

What was strange was that he did not seem to know what to do – not even what he wanted to do. A shocking male presence in the small pink-tiled space of the bathroom, he had her in his hands and did not seem to know what to do with her. When he started to move his hairy face towards hers, without thinking, with a sort of instinct, she sank her teeth into his forearm – he was pinning her shoulders to the wall – and immediately tasted his blood in her mouth like an old iron nail. He yelped and unpinned her, and she pushed past him and locked herself in her bedroom, from where she phoned the police.

She would not leave her room while he was still there – and for some reason he was still there when the police arrived, at speed and with wailing sirens. She threw the keys out the window and they let themselves into the house, where they found him still sitting on the linoleum by the toilet, holding the wound on his arm. (The puncture marks made by her teeth were plainly visible in the pale meat of his forearm, like a pair of dotted parentheses in a purple bruise.) He did not seem to understand what had happened, or what was happening.

Now, Melissa told James, he was indeed in a cell in Thamesmead Police Station, awaiting trial for a number of quite serious offences. Her parents had been to see him. A solicitor had appeared from somewhere. Michael himself seemed to be in a state of shock – he had not said a word since the police found him sitting next to the toilet, pathetically nursing his hurt arm.

'He's got an appointment with the psychiatrist this afternoon,' Melissa said.

'The psychiatrist?' James said, starting to understand that this was probably the end of Professional Equine Investments.

There was however one loose end – Absent Oelemberg.

Together, he and Freddy own half the horse. The other half is owned by her trainer, Simon Miller, who Freddy met in a Fenland pub one Saturday last November. Freddy told him he had owned horses in the past (which he hadn't), and Miller, who was not totally sober, said that one of his owners had just died, an old fellow name of Maurice something. He had owned a half share in an ex-French mare in the stable and, if Freddy was interested, the heirs were looking to sell. When Freddy said he was interested, Miller went further and hinted that he was hoping to land a 'nice little touch' with the horse, who had not yet run in the UK.

The next morning, Freddy phoned James. He told him that he, Freddy, had an inexpensive opportunity to own a horse in training with 'one of the top jumps trainers in the country'.

'Who's that then?' James sounded sceptical.

'Simon Miller,' Freddy said. He was using his this-is-serious-now voice. 'We have to move fast on this, though.'

'We . . .?'

'Miller wants ten grand for a half share.'

'A half share? Who owns the other half?'

'Miller does. He says he wants to hold on to half himself. He knows what he's doing. He's pretty shrewd,' Freddy said. 'And there's something else. You'll like this. He's hoping to land a touch with her early next year.'

Freddy explained what Miller had told him in the pub the night before. Miller had been so drunk that it had taken a long time for Freddy to work out what he was saying. Essentially it was this: Absent Oelemberg was a smart ex-French mare – 'a useful tool' was the expression Miller had used, slurring it so egregiously – *eryoofustoowil* – that at first Freddy had not even been able to make out what the words were, let alone what he meant by them. What he seemed to mean was a horse who would win her share of handicaps. Freddy had pretended to know all about the handicapping system, and fortunately Miller was much too drunk to notice that he had had to explain it to him from first principles himself. His plan for Absent Oelemberg was to ensure that she did not show her true ability in her first few races – she would then be assigned a handicap mark which was too low, from which she would therefore be able to win easily. And since she would have performed so poorly until then, the odds available on her in her first handicap would be very long. Thus you would have a horse at very long odds who you knew would win easily.

'Well?' Freddy said expectantly.

For some time, James said nothing. Thoroughbred ownership was an interesting prospect. On the other hand, this was Freddy on the phone on a Sunday morning, sounding like he was still drunk, with a proposition put together with a very drunk stranger in a pub the night before. It was not exactly investment grade. Not exactly triple-A. And James would unquestionably have said no, were it not for the embellishment of the touch. What Freddy understood was that James would see the touch as something he would be able to use for Professional Equine Investments.

Still, he slept on it.

Then the next morning he phoned Freddy and said he was prepared to put in his share. And Freddy said that actually he would have to put in the whole £10,000 because he – Freddy – was skint at the moment. He would pay James back with his winnings, he said, when the touch went in, and since it had been Freddy who found the opportunity in the first place, when he had let him sweat for a few days, James lent him the money.

They went up to Cambridgeshire the following Sunday and stood in the stable yard, trying to look as if they knew what they were doing, Freddy fiddling with a hip flask, while Miller's 'head lad' – despite the youthful-sounding moniker, a middleaged man – led the mare out of the stables and into the middle of the slurry-puddled, straw-strewn yard. She seemed fine – that is, there was nothing obviously wrong with her. She was quite unusual-looking. The visual effect was of a blackish-blue flecked with snow. And she was surprisingly small. She shook her head, tinkling the tack.

It was a frosty morning, and they were tired. Miller had insisted on meeting at eight. He stood there, taciturn, small eyes sly under a tweed peak, watching them while they watched the mare. (Ladylike, she lifted her tail and let fall a small heap of shiny manure.) He had been suspicious of Freddy at first. The morning after their meeting in the pub, up at half five as usual and monstrously hungover, he had foully berated himself for speaking so freely to a stranger – a stranger, what's more, who had plied him all night with whisky and pints, while finding out more and more about his operation on the pretext of being a potential owner. That was what all the snoopers said. If something seems too good to be true, he told himself, his head throbbing as he watched the lads and lasses taking the string out – it was a foul winter morning of horizontal sleet, not properly light yet – it probably is. And that this funny-looking posh fellow from London would just show up and pay £10,000 for a half share in the mare did seem too good to be true. And yet here he was, a week later, with his mate, and the money.

'What d'you think?' Simon said, eyeing them.

James stuck out his lower lip and nodded appraisingly. Freddy had a nervous swig from his hip flask.

The transaction transacted, they went into the house and had a heart-stopping fry-up prepared by Mrs Miller. It was an awkward meal. When James asked about the name Absent Oelemberg – what did it mean? – Miller just shook his head and said, 'No idea.'

'It's probably French,' James suggested politely.

Miller shrugged and went on feeding his smooth, fat face.

In London, Michael was being arrested.

*

The mare's first run was in late December, in a novices' hurdle at Huntingdon. (Though Professional Equine Investments no longer existed, and she would have to be sold, James had decided to land the touch first. Now that the service had failed he needed the money more than ever. He would be staking every penny he had on her, and he hoped to win enough to live on for a year or more, while he worked out what to do next.) Huntingdon was Miller's local track. He had informed his new owners that it was where the touch would take place in March, and he wanted her to have run poorly there on at least one previous occasion. He also said that they should 'have a few quid on'. When they looked at him in surprise, he said, 'She won't be winning. Not today.' He said they should put the money on over the Internet, where it would leave indelible traces, so that when it was time to land the touch, if the stewards had any questions, they would be able to prove that they always followed her, win or lose. And in December she did lose. In the leathern privacy of his Range Rover, Miller had told them she wasn't fit, and she looked unhealthily exhausted as she trailed in last with her tongue lolling out of her smoking head and the jockey standing up in his irons. His name was Tom. He was a stable insider, the son of Miller's head lad. Later, in the pub – not the nearest pub to the track, an obscure village pub twenty miles away somewhere in the stunning flatness of the Fens – James noticed him whispering something to Miller, who nodded and patted him on the back.

Her next run was two weeks later, also at Huntingdon. She was twenty to one that day (James still had his few quid on) and she finished tenth of twelve. Miller was not keen to talk about what measures he was taking to make sure she performed so ignominiously, and anyway James had other things on his mind, or one other thing – this woman he had met at Toby's wedding. The previous night he had taken her on the lamplit tour of the Sir John Soane Museum in Lincoln's Inn Fields, and then for dinner.

It was nearly midnight when he walked her to the tube at Holborn. (She had declined an invitation for a nightcap at his flat.) They stopped on the pavement at the station entrance.

'Well . . .' he said. 'I hope . . .'

'Can I kiss you?'

It was so sudden that he just said, 'M-hm,' and she stood on tip-toe and kissed him wetly on the mouth.

A few moments later the Saturday-night hubbub of station and street swam back. 'I'll see you next week,' she said.

'Okay . . .'

She went into the lightbox of the station, and he watched her through the snapping ticket barriers.

The next morning he was up early to take the train to Huntingdon.

The mare has not run since that murky January day. There was a scare when the meeting at which her final prep run was supposed to have taken place, at Fakenham, was abandoned due to waterlogging. That was while he was in Marrakech. Miller had said he would enter her for something else.

'Fontwell, Wednesday,' Freddy says.

'Fontwell?'

'It's in Sussex.'

'I know. What race?'

Freddy shrugs. 'He did tell me,' he says. 'Some novices' hurdle. Do you want to get something to eat? A kebab?' There is a kebab place on Earls Court Road that Freddy particularly likes. He is on first-name terms with Mehmet and the others there.

'No, I can't,' James says, looking at his watch.

'Why not?'

'I have to meet someone.'

5

He has been waiting for this moment, the moment when he sees her, for nearly a week now. She is already there, sitting at a small table with a vodka and tonic. And something *is* up – when he tries to kiss her she moves her head to the side, though not enough to prevent their lips from smudgily touching. She seems unnaturally still, except for her eyes, which are nervously mobile. When he touches her she hardly seems to notice. There is, however, something strangely playful about all this. There is something strangely playful about the impish S-shaped smile which sits in her small lips while he talks. That is probably why he is not worrying, not even about her visitor of yesterday night, whoever he was. Why he is even enjoying it. Why it is even exciting him. There is even something playful about the way that she will not let him kiss her on the mouth. Whenever he tries – and leaning towards her, he tries often – she smiles and turns her face away. They stay in the pub for two drinks – she has another V & T – and then she says she wants to get something to eat and they walk to a noodle place she knows on Upper Street.

There, things are less playful. She seems sadder. She drinks water. They share a platter of fried pastry parcels. They each have

a deep bowl of soupy noodles. They still only talk about insignificant things – for some reason, he is explaining to her how the
stock market works. Though she lets him take her hands in his,
she looks down at her empty soup bowl when he does. He notices
her rosy, tattered cuticles – they are even worse than usual. Her
hands are usually a fiery pink, weathered by soap and water, wrin-
kled on the knuckles, the nails snipped very short. So different
from her feet, which he has told her more than once are the pret-
tiest he has ever seen – small and smooth, with soft pretty toes,
and the same even ivory hue all over.

When he tries to kiss her, she turns her head away again.
There is nothing playful about the way she does it now, and for
the first time he looks pained and says, 'What is it?'

Instead of answering, she asks him whether he wants to see
the photos she took in Morocco.

'Of course,' he says.

Outside he puts up the umbrella. They have to squeeze
together to fit under it. They have not been in such proximity
all evening and he smells the faded scent of the perfume – so
familiar a smell, lingering in woollens – that she put on in the
morning when she went to work. It is only a short walk to her
flat. They have made this ingress together many times. They
know what to do. He shakes out the umbrella and takes off his
shoes. She turns on some lights and starts to make mint tea.
When he puts his arms around her, however, she looks at him
quizzically, as if it is something he has never done until that
moment. 'Why won't you kiss me?' he says.

'I just won't.'

'What do you mean you just won't?'

She leaves the kitchen with the mugs.

'What do you mean you just won't?' he says, sitting down next
to her on the sofa. When he tries to, she sucks in her lips and

shakes her head. She laughs, and lets herself flop over to the side, so that she is half-lying there. 'I don't understand,' he says, leaning over her. 'What is it?'

Looking up at him, her eyes move like insects on the surface of a pond, with quick little movements, this way, that way, unable to stay still. 'Why don't you ask me some questions?' she suggests.

'What sort of questions?'

She shrugs with mock secretiveness and for a moment makes her eyes very wide.

'What sort of questions?' he says again.

She sighs, and lets her head loll on the velvet of the sofa. He is looking at her face from a strange perspective, more or less up her nostrils. She is looking up into the tasselled pink lampshade on the table next to the sofa. 'I don't know,' she says. 'Just . . .'

'What?' he says quietly. 'What is it? Tell me.'

She does not tell him. She pushes him off her and says, 'I'm going to get ready for bed.'

'Okay,' he says, propped on an elbow. 'I'll watch you.'

'If you want.'

'I do.'

He follows her upstairs. There, however, she takes her pyjamas from under her pillow and leaves him on his own. Eventually he lies down and stares at the ceiling. That this has something to do with the man who was here last night is obvious – it was obviously a significant visit, and if it was significant, he is pretty sure he knows who it was. In her pyjamas now, she takes a hairbrush from where her things are laid out – her perfumes and make-up, her lacquered pots of junk jewellery – and starts to sweep her hair. She holds it out to the side and sweeps it vigorously. 'Are you going to stay?' she says, lifting the duvet on her side.

'I'll stay for a while. Hugo's at home. Otherwise I'd stay the night.'

'M-hm.'

They lie there for a few minutes in the lamplight – her under the duvet, him fully dressed on top of it. Then he jumps up, takes everything off and joins her underneath. His eagerness, maybe, makes her laugh kindly. 'You like being naked, don't you,' she says. 'I saw Fraser yesterday.'

To hear her say it is surprisingly painful.

'I know.'

'You know?' she says, sitting up.

'I heard him. When we were talking on the phone.'

'You heard him?'

'Yes.'

'What did you hear?'

He tells her.

'Why didn't you say something?'

'I didn't know it was him. I didn't know who it was.'

He tells her that he noticed the way she lost the thread of what they were saying on the phone, that he heard the tension in her voice. She laughs when he tells her these things. And the way he tells them is *meant* to be funny – it is meant to turn the whole thing into a harmless farce – and he laughs too. She says, 'I'm so sorry, James. It was so unlucky he walked in just when I was talking to you. I heard the doorbell and I had this whoosh of adrenalin, and then when I heard him talking to Summer, I wanted to hear what they were saying. I'm so sorry. I'm sorry if I sounded tense. I'm sorry it was so obvious.'

'That's okay,' he says, still quite lightly.

Then, 'Why was he here? What happened?'

She sighs and flops onto the pillow.

Overhead there is an old-fashioned ceiling fan with wicker

blades – like something from a tropical hotel, pre-air conditioning. It was there when she moved into the flat. She never uses it, does not even know if it still works. 'He phoned me in Morocco. The day we were supposed to go to the mountains. That morning.' She says they hadn't spoken for a year, that she was surprised and upset. 'I mean it was upsetting,' she says. 'He said he was just phoning to say hi. I said I was in Morocco. He wanted to know what I was doing there. I said I was with someone and told him to leave me alone. That was it. I *was* upset, though. I'm sorry if I seemed . . . upset. Or out of sorts or something.'

Lying on his back with his left arm under his head, he puts his other hand pensively inside her pyjama trousers and strokes her pubic hair. 'That's okay,' he says.

He is trying to remember that day. Exactly a week ago. The hour at the poolside, the warm wind stirring the line of palm trees, the shadow of the hotel on the water . . .

'I thought you went to the mountains,' he says.

Surprisingly, she laughs. 'No, of course not.'

And that night, the terrace on top of the hotel in the Nouvelle Ville, over the thick smog of the town. The hotel turned out to be a sort of whorehouse. They saw one of the men who worked in their own hotel making for the lift and its full ashtray with two fat whores . . . Yes, she had been upset. He thought she was upset with him for making them miss the minibus to the mountains, and then taking her to a whorehouse. In fact, it had been something else entirely. Nothing to do with him.

She says, 'A few days ago he phoned me again. He said he wanted to see me. I told him I didn't want to see him. He insisted. He said he had something to say. So yesterday we went for a drink.'

'What did he say?'

'He said . . . he wants to try again.'

They lie there in silence.

'And what did you say?'

'I said . . . I said . . . I said I'd think about it.'

She turns her head on the pillow. He is just lying there, staring straight up. 'Are you crying?' she says softly.

He shakes his head.

'I said I'd tell him within a week,' she says.

He is seeing the ceiling fan with a strange intensity. It is as if the whole world has shrunk to that old fan – its off-white wicker blades, its thick stalk, the plastic housing of its motor, and the weighted string of tiny stainless-steel spheres that hangs from the housing.

'I don't need a week, though. I know what I'm going to tell him.'

'What are you going to tell him?' And then, feeling a need to justify himself, such is his sense that Fraser King has some sort of primacy over him in this situation, 'I think you should tell me if . . .'

'Of course.'

Still, she does not speak for a few seconds.

From the start he has frequently had the sense that she is measuring him against Fraser King – measuring him in every way, from the most obviously physical to the most ineffably emotional – measuring him, and finding him wanting. There have been times when seeing her lost in thought – for instance on the Eurostar as it left Lille Europe – he experienced the precise, painful feeling that she would prefer to be there with Fraser King than with him. That she would prefer to be *anywhere* with Fraser King than with him. And yet now she is telling him, in effect, that this is not true. Hearing her say it, he feels a hint of euphoria. Fraser King is no longer a factor. Everything is now okay.

It is a feeling that lasts only a few seconds, until she says, 'I don't think we should see each other for a while.'

And when that elicits a prolonged silence, 'I'm sorry.'

He turns to her and sighs and they smile wistfully at each other.

She lets him slip his arm under her neck and snuggles up to him. The way she does this makes him improve his prognosis. When she says she does not think they should see each other 'for a while', what he now takes her to mean is maybe a week or two – until she has told Fraser that she intends to turn him down. Poor Fraser.

'I'm sorry, James,' she says.

'I understand.'

'Thanks for being so magnanimous.'

'That's okay,' he says. (She laughs.) Easy to be magnanimous when he is the one in her bed. He says, 'When you say a while . . .'

'Mm.'

'What do you mean?'

She shakes her head – he feels it move in the hollow of his neck. 'I don't know,' she says. 'I just . . . I don't know. Sorry.' And as if it were part of the apology, she strokes his leg with her foot.

Still studying the ceiling fan, he twists a lock of her hair around his finger. Then he turns onto his side, and studies her face. She submits to this study with a small smile. For the first time that night she does not try to move away when he kisses her on the mouth. Indeed, she even opens her mouth, and there is an immediate surge to heart-hammering intensity. She does not let this last long, however. He encircles her with his arms and squeezes her. She squeezes him too, and for a long time they lie there like that.

'Should I turn off the light?' she whispers.

'If you want.'

With a sudden twisting movement she turns and sits, takes a sip of water – with water in her mouth she offers him the glass, he shakes his head – and switches off the light.

*

It is still dark when he leaves the bed and feels for his things, which are mixed up with hers on the floor. He has a terrible feeling that he is neglecting poor Hugo – who, having spent the night unexpectedly on his own in Mecklenburgh Street, must urgently need a walk. That is why he is standing there in the dark, even though to all intents and purposes it is still night outside and he has not slept much on the thin pillows, frequently waking to look at the time, in spite of the fact that the alarm was set. Then it went off – loud and shrill – and he sat up while she struggled, still essentially asleep, to make it stop.

He is feeling for his things on the floor when she turns on the light. She puts a hand over her eyes. 'No, it's okay,' he says quietly, doing the same. 'I don't need the light. Thanks.' His mouth is thick and faecal-tasting. He is sweating. It is too hot for him here, where the storage heater seems impossible to switch off and leaks nasty heat all night.

When he is dressed he sits on the edge of the bed, wondering whether she has fallen asleep again. She has not – as soon as she feels his weight on the mattress, she sits up, and seems to prop herself on an elbow.

'Okay, I'm going,' he whispers.

'Okay.'

He kisses her, lightly touching her lips with his own. Her lips are sleepily warm. Her whole face, which he can hardly see, is sleepily soft and warm. He kisses her again, and is just standing up to leave when she says, 'James.'

'Yes.'

'So . . . What are we going to do?' she says. 'Just carry on as before?'

For a few seconds he says nothing. 'Yes, I suppose so.'

This time it is she who does not speak for a few seconds. 'Okay,' she says eventually. 'Nothing too intense, though.'

He is not sure what she means by this. 'No,' he says. 'Nothing too intense.'

'Okay.'

'Sorry to wake you up.'

'That's okay.'

She hears him tiptoe through the squeaking hall. There is a suspenseful silence while he puts on his shoes and jacket, then she hears the front door swing open and shut. Twice. In an effort to be quiet, the first attempt was too tentative.

2

I

S he is half an hour late for work, and striding across the
lobby she sees immediately that Carlo is upset. 'I'm sorry,
Carlo,' she sings, while still out in the open space, under
the shimmering spectrums of the two-tonne chandelier. He just
shakes his head and skulks into the staff cloakroom. For a few
seconds she stands at the front desk, paying down the oxygen
debt of her hurry.

Then she follows the small Italian into the staff cloakroom.
In the mirror, she sees what a mess her hair is, how pouchy her
eyes look.

Carlo is shrugging on his smart blue overcoat.

'I'm sorry,' she says flatly, as if it were a final offer.

'S'okay,' Carlo says, without looking at her. He straightens his
scarf. 'You owe me though.'

Throughout the morning the huge hotel empties. The lifts
ping. Porters push trolleys loaded with luggage. Taxis swarm on
the manicured forecourt. The doormen endlessly open the doors,
while from the windows of the top floor the waiters have no time
to look out over the massed treetops of the park, pushing west-
wards for over a mile into the indistinct distance.

At about eleven, when things up there have finally quietened

down, Ernó – the Hungarian waiter, her silent suitor – steps out
of the lift with something in his hands.

'Is that for me?' she says, matter-of-factly.

'Naturally,' Ernó says, under the innocent impression that this
is just an elegant way of saying yes.

'Thanks. That's very sweet of you.'

'Nothing,' he says.

She puts the coffee under the summit of the desk and stares
out at the long perspectives of the lobby. The shimmer of
its spaces, of the chandelier – an inverted wedding cake, listlessly
iridescent – seems superannuated. Its luxury seems stale. The
little shops in the neglected, marble-floored passage seem frumpy,
superfluous, survivors from a time when only the shops in luxury
hotel lobbies were open on Sunday, or even Saturday afternoon.

She has lunch in the subterranean warren of linoleum passage-
ways the public never sees, and it is sitting there in her sober
work clothes that she starts to think properly about what has
happened. She feels uneasy. When she said, 'I don't think we
should see each other for a while,' that was what she meant, and
yet somehow it is not how things seem to have been left. She
shouldn't have had sex with him, of course. Probably she should
not have let him stay the night at all. Should not even have let
him kiss her. It had been her intention not to let him kiss her.
She had felt sorry for him. She had felt sorry for him when he
said, in that oddly simple way of his, 'Why won't you kiss me?'
There is something about him that tugs at her heart. ('Why won't
you kiss me?') So yes, she felt sorry for him. That was not the
main thing, though. The main thing was that she seemed to find
it impossible *not* to kiss him when he was there, in front of her.
His mouth. The way that kissing it her whole mind seemed to
melt . . . Pondering this phenomenon, she pours herself some
water. Her failure to hold to her intentions makes her wonder

whether she is wrong to want not to see him for a while. It makes her wonder whether that is in fact what she wants. Does she know what she wants? She does not seem to.

She finds it upsetting to upset people. That is her weakness. That is why she let him leave this morning thinking that everything would just go on as if nothing had happened. That is why the idea that maybe she was wrong to want not to see him for a while so easily tempted her as she sat propped on her skinny elbow in the dark and turned her face slightly away from his halitosis. She had nearly not said *anything*. Nearly not even said, 'James! So ... What are we going to do?' And then, oppressed by his silence − standing there like a sullen shadow − and her own sudden uncertainty, 'Just carry on as before?' She had not meant the words to convey the sense that that was what she thought they *should* do. She had meant them more as the sceptical starting point for a conversation on the subject. That was not how they had sounded. They had sounded like a straightforward suggestion, and he was obviously willing to take them as one. So he left, and she lay there for a few minutes, feeling that he had somehow been unpleasantly sly − which made her dislike him − and then she fell asleep.

She was hurt by his lack of emotion when she said she did not think they should see each other for a while. The way he was silent for a few seconds and then just said, 'Okay.' When he said that, she suddenly wondered what he felt. He did not seem to feel anything. And if he did, why did he not show it? Why did he not express it in words? Why did he not even try?

She pours herself some more water from the plastic jug and someone sits down at the table, as far away from her as possible. Ernó. When she looks in his direction, he just nods. They do not speak to each other, not even a few pleasantries, which seems odd. He must be ten years younger than her. He might be no more than twenty. Sometimes she thinks that if he simply walked up to her and suggested they take the lift upstairs and have sex in a vacant room – as he presumably wants to – she would just say, 'Yeah, okay,' and start setting up a suitable key. The trouble is, if he did that, he would no longer be Ernó, with his shy, lusty innocence. His unspoken, obvious longing. He would be something else.

'How are things today?' he says suddenly.

It is a tedious question and his tone is tediously sincere and she just shrugs and says, 'They're okay. Fine.' He has no sense of humour, or does not seem to. 'I'll see you later,' she says, and stands up with her tray.

'Okay, see you,' he says.

She smiles at him.

Well, she 'smiles' at him. It is a smile she sometimes does – a momentary flexing of her mouth – which does not even pretend to be sincere. To that extent it is, in its way, a sincere expression. It expresses *something*. She knows this, and wonders as she leaves and wanders up to the lobby, what it does express. She tends to do it when she is nervous, when she does not know what else to do. It is a sort of surrender to the pressure of social niceties, to the pressure of pretending – a sort of helpless shrug.

She starts to walk up the service stairs, with their strip-lit landings. She finds it impossible to pretend. She is not sure why. Other people seem to be able to do it so easily. Once – and they have been together just long enough for there to be 'once' – James said it was impossible for him to imagine her acting, acting in a play for instance. Impossible to imagine her playing someone else. If she had to, he said, she just wouldn't take it seriously, she'd turn it into a joke. It was not something she had thought about. He was very pleased with himself for having had what he thought was an insight into her personality – and one which she had not had herself. She is still sometimes astonished that anything much has happened with him at all, after that first – or was it the second? – night at his flat. The *fiasco*. That was the word she used for that episode of pure sexual misery, which a sort of politeness had led her into. It was a problem, the way she let men polite her into things. And that night, when he was suddenly all over her in the hall of his flat, it was a sort of politeness which pressured her into letting him do what he wanted with her – a feeling that perhaps it would not be *polite* to stop him, that he might be offended, that there might be a scene, with her somehow in the wrong. When she thought she was pregnant the following week and he seemed unable to understand what she was suffering, she hated him as much as she had ever hated anyone. He was in his own world and seemed to have no understanding of hers – and *no interest* in having such an understanding. That was what she found so strange. His two-dimensionality. He was, however, the first man she had felt a strong attraction to since Fraser, and she had started to fear that she would never feel very attracted to anyone else again. That was probably what had made the *fiasco* so painful – it had been surprisingly painful. And that was probably what had made it so hard just to end it, as for a week afterwards she had fully intended to, even when it turned out that she was not pregnant.

She visits the Ladies, and while she is in there she tries to tidy up her hair. She splashes water on her pasty face, and nurses her shot eyes. Then she takes up her post at the front desk and stands there facing the hours of the afternoon. From the heart of the lobby, the huge London outside and the weather, which is increasingly wild, seem like another world. It is difficult not to think of Fraser here. It was here, in this lobby, that she met him. It was this time of day. An afternoon like this one – a dark sky through the distant, attended doors. He had been hanging around for some time, since the morning. First outside. Then, when the downpour arrived, in the lobby. He was not the only photographer; there were a few others, all waiting for someone upstairs – she did not know who. The sort of person they were waiting for never used their own name, so to look at the long list of people staying in the hotel was pointless. She had not been given any special instructions; there were no special security people in evidence.

The photographers were matey with each other, but it was obvious from their eyes – she had plenty of time to watch them in the quiet hours of the early afternoon – that they were plotting against each other too. (As he later explained to her, any edge over the others, however marginal, might make the difference between a massive payday and a total waste of time. The point was – if they all got the same shots, they would all be worthless.) He was the most talkative. He seemed the happiest – he was always smiling, and made the others laugh. He was also the tallest. And also, she noticed, the most determined. It was he who quietly detached himself from the others and tried to slip into the lifts, until he was spotted and held up his hands like a football player. When he tried it a second time the security guards evicted him from the lobby. She found, standing at the desk, that – while she had watched its noisy slapstick progress with a sort of smile – she did not welcome his eviction. The lobby seemed more tedious with him not there. And something had happened as he was being ejected – their eyes had momentarily met and, from the middle of his melee with the security men, he had smiled at her. She was not sure whether she had smiled back. There might not have been time. The other paps did not entertain her. They stood in a little sour-faced huddle, pacing up and down the strip of marble to which they were now limited – the security guards had seemed to want to throw them all out, there had been a long negotiation – and not speaking much.

It was several hours later that she suddenly found herself facing him. She had more or less forgotten about him, though the other paps were still there, on their strip of marble. They had been there for such a long time that she no longer noticed them. And she did not have time to notice them. It was early evening and the lobby hummed with purposefully moving people. She turned to the next person waiting there. 'Hello,' she said, and only then saw who it was. To her irritation, she immediately felt nervous. He too seemed nervous, however. When he smiled – and he was smiling nervously at her – his eyes shrank to laughing slits. He was in his mid-forties probably and his face was pleasantly weathered. It was the face of someone who smiled a lot, and who spent a lot of time outside. 'Look, I'm sorry about this,' he said. Was he American? 'And I quite understand if you call security on me straight away.' She did not move. 'But I really need this shot and there's no way I'm going to get it out there.' No, not American – he had just said what sounded like 'oot there'. He tilted his head quickly in the direction of the doors, and through them the sodden London evening, still just streaked with light, where a mush of fallen plane seeds and soppy leaves was choking the drains of Park Lane. It was October. 'So I was wondering,' he was saying, 'if I could wait in there for a bit.' He had noticed the staff cloakroom, a door to the side of the front desk, the wood of which discreetly matched the wood of the section of wall in which it was set, with a sign saying, 'STAFF ONLY'. Or maybe he knew about it already. He was probably very familiar with the layout of the hotel. This was probably not the first time he had done this. 'I quite understand if you say no,' he said. 'I don't want to get you in trouble.'

And of course she would get in trouble if he was found in there.

'Okay,' she said quietly.

She let him into the cloakroom – 'Thank you so much,' he said – and went back to her post at the desk.

An hour or two later, she went into the cloakroom herself. It was windowless, and except for a hanging-rail with some wire hangers – one of which held her coat – and a few stained chairs withdrawn from public service, it was empty.

He was on the phone. As soon as he saw her, he said, 'Listen, can I call ya back? I'll call ya back. Okay.' He smiled at her. 'I don't know how to thank you for this,' he said. 'My name's Fraser, by the way.' He stood up and held out his hand.

She shook it and told him her name.

'Who are you waiting for?' she asked.

He said the name of a very famous singer, an American. 'She's checked in as Jane Green,' he said. 'She's staying until Friday or Saturday. It's supposed to be a secret that she's in London. She's here to see . . .' He named a film star, also American. This film star was famously married to someone other than 'Jane Green'. 'He's shooting a film in London. She's here to see him, and nobody's supposed to know. A shot of them together would be . . .' He laughed. 'Priceless. Just priceless. I don't imagine they'll be seen in public together, though, and just a shot of her in London would do almost as well.'

'If you're in here,' Katherine said, 'how will you know when she comes down?'

He said he had a spy on the hotel staff who would phone him when she was on her way. Then he smiled and said, 'I know it's silly. All this skulduggery.'

'Who's your spy?'

'I shouldn't say.'

She shrugged and was about to say, 'Okay,' when he said, 'Can you keep a secret?'

'Sometimes.'

He laughed. 'Sometimes?'

It was strange – she had never been so aware of her own pulse in her life. 'If you don't want to tell me . . .' she said.

He did tell her. The spy was a man. She knew his name, knew him by sight – one of the senior security staff, who would presumably be able to see 'Jane Green' and her entourage emerge from their suites on his wall of CCTV monitors in the sub-basement.

'Do you pay him?' she said.

'Oh,' he said, still squinting as he smiled. 'That is a secret, I'm afraid.'

He said that he wanted to be a landscape photographer. This was the next day – he and the other paps were still there. There had been no sign of 'Jane Green'. He said that he loved nothing more than to travel to remote places – northern Norway, Kamchatka, Patagonia – and spend a week or two in the wilderness taking shots of nature. That is, Nature. He talked of walking for days, or even weeks, through unpeopled mountains to find the perfect shot; of setting up the equipment and waiting while the sun, in its own sweet time, moved into position. Then the exposure, a fraction of a second. That fraction of a second was the whole point. It was what justified all the waiting, the walking, the weeks of sleeping under nylon. That fraction of a second was all that mattered. It was something, he said, that made you think about the nature of time.

She had not expected this. Now, incredibly, he was saying something about T. S. Eliot's *Four Quartets*. 'Yes, I know them,' she said, and smiled imperceptibly as she thought – *A philosopher pap! A philosopher King!*

'Do you know Ansel Adams?' he said. 'Do you know his work? The stuff he did in Yosemite?'

'I've heard of him,' she said. Her heart was pounding.

'I'd like to do stuff like that . . .'

'Are you married?' she said, surprising herself.

The question took him by surprise too. He smiled and looked at the thing on his thick finger. 'I was,' he said. 'Well, strictly speaking I still am. We're separated. Why?'

She shrugged. 'Do you live on your own?'

'Yes, I do,' he said. 'Unfortunately. I wish I didn't.'

He was looking her in the eye when he said that. In the frayed, neglected space, she felt her pulse swell with terrible energy in her throat. For the past twenty-four hours it had been like that.

The next morning she was late into work. She had been to the doctor – the incessant heavy tambour of her heart had started to frighten her. He made her unbutton her shirt and placed the heatless milled-steel head of his stethoscope on the skin where it started to slope into her left breast. He pumped up the sleeve of the sphygmograph until it was fiercely tight on her arm. He said it was nothing serious, and prescribed her some pills.

The paps were still there, on their strip of marble. Fraser was with them now – the security men seemed to have forgiven him – and to her surprise she found herself swerving off her path towards the front desk and walking up to him. She had no idea what she was going to say. Stepping away from the others, he spoke first. 'Morning,' he said, smiling. He looked at his watch. 'Late, aren't you?' The other paps eyed her with interest – the shortish skirt, the slightly saucy shoes. She had taken time, that morning, to decide what to wear.

'I've been to the doctor,' she volunteered.

'Nothing serious, I hope.'

She shook her head. 'Any sign of Jane Green?'

'Not yet,' Fraser said. He was still smiling.

She stood there for a few seconds.

'Well . .' she said.

The fact was, now that the security men were willing to have him in the lobby, there was no point him hiding in the staff cloakroom.

'I'll see you later,' she said, and walked the twenty metres, under the twinkling inverted wedding cake, to the front desk.

She wondered whether she *would* see him later. For the next hour or so her eyes kept sliding towards the posse of paps. He was never looking at her, though two or three times her eyes met those of one of the others – a younger man, with well-gelled hair and pointy sideburns, and white leather shoes that were pointy too. Eventually she stopped looking, fearful of meeting the pointy-shoed man's eyes again.

Feeling slightly low, she went for lunch and when she got back, she found him – him is Fraser – sitting in the staff cloakroom.

'I know I shouldn't be in here,' he said.

'That's okay.'

'It's just,' he went on, 'if I'm in here, I'll get a different shot from the others.'

'Okay,' she said. She was staring at him. Her heart was walloping again.

'They're all going to have the same shot,' Fraser said.

'Yes.'

'If I'm in here, I'll get something different.'

Yes, you just said that, she thought.

She hoped all this stuff about shots was just a silly excuse to come and see her. However, he was now saying that if his unique shot was somehow superior to their set of very similar shots, his would be the one all the papers would take.

'I understand,' she said shortly. She wished he would stop talking about it.

He smiled.

Then she said, 'What if she gets smuggled out through the kitchens or something?'

'Oh, she probably will be smuggled out through the kitchens,' he said.

'She will?'

'Yes.'

'Then why are you all here, in the lobby?'

'We're not,' he said. 'There are – what? – five of us here? We're the awkward squad. We're taking a punt. We're hoping she'll try to wrong-foot the pack by just walking straight out through the lobby.'

'The pack?'

'Most of the others are outside.' He smiled. 'You think I'm making this up, don't you? Have a look then. Do you want to have a look? Let's have a look.'

It felt strange to be walking somewhere with him, to be out in the wind and traffic of Park Lane. Turning into the street at the side of the hotel, they passed the sombre entrance of the 'State Rooms', and further on some of her fellow employees smoking in a sticky doorway. They traversed the moaning out-vents of the heating system, and a vast expanse of steel shutter. Then they turned into Park Street, and saw several dozen photographers – a hedgehog of telephoto lenses on the pavement opposite the service entrance, marshalled by a lone, tired-looking policeman.

She laughed with surprise.

He made her laugh with stories of the exploits of sweatily desperate paps. He told her the story of a friend of his, Ed O'Keefe, who used to work for a national tabloid and was sent by his editor to doorstep Ian Hislop in the village where he lived. He was told to get a shot of Hislop laughing to illustrate a piece on a natural disaster. He arrived in the village on Friday afternoon. There was no sign of Hislop. Nor was there any sign of him on Saturday. Finally, on Sunday morning, he emerged. He was on his was to church and he said, 'Who the fuck are you? What do you want?' Ed O'Keefe explained that he just needed a shot of him smiling. Hislop told him to fuck off, and went on his way. For the next week, Hislop wouldn't stop scowling, and finally poor Ed – unwashed, unshaved, and sore from sleeping in his car – headed back to London to face the wrath of his editor. Then, just as he was leaving, his engine started spewing smoke and exploded, and Hislop, who was watching him leave, exploded wth laughter, and, ignoring the flames, the quick-thinking pap whipped out his Nikon and got the shot.

'Sangfroid,' Fraser said. 'Should've been a war photographer.'

She smiled. She looked at the time. It was twenty past eight. She had finished work well over an hour ago, and she was still there, in the institutional light, listening to him.

'I suppose I should go,' she said.

'Okay.'

She didn't move, though. 'How long do you stay here? Do you ever go home?'

'Never,' he said, smiling.

She looked at him sceptically. 'Well, I'm going home,' she said. She stood up and started to put on her coat. He watched her. 'You can stay here if you want.'

'If that's okay.'

'M-hm.' She opened the door, letting in noise from the lobby. 'I'll see you tomorrow then.'

'Okay,' he said. 'Sleep well.'

'You too. If you do sleep.'

It was hard to say whether the pills were having any effect on her heart. It was still thumping with unwarranted force as she walked to the tube station. She wondered why he still wore his wedding ring if his marriage was over.

The next day, in the middle of the afternoon, someone phoned him on his mobile. Something short and to the point. 'Yes, okay,' Fraser said, and hung up. 'She's on her way down,' he said, starting to prepare his equipment.

'Through the lobby?'

'Possibly.'

There was nothing unusual happening in the lobby. The other paps – standing in their notional pen near the entrance – did not seem to know that their long days of waiting were almost at an end. When one of the lifts pinged and the doors parted, Fraser moved urgently forward. It was not 'Jane Green'. The other paps had noticed him, however, and were themselves now starting to prepare. Though life in the lobby went on as normal, the sudden tension of the paps seemed to be spreading to other people. The security guards sensed that something was afoot – they seemed to be moving into position, in fact – while some of the doormen and porters had stopped what they were doing and were trying to see what it was that had unsettled the paps. This in turn had some of the more perceptive members of the public doing the same thing. She stood at the front desk and watched the numbers over the lift doors slowly descend.

When it happened, it happened quickly. Two lifts pinged simultaneously and some people poured out of each. At first this tightly knit dozen merely walked, quickly and with purpose, towards the doors, where two long silver Mercedes had pulled up outside. When the paps fell on them, however, they started to move faster. There was suddenly a lot of shouting. There was pushing and shoving. The paps had scattered from their pen and were everywhere. As soon as the lifts opened, Fraser had sprung forward and was now where the fighting was fiercest. Other paps were walking backwards towards the doors, firing off flashes as they went. And they walked straight into still more paps, arriving at a sprint from their futile vigil in Park Street. These ones too were snapping as soon as they arrived. Voices were shouting Jane Green's real name. Shouting, 'Over here! Here!' Katherine heard one man shout, 'Oi! You fucking whore!' (Fraser would later explain, when she mentioned it, that this man had not meant anything nasty – he had simply been trying to get her attention and perhaps provoke some sort of interesting facial expression.) It had turned into a scrum in the vicinity of the doors. As they poured into the lobby, the influx of sweating, panting paps from Park Street was pushing against the security guards and Jane Green's now furious entourage. There was even a policeman involved. Some hapless members of the public were knocked over as the scrum wheeled to one side. More security guards arrived at speed, sprinting through the lobby in their blue blazers. A pap was knocked over too – his camera, which may have taken a kick, went skittering over the marble. Immediately he was on his feet shouting threats to sue, but by then the entourage had forced its way out, and moments later the two Mercedes were pulling away, even then being pestered by paps on foot, stumbling through the flower beds in front of the hotel, holding their cameras over their heads to fire off a last flickering fusillade as the mopeds appeared from nowhere and tore off into the traffic in loudly nasal pursuit.

Fraser was triumphant. His face was shining with joy. She loved that. She loved the way his face was shining with joy. It made her feel joy herself. Needless to say, her heart was pumping frenziedly. Flushed with victory, having spontaneously picked her up and spun her around – she shrieked, then laughed – he was showing her the shots he had taken. Throughout the whole mad half-minute – or maybe it was even less – she herself had not seen 'Jane Green'.

And now, excitably, Fraser was saying something else.

'What?' she said. She had not heard. There had been some furious shouting – a pap and a security guard were still having a private feud.

'I want to buy you a drink,' he said. 'What time do you finish work?' His face was still shining with joy.

'Eight,' she said.

'I'll meet you here at eight. Okay?'

'Okay,' she said, and he jogged off, whooping and waving to some of the others.

He was early. At ten to eight she saw him waiting in the lobby. No longer in his photographer's fatigues, he was wearing a suit with an open-necked shirt and two-tone shoes. (Those shoes made her smile.) And he looked touchingly nervous. He was nervously pacing.

As soon as they were out of the hotel he surprised her by lighting a cigarette. A Silk Cut. It seemed an effeminate choice of smoke for him. He offered her one and she shook her head. Then she said, 'Yes, okay.' He lit it for her – together they made a tulip of their hands in the fresh night wind. She was so intensely aware of the points at which their fingers were touching that for a second she felt slightly faint. The frail flame steadied. They started to walk towards Hyde Park Corner. 'I don't really smoke,' she said.

'No, me neither.'

He told her that a London tabloid had snapped up his pictures of 'Jane Green', and they were selling well in other territories too.

'How much for?' she asked.

'Quite a lot.'

'How much?' she insisted.

'No,' he said, 'not that much.' He was smiling, very pleased with himself. 'Enough for a drink in one of these places.'

They went to one of the other handsome Park Lane hotels for their drink, and there, in the very first lull, with her poor heart moving into overdrive, she lifted her eyes to his and said – 'I find you very attractive.' It was not the sort of thing she was in the habit of saying to men she had only just met. It was not the sort of thing she was in the habit of saying at all. That she said it was part of the intense strangeness, the strange intensity of those days. It was what she was thinking, and she felt a sudden vertiginous freedom just to *say* it. So she did.

For a moment he seemed less sure of himself. There was in his smile for the first time a shadow of self-doubt. It was not *what* she had said – that or things like it he had heard many times. It was the essentially unflirtatious way that she said it. She said it as if it was something important. She looked very serious. It was very intense. He smiled – the shadow of self-doubt – and seemed to be about to say something himself, he was not sure what, when she leaned through the elegant light and kissed him.

Without saying a word, she then placed herself entirely in his hands, and he seemed happy to take the initiative. The luxurious mojitos finished, and paid for without her noticing when or how, she found herself in a throbbing taxi, then in a street somewhere south of the river – perhaps Battersea – then in a tiny lift, and then in an equally tiny flat, then on a sofa that seemed still to wear the plastic wrapping in which it was shipped, with his tousled head between her white thighs (his hair was thinning on top), and then naked on an enormous bed, and all the time her heart was pounding. He would not let her lift a finger. She loved the way he would not let her lift a finger, the way he let her lose herself again and again in her own passivity. Her fantasies were mostly fantasies of passivity, for instance of medical examinations, of white-smocked professionals straying from their task and starting to touch her in ways they were not supposed to.

'You're too smart to work in a hotel lobby,' he said. He was propped on his side, peering at her in the imperfect darkness of the London night.

'I know,' she said, and then laughed – *Ha!* – at her own immodesty.

'Of course you are,' he said. 'So why do you? You went to university?'

She nodded.

'Which?'

She told him.

It made him laugh. 'Jesus!' His smile shone. 'That's quite intimidating!'

'Is it?'

'So why do you work in a hotel?' he said.

She said she wanted to set up a small hotel, somewhere near the sea, and she needed some experience of hotel management. That was why.

'That's very sensible,' he said. 'Most people would just get on a plane somewhere and fuck it up.'

'I know,' she said. This time she did not laugh.

'How long have you been working there, in the hotel?'

'A few months.'

'What did you do before?'

'I worked in publishing . . .'

She had taken his flopping penis idly in her hand – or it seemed that she took it idly. In fact, she felt quite self-conscious, and she just held it as in slow pulses it started to stiffen. 'I worked in publishing,' she said. He seemed to have no further questions.

Still feeling quite self-conscious, she moved on the mattress until her flaxen hair spilled onto his furry stomach.

Some time during the night, when she went to the loo, she opened the fridge in the tiny kitchen. It was entirely empty – not even milk. It had the pristine white look of a display fridge in a department store. It was then that she noticed there were no covers on the duvet or the pillows. In the morning, while he showered, she started to wonder about these things. The flat had a totally unlived-in feel. It seemed to be very new. In the living room there was nothing but the sofa, still in its plastic wrapping, and a TV – its packaging too was still there. The kitchen was equipped with two mugs, one plate, one knife and one spoon. The oven had never been used – it still had pieces of polystyrene and an instruction manual in it. The expanse of built-in storage space in the bedroom was empty. She was looking into this surprising void when he put his arms around her waist and picking her up, spun her once, twice – she squealed, her legs kicked and flailed – and fell with her onto the bed.

'Why isn't there anything here?' she said.

'What do you mean?'

'I mean those cupboards are empty. There's nothing there. Don't you have any clothes?'

'Clothes? What do I need clothes for?'

'And there's nothing in the kitchen. Not even a kettle.'

'I've just moved in,' he said, more seriously. 'That's obvious, isn't it?'

'Where are all your clothes then?'

'They're somewhere else. I'm moving my stuff here next week. What's the matter?'

She did not press him.

Instead, she went and had a shower. There was only one towel and it was already quite wet. While she was using it, and looking at herself in the steamy mirror, he shouted through the door, 'Do you want to go out for breakfast, or do you want me to go get some stuff?'

'Go out!' she shouted back. She brushed her teeth with his toothbrush, and daubed some of his deodorant under her arms.

He was smoking a Silk Cut in the kitchen with the little window open, using the sink as an ashtray. 'Okay?' he said, smiling.

As they went down in the tiny lift – the flat was quite high up, had a view over the huge normality of south London – she surprised herself again. She said, 'I'm in love with you.'

* * *

The past. As if someone had forgotten to lock its cage and it had slipped out, looking for her. It is on the loose now. It is at large in the lobby. It is there with the multilingual louche *flâneurs* who populate it at this hour of the day. Half past four, p.m. She stands there next to an enormous vase of flowers, staring out at the public luxury.

For a while, months, they met in the flat in Battersea. It soon emerged that he was not in fact separated from his wife – not physically, though he insisted they were 'emotionally separated', that when he had told her he lived on his own, it was in a metaphorical sense true. He said he hated his wife. (And she was shocked by his use of that word – she had never hated anyone.) In a strictly literal sense, however, they did still live together, with their two daughters – and *for* their two daughters – in the house in Sevenoaks. The flat in London was a pied-a-terre, that was all. He was often on jobs – 'stake-outs' – that made it imprac- tical for him to trek all the way to Kent every night. The 'Jane Green' job had been such a 'stake-out'. Mostly they were neither so interesting nor so profitable. Typically they involved loitering outside a fashionable nightclub in Mayfair, hoping to snap a Premier League footballer or someone from TV, or if you were very lucky one of the junior Windsors. Or spending days at Heathrow like a stranded traveller, eating junk food and eyeing up incoming flights from JFK and LAX. That was the sort of thing he mostly did. He said he hated that too. He hated his life, he said – how it had turned out. 'How did it happen like this? I didn't *want* it.' He meant the marriage, the job. (On the plus side, he did make a lot of money. For the 'Jane Green' pictures alone, he eventually told her, he was paid £50,000.) He said, as they lay naked on the mattress in the still unfurnished flat, that he wanted to change everything. He just needed some more time. Then he would leave his wife in Sevenoaks and live with *her* in London; he would stop papping and start Ansell-Adamsing. Then they would travel together to the wild, pure places he told her about. Then everything would start anew.

She lived for the two nights a week she spent in the flat in Battersea, and the occasional minibreak – there were minibreaks, there were weekends away. When they met in London she would wait in the flat. She had her own key. She would wait in the kitchen smoking, or in the living room with the TV on. He was usually late. It might be midnight, one o'clock. Then he showed up smelling of the kebab he had eaten, sometimes flushed with success. He opened a bottle of wine and she listened while he told her about his evening's adventures. Then they had sex. The next day, at lunchtime, he took the train to Sevenoaks. It wasn't always exactly like that. Sometimes he didn't have a job to do and they would spend the whole evening together.

Finally, on New Year's Day, she told him she would never see him again unless he left his wife. 'What are you talking about?' he said. He was in a windowless hotel bathroom in Florida (a family holiday), whispering into his phone while the extractor fan and the shower made noise. 'You *know* that's what I want. You know that's what I want to do. It's just a matter of time. You know that . . .'

He thought he had talked her down, but in London a few days later – they were walking in Battersea Park – she said the same thing. She said he had until the first of February to make up his mind, and until then she wouldn't see him. He pleaded. He phoned, he turned up in Caledonian Road, he tried to make her see things from his point of view, the kids, the *kids* . . . Though she wouldn't listen, she did not know what she would do if he said he wouldn't leave his wife.

He did leave her – in March, a month late – and she must have found Katherine's number in his phone. She phoned her and swore at her in impeccable RP – she sounded surprisingly posh – for twenty solid minutes.

In April she left her flatshare over the shop on Caledonian Road and moved in with him in Battersea. He was still papping, though he had started to spend a lot of time poring over atlases, trying to work out where to take his first shots of Nature. There would be no more papping for him then. In the end – the fact that they would be travelling in winter effectively excluded the northern latitudes – he settled on Mauritania. She took two months' unpaid leave and they left London on 2 January in an old unheated Land Rover and headed south through France and Spain. They lingered a few days in Marrakech. Then pressed on through the Atlas Mountains, where they spent two memorably idyllic nights in a stone hotel within earshot of a waterfall – and then south, south, towards the Sahara. There were a few weeks in the Mauritanian desert, a picture-book desert of peach dunes neighbouring the dark blue Atlantic. Fraser took his photos, and then they went further south, over the frontier into Senegal. (Where he almost lost his equipment and plates to some venal khaki officials.) For a while they hung out at a place called Zebra Bar near the city of St Louis – some huts in a national park on a marine lagoon, and a fridge full of beer. A population of intriguing transients. Fraser was popular there. He loved it and for a few weeks he was king of the place and she was his freckled queen.

Then they went on to Dakar and stayed out late in salsa clubs.

And then on.

And on.

They left the Land Rover in Burkina Faso and flew back to London in April.

He had opened a different sort of world to her – it wasn't anything he did so much as something in what he *was* – a world of immediate feelings; and with them the sometimes troubling sense that they were the only thing that was of any value, that finally they were what life was.

Later that year they were married. If there was to be a wedding he wanted it low-key, which it was. A London registry office on a Saturday afternoon. His mother, over from Saskatchewan. Her parents. A Swedish aunt. A few friends.

His photos were not a huge success. He had exhibited them over the summer, and sold a few prints, but it was obvious that he was not going to be able to make a living from them, and he had to look for other sorts of photographic work. (As for her, she was still working in the hotel – she had been working there for more than two and a half years, and was now a shift manager.) Fraser was depressed that his attempt to be Ansell Adams had failed. He said he was too worn out for papping. That was a 'young man's job'. They didn't have much money. He sold the place in Battersea and they took out a joint mortgage for a flat on Packington Street in Islington.

She had always imagined a house in some nice white-stuccoed nook of north London. Trees in the street. Family Christmases. What she had was not quite what she had imagined, but Packington Street passed for a white-stuccoed nook, just about. Fraser said it was the worst possible time. They were just scraping along as it was. They needed her income. And there was no hurry – she was only twenty-nine. Every second weekend his daughters stayed with them. He picked them up from school on Friday, and his wife picked them up from Packington Street on Sunday afternoon. She stayed outside, usually sitting in the car – except for that once on the phone, she and Katherine had never spoken.

He started finding more work. He seemed to have found a source of more lucrative product work, high-street fashion stuff. He had shots of posh parties in *Tatler* – Lord Something So-and-so's twenty-first, the bar mitzvah of a north-London billionaire's son. He was often out late on these jobs, and was sometimes away overnight.

She was very strict with herself. He himself had once told her, while he was still living in Sevenoaks, that even if he did leave his wife, she would never trust him. Not the way things had started. She knew from her own experience what he was like. She often thought of those words. Her memory of him saying them, of the self-satisfied melancholy smile on his tremendous face was precise. They had made a powerful impression on her. However, she insisted on trusting him. She *had* to trust him. What was the point otherwise? To freely enter into this situation and then spend a lot of time *not trusting him* – that would be insane. She had known what she was doing, and in doing it she had taken a decision to trust him. So she did. She trusted him.

*

When she leaves the hotel at the end of her shift it is nearly dark outside, the western sky over the park still just streaked with wet blue light – she sees it through the trees – as it was on the afternoon that she first spoke to Fraser, over four years ago. She walks quickly to the tube station. When she saw him on Sunday he did not look well. He looked surprisingly old and paunchy. He looked out of shape. Having exchanged a few words with Summer, he stood there waiting, staring at the floor, while she finished her phone call – she was trying to hide the fact that her heart was palpitating from him and also from James on the other end of the line. When she had finished with James she snapped her phone shut and said, 'Hello.'

'Hello,' he said.

She stood up. 'Do you want to get a drink then?'

'Okay.' He shrugged, seemed unenthusiastic.

'That's what you said you wanted,' she said. 'You said you wanted to have a drink.' That was what he had said. He smiled – the smile wasn't quite there. 'Sure. Let's do that.'

Watching her put on her coat, he said, 'You look nice.'

She ignored that – though her heart seemed to hit a pothole – and they left (she shouted up to Summer that she wouldn't be long) and walked in silence to the Old Queen's Head, where they often used to go for quiet drinks on Sunday nights . . .

She stands on a fully freighted escalator at King's Cross, one of thousands of people in motion, tens of thousands. The *formiche di Londra*, Carlo calls them. And one of the *formiche*, lost in her thoughts, she transfers from the Piccadilly line to the Northern for the single stop to Angel.

The flat is empty and unlit. Summer is out. She will probably not be home tonight.

She has a long bath, and opens a pack of supermarket tortellini, and phones her mother and tells her that she has seen Fraser and wishes she hadn't. Then, in her turquoise kimono, with her hair in a towel, she watches television for an hour.

Lying in bed, she opens the poetry anthology that lives on the night-table and, as she sometimes does last thing at night, takes the first poem she sees. She is pleased that tonight it is a short one.

> Ah! Sunflower, weary of time,
> Who countest the steps of the sun,
> Seeking after that sweet golden clime
> Where the traveller's journey is done;
>
> Where the youth pined away with desire,
> And the pale virgin shrouded in snow,
> Arise from their graves and aspire;
> Where my sunflower wishes to go.

She switches off the light. When she is half-asleep, however, she hears her phone, muffled somewhere in the flat. She does not move. Sleepily she wonders whether it is James, or Fraser, or someone else.

Simon Miller wakes at four. Though it will not be light for more than two hours, he has things to see to. Leaving Mrs Miller to sleep in – she were a lazy so-and-so – he pulls on his jeans and prowls downstairs. In the kitchen he switches on the overhead light and, still squinting painfully, sets matchflame to Marlboro Red. Then he starts to make his tea. He has five runners entered at Fontwell Park this afternoon, a large number for a small stable like his – he has had to hire an extra horse transport – and there are preparations to see to. He opens the yard door and standing shirtless under the lintel puts on the floodlight. Floodlight were right. The fockin yard is under water. With filthy weather like this down in Sussex, it's a short odds-on shot, he thinks, that Fontwell will be off. He'll still have to pay for the horse transport. He'll still have to see to all the paperwork that sending five horses to the track involves. There's an inspection scheduled for later, until then he just has to assume the fockin thing is on.

When the light struggles up the rain has stopped and the old farmhouse looks sullen in its hollow. The stand of nettles shivers in the wind. In the tackroom the neon lights are on. The lads and lasses are up and taking out the string.

'What you reckon, Piers?' Simon says, sunk up to his ankles

in the ooze of the yard mud, so that his thick legs seem to thrust from it like young trees. 'Will it be on? What do you think?'

And patient, pale Piers *does* think – he thinks as if he is trying to work it out, as if it was possible to work it out logically. From his vantage point in the high saddle – he is on Mr President, smoking a cigarette while he waits for the others – he looks up at the laden sky. He looks at the flat ploughed fields. 'Don't know,' he says finally.

'Yeah.' Simon nods. 'That's what I thought.'

'There's talk,' Piers says, still with his eyes focused somewhere near the horizon, 'about a heavy-ground Festival.'

'I heard that. I heard that.'

'What with all this rain.'

'That's right.'

The others are filing out into the twilit yard. Among the workriders are several of Simon's offspring, and Piers's son is on Absent Oelemberg, her profile looking like a shadow or silhouette in the frigid half-light. Warren Andrews, the stable jockey, is next, slouched over the withers of his mount. Handsome despite the slaloming nose, Indestructible Warren is the veteran of very many nasty falls. Snapped legs, smashed arms, pierced spleen, punctured lung – he knew what it meant to be mashed into hospital fodder by a storm of pummelling hooves. He is a famished, saturnine figure first thing in the morning. He struggles increasingly with his weight, and needing to do ten stone ten at Fontwell today, he spent most of yesterday in the makeshift sauna he has (an oil-drum filled with stones in his shed), eating nothing except a few Ryvita.

Simon smiles at one of the lasses, a plump teenager in jodhpurs on Mistress Of Arts – Kelly, the daughter of the local farmer from whom he rents this land. In spite of being the fattest workrider, she is the only one who wears jodhpurs. Them, and posh boots, and a purple velvet helmet. Proper little madam, Simon thought, when she first walked into the yard. 'Alright, Piers,' he says, and the head lad moves his mount into a walk and leads the slopping string down the lane. When they have left, Simon heaves himself into the old Land Rover, into its comfortless smells of cold oil and suffering canvas, and follows them to the new all-weather gallop – you need them nowadays – on the other side of the swollen stream.

*

It is eight when he steps into the hot kitchen. Mrs Miller has made his fry-up – the plate is waiting in the Aga – and the *Racing Post* has arrived. When he has eaten, he takes the paper and two Marlboros to the lavatory.

He is still in there twenty-five minutes later when James phones. 'Oh, she's fine,' he says, when James asks after Absent Oelemberg. 'Fit as a flea, she is.'

'She *is* fit this time?'

'She is.'

'So . . .' James says. 'If she's fit . . . How will you stop her winning?'

'You don't need to worry about that,' Miller says, smearing out the second Marlboro in an ashtray stuck on the toilet-roll holder.

'She's not going to win then?'

A short silence. 'I wouldn't have thought so.'

When James presses him on *how* he plans to ensure this, however, Miller just says, 'Look – you let me worry about that.'

'Okay,' James says. 'I'll let you worry about it. I'll see you at the track then. About two o'clock.'

James tries Freddy – who does not answer – and walks Hugo.

When he tries Freddy again an hour later on the way to the tube station, and he still does not answer, he starts to suspect that he will have to travel down to Sussex on his own.

Which is indeed what happens.

The train disembogues from London under an empty March sky. In the middle of a weekday the platforms of south-of-the-river stations are quiet. Nor is the train full, though there are a few other people obviously on their way to Fontwell Park – mostly old men with *Racing Posts*, and soft sandwiches in Tupperwares, and Thermoses. It has been some time since James has seen a Thermos. Watching an old man pour some tea – or whatever it is – into the plastic mug that doubles as a lid, he thinks of the large tartan one they used to take on family outings in the Seventies. Often he thinks of Katherine. His sense, when he left her flat yesterday morning, that everything was essentially okay has lost much of its positive force since then. It is now as faintly evanescent – there one moment, not the next – as the sunlight on the nodding thickets of withered wild lilac on either side of the tracks, so faint sometimes that it is imperceptible. She did have sex with him on Monday night, when all was said and done. After all the palaver, she did do that. On the other hand, he has not heard from her since, which makes him wonder, as the train winds its way through the post-winter, pre-spring landscape, whether perhaps, when she said she did not think they should see each other for a while, that was in fact what she meant.

3

The next morning he still has not heard from her. He walks Hugo. The quarter is full of students. On every street, interrupting the sombre London terraces, stand the structures where they study. More than in the past, he sometimes wonders how his life might have turned out if he had been a student himself, if he had not been so impatient, straight from school, to make some sort of mark on the world, and money. Indeed, while he was still *at* school he had started a salted-snacks wholesale business. North-London newsagents were his trade. He had his own van and he drove it himself, with special permission of the headmaster, who liked his entrepreneurial spirit, and singled it out on Speech Day as being a source of pride to the school and of value to society at large – the year was 1987. Perhaps encouraged by this head-magisterial shout-out in the humid marquee, the summer after his A-levels, instead of taking the usual path to university, he invested his profits in a takeaway-pizza franchise in Islington. Needless to say, he did not imagine spending his life as the proprietor of a pizza-delivery outfit. He was always on the lookout for something new. And then it turned out that one of his employees needed money to finance a film . . .

On Friday and Saturday nights, when they were open till two, he drove the staff home himself. Eric Garcia, who lived somewhere up the Holloway Road, was usually the last to be dropped. An introverted young man a few years older than James, he had a wide mouth and skin that was somehow simultaneously pallid and olive. He looked, James thought, not unlike a chameleon. He was about as talkative as a chameleon too, and not wanting to sit in silence while they travelled together in the front of the van, James would prod him with questions. 'Any plans for tomorrow?' he said one night.

'Probably writing,' Eric said, staring through the windscreen. 'Yeah, writing.'

The light moved to green. 'Writing what?'

Eric muttered unintelligibly.

'Sorry?'

'Just, um . . . mn . . . nm.' Eric seemed to be looking for something that had fallen down the side of the seat.

'Sorry, I didn't hear . . .'

'Screenplay I'm working on,' Eric said. 'You know, developing . . . nd . . . yeah . . .' His voice trailed off.

'A screenplay?'

'Mm . . .' He nodded.

'What sort of screenplay?'

It was a thriller, Eric eventually said.

When he sat down with it a few nights later, James very much wanted to like Eric's screenplay. Eric even had a director lined up – Julian Shoe – and the following Sunday they met to discuss the project.

With a smile on his bearded face, Shoe did most of the talking. Garcia studied the froth of his pint and piped up only when he was invited to speak. 'I met Eric through post-production on my short, *The Jokers*,' Shoe said, 'and he did some special effects, and he had some post-production contacts, and had worked at – was it Harry's?'

Garcia looked up from his pint. 'Er – yeah – Harry,' he said. 'Paintbox.'

'Yeh, that's it.'

'Harry,' said Garcia. 'Harry, yeah.'

'So I needed special effects and I was introduced to Eric. And he helped finish the special effects, and he had written this wicked script, and you know, when it was time to think about doing a feature we were both of a like mind towards . . . you know, trying that venture.'

James nodded. Shoe was, he thought, quite impressive. He had presence – sitting next to him, Garcia seemed on the point of disappearing. He seemed faint and substanceless, like a film projected in a sunny room.

They were waiting for James to speak.

Though he let them wait for a minute, though he took a slow pull of his Bloody Mary, his mind was made up. They needed money to make their film; that was the purpose of the meeting. That was why Shoe wouldn't stop smiling, why Garcia was so nervous. James had told him that he had money to invest, which was not strictly true – he would have to mortgage the pizza place.

Shoe sighed and said, 'We've been to every funding body in England.'

'Yeah?'

'Yeah.' He shrugged. 'You know.' He was still smiling, wryly now. 'It just seems nobody wants to help low-budget film-makers, for some unknown reason.'

Garcia said, more or less to himself, 'No, I know the reason. It involves *money*. People just don't want to give *money* to in-experienced film-makers.'

'Look, this is a money-making venture we're in,' Shoe said, with fresh impetus, looking James in the eye. 'You know. Film-making. It's about making a profit, ultimately. We understand that. I don't think a lot of people in the British film industry understand that. You find this really snooty attitude in the British film industry, that just because we're not ashamed of wanting to make money, people don't take us seriously. And then you look at American films, and the success of them.' He shrugged exasperatedly. 'You know.'

The film was made for not much more than £20,000. While James wondered where the money went – it did not seem to be up on the screen – Garcia and Shoe showed every sign of being pleased with what they had made; and probably feeling his inexperience, James was inclined, throughout the long and expensive process of post-production, to doubt his own intimations of mediocrity. And he wanted to doubt them. He very much wanted to doubt them.

In May, they took the film to Cannes, hoping to find a distributor there. It was shown twice in the south of France, in a screening room under the monstrous concrete molar of the Palais du Festival. They were not staying in town, in one of the luxury hotels overlooking the sea. Instead they had a mobile home in the Camping Belle Vue, somewhere miles inland. The place had a pre-season feel. The weather was tepid. The swimming pool was still under wraps, and most of the other mobile homes were unoccupied. A few tattooed pensioners in trunks promenaded under the trees, or sat in folding chairs in front of their mobile homes, or watched television inside them.

On their first evening there, James left the silent, frightened Garcia, the sulky Shoe, and went into town on his own. He parked on a meter near the station, and set out on foot for nowhere in particular, except that through some instinct he seemed to be making for the sea. Other than the ubiquitous posters, the only sign of the film festival were some tired-looking men porting video equipment through the streets. It was early evening. As he neared the seafront there were more people in evidence. Most of these people, however, were walking the other way, and when he stepped onto the windy esplanade, under the tall palms and umbrella pines, it seemed to be emptying. The African hawkers were still there with their trays of watches and lighters, but even they were sitting on the lawns under the trees, smoking. Out on the water the yachts and the superyachts, though starting to fade into the smudge of the horizon, had not yet switched on their lights.

In the mothy twilight of the *hôtel de plein air*, Garcia and Shoe were finishing off a litre of warm vodka, taking the stuff out of mugs, mixed with warm orange juice. Shoe kept slapping his large white legs – he was wearing shorts – as the invisible mosquitoes went for them. 'What are we doing for dinner?' he said when he saw James, though he was inspecting his own legs when he said it. 'I'm starving.'

'I've eaten, mate,' James said.

'Oh. Well what about us?'

'Take the van. Get something. Whatever.'

'Can't take the van.'

'Why not?'

Shoe held up the Smirnoff. 'I'm too pissed,' he said.

'Well . . . you should have thought of that.'

'I thought you'd sort something out.'

'Why?' James laughed sourly and went inside.

Shoe had turned out to be a lazy prima donna, always whining about something – he had made a fuss about not staying in a proper hotel, for instance – and leaving all the promotional heavy-lifting to James.

No one showed up to the first screening. The slot was a poor one – two o'clock, when everyone was still lingering over liquid lunches or taking siestas in their seafront hotels. Still, it was a sad moment when they told the indifferent projectionist that he might as well take the film off the spools. And while Garcia and Shoe got morosely smashed, slumped in cane chairs in the British Pavilion, James spent the whole afternoon – it was humid and hazy – schmoozing strangers to ensure that the same thing did not happen the next day.

In that, he succeeded. Half a dozen industry types turned up to the second screening, and all left within ten minutes.

So that was that.

Except, for James, there was a postscript.

On their last night one of the Hollywood studios hosted a junket in the Chateau de la Napoule, to which he had managed to wangle spare invites from someone in the British Pavilion. Still locked into his promotional mindset, he moved through the party, sweating in the dinner jacket he had optimistically packed, and trying to set up an interview for 'the talent'. The place was full of would-be showbiz journalists, with their microphones and hot little lights, and squinting into one of these lights Garcia and Shoe played for the last time at being in the movies. Their interviewer was a young woman dressed for a party, in figure-hugging black with a peach silk rose on her shoulder. She was not English; her voice had a very slight foreign intonation. Probably she was Scandinavian, though she did not look Nordic. She was short, and her hair, except for some silvery threads, was dark and wiry. Her eyes were topaz. 'And how did you go about getting actors?' she said.

'Just rang up agents,' Eric answered, drunk. 'Just rang up agents. Spoke to people. Agents . . .'

She looked uninterested. James had only just managed to persuade her to interview his men, and they were not making a strong impression. Garcia, in particular, was all over the place.

'And . . And what sort of reaction have you had?' she said, shifting a lock of hair from over her eye.

Standing off to the side, in the shadows, James looked at his polished shoes. There was a pause. He looked up. Julian was smiling steadily. 'Well, put it this way,' he said. 'We've had only one person – of all the people who've seen this film here – we've only had one person who actually hated it.'

The interviewer laughed tactlessly, and James found himself liking her. 'What did they say?' she said.

There was another pause.

'They weren't very polite,' Julian said. 'Let's just say they weren't very polite . . .'

It had been an American, who stood up no more than ten minutes into the second screening and muttered, 'Thanks for wasting my time.'

To which Shoe, with hurt British fury – 'Thanks for giving us a fair shot.'

'I have given you a fair shot,' the American said, making his way noisily to the exit. 'This is the worst picture I've ever seen here. The worst. Saying something.' Which elicited some nervous laughter from the other members of the audience. The heavy sound-proof door thudded to – and then, following an interval of perhaps a minute, the whole place emptied out.

'And,' said the Scandinavian interviewer, struggling for questions, 'what would you say about independent production?'

'It's excellent.' Garcia.

'Why?'

Garcia laughed as if it was a stupid question. 'Nobody can argue with us. You know, if they tell me I can't write . . . There's the proof. It's there, on the screen. If they tell Julian he can't direct . . . If they tell James he can't produce . . . There's the proof . . .'

'James?'

They turned to him.

He smiled warily – and immediately Garcia and Shoe were pulling him into the white light, were holding an arm each, ignoring his modest protests. He no longer wanted to be publicly paraded with them. They embarrassed him now. And the small Scandinavian interviewer was quite attractive, in a pixie-ish way. Garcia's arm was heavy on his shoulders; Shoe was still holding his left wrist.

'This is James,' Garcia said, showing a leery smile. 'Say hello, James.'

'James's the money man,' put in Shoe.

'Thanks, Julian,' James said, freeing his wrist. He wanted to shrug off Garcia's ponderous embrace too, but decided that any attempt to do this – if it led to a scuffle – might just make things worse. Smiling faintly, the interviewer was looking at him, twisting a strand of her tough hair around a finger. 'Well I would be the money man,' he said, trying to make light of the situation. 'If there was any.' He noticed that she had exquisite skin, exactly the shade of very weak and milky Nescafé.

He was pleased not to have to spend another night in the mobile home with Garcia and Shoe, who snored so sonorously that the people in the next-door home had insisted on being moved. The *hôtel de plein air* was a low, humid spot, pleasing to mosquitoes, where the turf was squelchy underfoot and the duckboards in the showers were mildewed and black. Not that Miriam was staying in the belle-époque elegance of the Carlton. She had an overpriced shoebox near the main-line station, within earshot of the platform tannoy, especially in the quiet of the early morning, through open windows. It was at such an hour that James walked through lemony sunlight to where he had left the van, with his silk-lapelled jacket over his arm.

Shoe was sitting on a white plastic chair on the smear of concrete that passed for a terrace in front of the mobile home. He was wrapped in towels, even his hair. Walking down the hill, James was surprised not to stir with irritation at the mere sight of him sitting there, towel-headed, his narrow beard still damp from the shower.

'Morning,' he said.

Shoe just nodded. He was on the phone. He spent several hours a day on the phone to his wife. For the last four mornings, James had listened to one side of an ill-tempered and seemingly endless dispute through the negligible partitions of the mobile home. This morning, however, he was pleasingly impervious to the self-importance and monotony of Julian's voice. He even felt sorry for him, to see him sitting there in his towels, negotiating some tired issue of matrimonial politics. He left him out in the mild morning air, and went inside.

There was no sign of Garcia, and when Julian finally tossed the phone down on the white plastic table, James stuck his head out and said, 'Where's Eric?'

Eric, Julian said, had vanished overnight. He had left a note. Initially, Julian had thought it was a suicide note. *By the time you read this I will be gone* . . . In fact, Eric had simply taken a train to Paris, and from there another to London. In the note, he said he had had to leave immediately – unable to stand another moment of slow-motion failure – and that he did not want to see either of them ever again.

It was nearly noon when they set out in strong sunlight, leaving the wreck of their hopes on the Côte d'Azur. They stopped for lunch at a motorway service station near Avignon – Julian eating his fill, as always when the production (i.e. James) was paying, loading his tray with starter, *steak frites* and pudding, wine, while James watched in silence. It was, however, a vacant and not a savage silence. In his pocket he had a piece of paper with Miriam's London number on it, and while Julian fed he stared out the window, at fleecy flotillas standing still in the shining monochrome sky.

*　　*　　*

The very springiness of the still air seems sad to him. Perhaps it is just the way the warming air, on these early spring days, is so sharp with transience. The end of something, the start of something new. Time. It is intrinsically sad. Last night, for instance, James had woken in the dark to hear Hugo lapping at his waterbowl in the kitchen, and for some sleep-fuddled reason he had thought – *Many years from now, when Hugo is long dead, I will remember this specific moment, in the middle of the night, and the sound of him lapping innocently at his waterbowl.* And with a start of sadness it had seemed to him that Hugo *was* long dead – how short his life was! – and that he was hearing the sound of his thirsty lapping from a deep well of time. He unleashes him. St George's Gardens is a little graveyard. Daffodils sprout eagerly between the tombs. Hidden behind the School of Pharmacology, it is usually very quiet – this morning, the only other human presence is a man tidying away last year's leaves. Hugo trots over to a white stone obelisk, and pisses on its pitted plinth.

Somewhere, in one of the trees, the first tit of spring is singing. He stands there listening to its song – its up-down song. Two notes, starting on the higher one. Up-down up-down up-down up-down up-down. It sings them in sets of five. The sound of spring in London. Up and down. Like the next few days. The next few days are up and down.

When he finally spoke to her, for the first time since leaving her flat on Tuesday morning, she sounded irritable. (That he took to be a positive sign, since it was not him she was irritated with.) She said someone was off sick . . .

'What, someone else?'

'There's a flu going round.'

. . . and she had been asked to do two nightshifts, tonight and tomorrow, starting at ten.

Testing the meaning of 'for a while' – as in, 'I don't think we should see each other for a while' – he suggested they meet in the early evening.

'Maybe.' she said, as if thinking about it. 'Phone me later.' (*Up!*)

He did phone her later, in the middle of the afternoon, and she seemed to have lost interest in the idea. She said vaguely that she wasn't sure what time she would be home – she was out somewhere – and that she would phone him.

Hours passed without her doing so. (*Down.*)

Five fifteen found him in a Spitalfields pub with Mike, a friend from his City days. When they were settled with their pints, James asked after his wife and kids. They were fine, Mike said. He had thickened since James first knew him. His wrists, his neck. Though he wasn't losing his hair – or not much –

somehow his head had an increasingly taut, polished look. He had taken, in the last month or two, to wearing a three-piece suit. (James was in nondescript mufti – designer jeans, a soft zippered top, Adidas.) Night was starting to fall outside on Commercial Street when Mike went to the bar for a second pair of pints and James tried Katherine again. When she did not answer he felt deflated. He started to tell Mike, in outline, what was happening. 'Yeah?' Mike said. Though not unsympathetic, the way he said it made the story seem insignificant. It made it seem as if next to his own unmentioned worries – London school fees, the state of the markets, the travails of a long-standing marriage – James's situation was essentially frivolous.

And though he was in fact a few years younger, James felt that Mike was older than him now, that he had managed the transition to a sort of maturity.

His phone let him know, in the usual way, that he had a text message. The message said – *I'm home! Where are you?*

'What is it?' Mike said.

James was staring at the screen of his phone. 'I've got to go after this pint, mate.'

'Fair enough.'

He phoned her as he walked under the heatless lights of Spitalfields Market – an empty space after dark, except for the metal frames of the stalls and their multiple pale shadows – and said he was on his way to Moorgate tube.

They met in the Old Queen's Head. 'I'm working later,' she pointed out, when he asked if she wanted a drink. He himself was quite tipsy from the two pints he had had with Mike, and perhaps also from the unexpected pleasure of her presence. (He put out his hand and touched her.) Whatever the reason, he was in fine form. He told her about Fontwell Park yesterday – upmarket pastoral, no shortage of men in green tweed suits and fedoras – and about Miller. Miller was one of the green-tweed-suit wearers. He looked, James said, like an ambitious farmer on about a million quid of EU subsidies a year.'

'And what happened to your horse?' she said.

'She fell.'

'She fell!'

Even later, James felt unable simply to ask Miller if the fall – and the nightmarish ten minutes that followed while the screens were swelling out on the track – was planned, was part of the trainer's plot, or whether it was just something that happened. He found himself unable even to insinuate that it might have been planned. It just seemed too shocking – that *that* was the way Miller had planned to stop her. And indeed, while the screens were still up and keeping their terrible secret, and James was standing there waiting for the worst with tears in his eyes, Miller had said, 'Wasn't expecting that.' Unfortunately, the way he said it, working a lighter, was not entirely persuasive. 'Normally she jumps super,' he said later, when the suspense was over. 'She's schooled super. Don't know what happened there.'

'No,' James said. 'No.' He tried to inject some scepticism into his voice. It was the most he felt able to do.

In the Old Queen's Head, Katherine looked at her watch – a pretty little Swiss thing – and said it was time for her to leave.

'It's only half eight!' he protested.

'I know. I have to go home, eat something, have a shower.'

'I'll walk you home then.'

It was a very short walk.

'How is she now, your horse?' she said as they walked.

'I think she's okay. I phoned Miller this morning. He said she was okay.'

He sat on a stool in her white kitchen, with its sash window overlooking the street, while she ate something. He seemed to have lost his pizzazz. He sat on the stool watching her spread pâté on toast. He just shook his head when she asked if he wanted some. They had sparkled in the pub. They had sparkled easily, without effort. It had seemed then that everything was okay. Now, in the kitchen, a question which it had been possible to ignore in public seemed to be pressing itself on them insistently. She was nervous and impatient with him, as if he had overstayed his welcome. He should not have lingered, he thought.

'I should be off,' he said.

Her mouth was full, and she just said, 'Okay.'

He went to the hall for his jacket. 'Okay?' he said when he had put it on.

'M-hm.' She had finished eating and was hurriedly tidying up, wiping surfaces near the toaster. When he went to kiss her, she seemed to spot something that needed seeing to on the floor and, stooping, started to mop the old linoleum. He just stood there, waiting for her to finish, until she laughed, while still mopping, and said, 'Sorry.'

'That's okay,' he said. 'When you're ready.'

Finally she threw the damp sponge into the sink and pushed a stray piece of hair out of her eyes. 'Bye,' she said.

Somewhat tentatively, he put his hand on the woolly swoop of her waist. She was wearing a long wool jumper. 'Will I see you this weekend?' he said.

'I don't know. If you want to.'

'I do want to.' To that she said nothing. 'Well,' he said. 'When?'

'I don't know. I don't know how I'm going to feel. After the nightshift. Phone me.'

'Okay.'

He pulled her towards him. She yielded to this pull, though if she was smiling it was the faintest smile he had ever seen – and then, seeming to withdraw even that, she lowered her face. He stroked one of her transparent eyebrows with the tip of his little finger. The neon tube over the sink was humming.

4

She visited him the next morning, straight from the nightshift. She had phoned in the small hours and said she would. For some time she had whispered into the phone while he lay there listening, half asleep. She told him she didn't know what she wanted or what she felt. That was why she had kissed him in the kitchen last night, kissed him properly just as he was leaving, her tongue in his mouth struggling, it seemed, to obliterate its own intransigent singleness.

He heard her shoes on the metal steps outside his window. For a moment she seemed to pause in the wet area. He sat up and inspected his watch. It was twenty past eight.

'It's sweltering in here,' she said, ignoring his total nudity, and heading straight for the living room.

'Is it?'

'Why don't you put some clothes on? And turn the heating down.' As she went through the hall she twisted the thermostat herself. He followed, shrugging on his dressing gown. 'How was it?' he said. 'The nightshift.'

She looked very tired as she stepped out of her wet shoes. With a small sigh, she sat down on the old wooden swivel-chair. Under her weight it too emitted a small sigh. It went with the stupidly huge desk. Its back was a padded U on little wood pilasters. Its seat looked as if it had taken the shallow impression of a sitting arse.

She said there were 'loads of hookers' in the hotel overnight.

'Hookers?'

'Yes, loads of them. I mean, up-market ones. You know, escorts.'

'There were loads of them?'

She nodded. 'I mean, I was expecting *some*.'

'How did you know they were hookers?'

'Young women on their own. Tottering out through the lobby in the middle of the night. Without looking at me. In dresses slashed up to the hip. Holding sparkly little handbags.' She laughed. 'It's obvious. I kept thinking of their parents,' she said. 'I imagine their parents never know.'

'No, probably not . . .'

'Some of those girls must make loads, seriously loads.'

'I'm sure . . .'

'Supposedly they're all saving up for something. They look quite sensible, most of them. Like the sort of people who have ISAs and things. I suppose it's just a way of getting where they want to be in life.'

'And the hotel doesn't mind?'

'There's nothing we can do about it!'

'Isn't there?'

'What can we do about it? We'd lose masses of business if we tried to stop them! Everyone would just go next door to the –'

'Everyone?'

'Most of our best customers.'

'I'm not surprised . . .'

'You would be,' she said. 'You think you know, but you don't.'

'I dont think I know,' he said. 'I *don't* know . . .'

'There's some VIP staying,' she said. 'Some African president, with a whole big entourage. Maybe that's why there were so many of them last night.'

'Which president?'

'I'm not supposed to tell you.'

She told him.

'I've never heard of him.'

'That doesn't surprise me.'

He laughed. 'What do you mean?'

'Honestly,' she said, 'I wasn't supposed to tell you.'

'Why not?'

'You mustn't tell anyone.'

'Who would I tell?'

'I don't know. Your friend.'

'Who?'

'The journalist. The one you set up the magazine with.'

'Freddy? He wouldn't be interested in that. I'm just going to feed Hugo. Do you want tea?'

'Yes.'

She examined a hole in the heel of her tights. She had just been saying whatever popped into her head. Just talking. Talking. Just talking. It was nice to talk like that. Drizzle pittered quietly on the skylight. The only light in the living room sank to it past high walls – it seemed to lie in the depths of a well, this subterranean hidey-hole full of heaped-up stuff. Only a few strips and squares of tired carpet, the colour of pale jade, were visible. The largest was in front of the TV, where there was the plastic tangle of a Playstation, one of those men's toys . . . She touched the orbit of unfeeling skin on her heel.

'What's this?' she said.

'What?' He put the tea on the desk and his hands on her shoulders. 'It's a grape stem . . .'

'Who's Izette?' The grape-stem was in an unsealed envelope, on which James had written *Izette*.

'She's South African,' he said.

'And?'

'And? And I'm selling that to her.'

'What?'

'The grape stem.'

'You're *selling* it to her?'

'Yes.'

He started to massage her shoulders. She shrugged him off and, turning to look up at him, said, 'What do you mean you're *selling* it to her?'

'I put it on eBay.'

She laughed. 'What are you talking about? Why does she want to buy it?'

'The shape, I suppose.'

He had found it one evening while eating grapes, and a few days later, in a spirit of experimentation more than anything else, he had quietly taken some photos and put it on eBay.

'What do you mean the shape?' Katherine said. 'She thinks it's miraculous or something?'

'I've no idea,' he said. 'It's her mother who's buying it. She saw it on the Internet in South Africa . . .'

'This is absurd!'

'Why?'

'Did you say it was miraculous or something?'

'No . . .'

'Did you say it was holy?'

'No,' he said. 'I didn't.'

'Who did?'

He sighed. 'I don't know. People on the Internet. I don't know who they are. There are various threads . . .'

'And how much are you taking from these people, these poor South Africans?'

He shoved his hands into the pockets of his dressing gown. 'A few hundred dollars . . .'

'*A few hundred dollars?*' she screeched.

In fact it had sold for more than two thousand. He said, 'What? I haven't lied to them. What are you so upset about?'

'What am I so upset about? It's *immoral*.'

'Why?'

'You're taking advantage of these people.'

'No I'm not . . .'

'You *are*!'

'I'm not. If they want to buy it –'

'It's a worthless . . . It's *worthless*!'

'They don't think it is.'

'*You* do. *You* wouldn't pay for it.'

'So what? I don't think it's holy. If I thought it was holy, I might.'

'Can't you see,' she said, 'that what you're doing is wrong?'

With his hands in his pockets, James said, 'No. I didn't say it was holy. I never said it was holy. I was totally upfront with these people. What they do with their money is up to them.'

She stared at him with her mouth open.

'They *want* it,' he said. 'There were hundreds of them.' That was true. 'The money's just a way of deciding who wants it most. Isn't it quite patronising of you,' he said, suddenly thinking of something else, 'to think you know better than they do how they should spend their money? They don't need you to tell them how to spend their money. Who are you to tell them what to do? They're free to do what they want with their money.'

'That's just a way of excusing your cynicism,' she said. 'You know what you're doing is wrong.'

For a moment the only sound was what was now a downpour drumming on the skylight. She stood up and slipped her feet into her shoes.

'You're going?' He sounded surprised.

'M-hm.'

'Why don't you stay here? You look exhausted. You're not upset, are you? This hasn't upset you?'

'No,' she said. She was putting on her white puffa jacket. 'I do think it's dishonest.'

'Why?' he said exasperatedly. 'It's not *dishonest*. Why is it dishonest?'

She thought about this for a while. 'Okay,' she said, 'it's not dishonest. It's not very nice, though. If they want it so much, and you think it's worthless, you should just let them have it.'

'Why don't you stay?'

She sighed. Then her shoulders slumped and she fell against him. He put his arms around her. 'Stay,' he said. 'You can sleep in my bed. I won't make any noise. I have to go out and do some things anyway. Okay? Okay?' She nodded – he felt her head move on his shoulder.

When he had put her to bed, wearing a set of pyjamas that he never wore himself, he took the umbrella and walked Hugo. The lights were on in offices and students hurried through the streets of Bloomsbury in hoods. He had some toast and coffee, and then a shower. All of which took place to the varying sounds of the rain – on the skylight, on the umbrella, pinging on the area steps, splashing in the mineral puddles of the melting area floor.

*

He was lying on the sofa with the TV on – the volume so low that at first the sound seemed to be off – waiting for the two-ten at Sandown, when she appeared in the doorway, wearing his tartan pyjamas and looking extremely muzzy. 'What time is it?' she said.

'Two.'

She moaned and smothered her face with her hands – she had only slept for five hours. Moving slowly, she picked her way through the stuff on the floor and lay down on the sofa with him. Lying there warmly squashed together, he put his hand inside the pyjama jacket and stroked her soft stomach. (*Up – very much so.*) There was a loud sluicing sound from somewhere in the same vicinity. 'Are you hungry?' he said. 'Do you want some-thing to eat?' She laughed and said she wanted to have a shower first and stood up shakily, tipping over with a squeal when she was halfway up and poking him with a sharp elbow.

When he heard the shower start – not a very vigorous sound – he stood up himself and took her a towel. She was standing in the stall, the plastic of which – limescaled and wet – was only partially transparent, with her wet hair trailing over her face and stuck to her white shoulders, and water trickling down her long pale body. It was not very warm in there. The only heating was a single elec-tric bar over the door, pathetically amplified by a piece of scorched tinfoil. He tended to turn it on an hour in advance, and feel its just perceptible warmth on his shoulders, like the weakest sort of sunlight, when he stepped out of the stall. Though it was too late now, he pulled the string that turned it on, noticeably soiled where his and other fingers had seized it innumerable times, and said, 'Here's a towel.' She started slightly. With her eyes shut she had not seen or heard that he was there. 'Thanks,' she said.

He watched the two-forty from Sandown, the novices' chase, while she sat naked on his bed drying her hair. When it was over, the winning trainer, Venetia Williams, talked to an interviewer about some Festival hopes of hers. 'One hopes,' she said, with a wistful smile, over the whine of the hairdryer. 'One hopes. Of course, if it doesn't happen one mustn't be disappointed. But one hopes.'

When she was dried and dressed, they went out and, holding each other tightly, traversed the windy tray of Brunswick Square. They had a late lunch at an Italian place on Lamb's Conduit Street. When they left the restaurant it was twilight. On the way home they passed the Renoir and had a look at what was on. All of which made him think, as they stood there looking at the programme, of another day when they had done exactly the same things. That Tuesday in the first week of February, when London was under a hard, dark frost. That February afternoon he had fed her forkfuls of strawberry tart while she looked through his limited selection of DVDs, finally and sentimentally settling on *Brief Encounter* – which he had never seen; it had been free with a Sunday newspaper. They had not been watching the film long, however, when he noticed that she had surreptitiously undone her jeans and had her hand inside them, and though she went very pink and smiled distractedly, she did not stop what she was doing. He said, 'I doubt this film has ever had that effect on anyone until now.' Which elicited a small hiccup of a laugh. Then he pulled the jeans first halfway down her thighs, then over her knees and finally free of her feet. The film plodded stoically on, oblivious to what was happening on the sofa. 'There's your train,' said Celia Johnson. 'Yes, I know,' said Trevor Howard.

'Squeeze my nipples,' said Katherine. 'It will make me have an orgasm. Use your teeth . . .' she whispered urgently. 'Your . . .' It overtook her in mid-phrase, a sudden open-mouthed expulsion of air from her lungs as she struggled to seize him with all four of her limbs, her shouts quickly subsiding into a series of soblike sounds, quiet sobs. She shuddered as some sort of aftershock seemed to tickle through her, and went limp in his embrace. They lay there for a minute until she sighed and with an exaggerated *mwah!* kissed him on the mouth. Putting her hand on it, she said she had to decide what word she was going to use for his . . . Well that was the point. She needed a word for it. All the existing words, she thought, sounded vulgar, were swearwords, or silly, or had a frigid medical neutrality. With such an imperfect vocabulary it was not an easy thing to speak of. She would have to find her own word, she said, with her hand on it. A private word. Of necessity, a private word.

As they had that afternoon in February, they had sex on the sofa, and she left at eightish, to do her second nightshift.

*

Saturday was Sunderland's Imperial Cup day at Sandown Park. The one o'clock train from Waterloo to Esher was full and most of the people on it were on their way to the track. There were loudmouths in office suits and tubby young women in tiny dresses despite the frost still lingering in the shadows of the trackside playing fields of south-west London. James spent the journey squashed in next to a man in his twenties, one of a party of men in suits and the only one of them to have a seat. His hair, plastered to his forehead at the front, was otherwise massively mussed up and stiffened with mousse. The tips of his tan winkle-pickers were medieval in their elongated pointiness. He might have had a hangover – his pale-lashed eyes were pink, and he was telling the others, in a strong hoarse voice, how much he had drunk last night.

It was a cold, sunny day at Sandown Park. From the stand, London was visible in the distance. It filled the whole horizon. James took the escalator down to the paddock to inspect the horses in the first, the novices' handicap hurdle. He was passing through the Esher Hall when he saw someone who looked familiar. It was J. P. McManus, the legendary punter, the patron saint of the winter game, standing there in the tatty hangar of the hall like any impoverished mug holding a plastic pint pot. Telling himself that if this man had the humility to hang out in the Esher Hall wearing a shapeless middle-management over-coat, then the least he deserved was to be left alone, James did not introduce himself or ask J. P. what he was on. (Probably nothing. His approach to punting was well known. It was a matter of *price*. Everybody knew that. They knew that serious pros did not look for winners, they looked for *prices*.) He just watched him for a minute talking shyly to some people he seemed to know, and then took the escalator upstairs.

Later, Dusky Warbler, a horse he had been following all winter, very nearly won the Imperial Cup. He was sent off at twenty to one, and James had £10 each way with one of the scarfed and hatted bookmakers in the huge shadow of the stand. It was a photo finish. The shrieking peaked as the two horses passed the line together. 'Pho-dagraph, pho-dagraph,' intoned an unflappable voice over the PA system. When a minute later the other horse was named the winner, there was some tattered shouting and the stand started to empty. Trooping downstairs to the winner's enclosure on the far side of the paddock, James was still in a sweat of exhilaration.

She thought he was in London. She wanted to meet now. He

explained that that wasn't possible – he was in Surrey – and she sounded frustrated when she said, 'Well when *can* you meet?'

They met at eight – or quarter past, he was late – in Mecklenburgh Street. She was waiting at the top of the area steps. She was, he thought, surprisingly smartly dressed. She was perfumy. Her shoes had a nice height of heel. The question was: where were they going to eat? As they walked through Mecklenburgh Square she put it to him. 'Where are we going to eat?' she said. The plan, it had been his idea, was to make an evening of it. (Hence the nice dress, the earrings, the heels.) However, he was tired – all that wintry fresh air and movement – and he didn't mind where they ate, as long as it was nearby. For some time he didn't say anything. Her heels ticked off the seconds. 'What do you feel like?' he said eventually.

'I don't want to have to decide,' she said. 'I want you to take me somewhere.'

'Okay.' They walked on in silence for a few steps. 'What do you feel like, though?'

'I don't want to have to decide!' she said heatedly. 'That's the point. I want you to decide.'

'Fine,' he said. 'I'll decide.'

They ended up nowhere more imaginative than Carluccio's. He suggested it when she started to show obvious signs of fed-upness. Her shoes were hurting her – she had not dressed to wander around for half an hour. And she was tired too, of course. They were installed at a table, furnished with wine and antipasti. He told her that he had seen J. P. McManus at Sandown. 'Who's J. P. McManus?' she said, eating a succulent olive, dripping spots of oil on the tablecloth.

She was talking about something else when he lost the thread of what she was saying. He was looking expressionlessly over her shoulder, out through the front of the restaurant – opposite was a line of terraced houses with fanlights and plain facades, like the ones on Mecklenburgh Street. Student flats, probably . . .

'What is it?' she said, turning in her seat to see what he was looking at.

'Oh . . .' he murmured. 'Nothing.'

'What?' she insisted, still looking over her shoulder.

'No, I was just looking at those houses on the other side of the street.'

'Why?'

'I once looked at a flat in one of them.'

'Oh. Did you take it?'

'No.'

'Why not?'

He shrugged. 'It wasn't very nice.'

She waited for him to say more.

He didn't.

Then the waiter floated up to them and they ordered some dessert. She suggested they take it home and have it there. So he asked the waiter to pack it up for them, and also to pay. This seemed to take a long time, and while they were waiting, he yawned, shielding his mouth with his hand.

When he had finished yawning, he smiled at her. She looked desolate. There were dark indents under her eyes. 'What is it?'

'We're just not having fun,' she said.

'What do you mean?'

'I mean, we're not having fun.'

'Aren't we?'

'We're like them,' she said. He turned and saw a man and a woman just sitting at a table, looking off in different directions. 'They haven't said a word to each other since they got here.'

'Then we're not like them.'

However, they started to walk home in silence.

'What is it?' he said. 'What's the matter?'

And she said the same thing – 'We're just not having *fun*! You yawned. That's not fun.'

'I yawned . . .?'

'When we were waiting for the bill. How fun is that?' she said, upset. 'That's not exciting.'

'So what if I yawned? I'm tired.'

'You're tired. Oh,' she said sarcastically, 'that's good.' She laughed in dismay.

'Yes, I'm tired.'

'Well . . .' She shrugged. 'Okay. You're tired.' They had slowed to a dawdle. Now they stopped. 'What do you want me to say to that?'

'You don't have to say anything.'

'Well . . .' She seemed at a loss.

'I'm tired,' he said. 'Why is that such a problem?'

She sighed.

She was stiff and aloof in his arms.

She said, 'It's a problem because . . . we're not having fun.'

'No, we're not. Not now.' Their foreheads touching, they were looking down at her shoes. 'Don't put so much pressure on things. You put so much pressure on things,' he said. She seemed to nod and they started to walk again, slowly. 'We're tired. That's all.'

Leaving her shoes in the hall, she went into the living room while he unpacked the dessert.

When he joined her, she was looking at something on the Internet. Whatever it was, she seemed very interested in it. 'You have some first,' she said, without taking her eyes off the screen. He did, and then passed it to her. 'What are you doing?' he said.

'Just . . .'

'What?'

He looked at the screen – it was nothing in particular, just news. He started to massage her shoulders. She moused a link and he unzipped her dress, first having to lift her hair to find the zipper's little tug. Then, while she muttered something about the news story she was perusing, he fiddled with the fasteners of her bra. Seemingly oblivious to this, she leaned forward to scroll down as he tried to pull the dress off her shoulder. That was physically impossible – it was supposed to go over her head. She still had her eyes on the screen when he swivelled her away from it, lifted her up – she squealed – and staggered next door, where they toppled onto the bed. For a few minutes they snogged and tussled in the mess of sheets.

He had just peeled off her tights when she sat up and smoothed her hair. 'I was looking at something on the Internet,' she said. Weltering there, half undressed, with a hard-on, he made a token effort to hold on to her. When that failed, he lay there for a minute or two staring into space and thoughtfully stroking himself through his trousers.

'I'm just taking Hugo for a walk,' he said. She was still on the Internet.

'M-hm.'

'I'll be back in a few minutes.'

'Okay.'

He did a slow lap of Mecklenburgh Square and found her at work with a toothbrush. (She was always fiercely energetic with a toothbrush in her hand, the head of her own was terrifyingly splayed and flattened.) She had tied her hair up. Her dress was still unzipped and the exposed skin, a wide tapering swathe the length of her spine, looked like old ivory in the forty-watt light. He kissed it while she washed her mouth out.

Her mouth was wet and minty. They were standing next to the bed, trying to kiss and undress at the same time, his jeans and shorts fettering his ankles. It turned out she wasn't wearing any knickers. Then he was supine on the bed with her astraddle him. She still had the dress on, though he was already inside her. From where his head lay he was able to peer in a haze of pleasure over the hairless plain of his torso, over the low hillock of his stomach with its one winding path of hair, to the site of that impossibly exquisite prehension. 'Is this nice? Is this nice?' she said. In a single movement she pulled the dress over her head and was naked. At the sight of her whole skin the pleasure intensified terminally. He put his hands on her working hips and swung her off him. And then he was over her, looking down at her, at her streaming tears, her oscillating midriff, the square prow into which he was . . .

His weight on her seemed to double from one second to the next. She felt the slippery warmth on her stomach and lower down. She smelled its white, polleny scent. His head sagged.

'I'm sorry.' The words emerged as a single exhalation.

'It's okay.' She stroked his hair. 'I'm sure you'll . . . have a second wind.'

He nodded, and kissed her soft nipple – which happened to be next to his mouth – though he was fairly sure he would not. He felt unimaginably tired. He felt as if he would be able to fall asleep instantly and sleep for twelve hours. However, she was waiting for him to do something, and the longer he just lay there, slobbering on her tit, the more utterly exhausted he would feel. He struggled to sit up. 'I'm sorry,' he said again.

'That's okay.' She was still lying there, her legs parallel to each other. Heatless semen slid down from the smooth shadow of her navel and matted the russet stubble of her pubic hair.

'Have you got something to wipe that up?' she said.

Leaning over the edge of the bed, he picked up his shorts.

His lack of desire, as he wiped her – wiped her stomach and

the seam of her pussy like an exhausted waiter wiping a table – was extraordinary. He felt like he would never want to fuck another woman in his life. In the last minute, the way he saw her had undergone a profound metamorphosis. He noticed the sanded soreness around her mouth, the zones of irritation – little livid spots – where she had shaved part of her pubic hair, the twofold meatiness of her sex . . . When he had finished wiping her he threw the smeared shorts onto the floor. Then he stepped into the bathroom and, holding his shrivelled prick, made water in the dark. When he had done that, he filled a glass from the kitchen tap.

She had pulled the duvet over her and was lying on her side with her face away from the light. It was with a sort of sad, shameful relief that he saw she had put on his pyjamas while he was away. 'Do you want some water?' he said quietly, and she sat up and took the glass.

*

The sound of rain splashing and trickling in the area. It was lovely to lie there in the warmth, still half asleep, holding her small body and listening to the rain. He would have liked to lie there for hours. For years. He listened to it intermittently pinging on the metal steps – sometimes it pinged several times in quick succession, sometimes there were long intervals – and whingeing quietly in the drain. She was wearing his pyjamas. He squeezed her and she whispered something. He stroked her instep with his foot.

She said 'What time is it?'

He did not want to move but he leaned over and looked at his watch. He had to stare at it for a few seconds in the semi-darkness. It was surprisingly late. It was nearly ten.

'Will you make some coffee?' she said.

He mumbled something and a minute later swung his long white legs out from under the duvet. He was pulling on his shorts when he said, 'Oh.'

'What?' she said.

'They're ...' He stopped.

'... stiff with spunk.'

'Yeah.'

It was at this point, pulling on the spunk-stiff shorts, that he remembered the wash he had put on yesterday morning, and that it was still sitting wet in the machine.

The music of the rain was less lovely now that he was no longer in bed. It seemed to lay siege to the flat's ill-lit interiors. Hugo greeted him in the hall, in the grey light that leaked through the small pane of glass over the front door. His white tail waved like a shredded flag. When he yawned the sound was like something moving on unoiled hinges. James patted his head, and scratched his ears, and in the windowless vault of the kitchenette put on the kettle. While it was heating up he opened a kilogram tin of offal and fish-meal and forked the pinkish paste into the St Bernard-sized feed-bowl. He washed the fork while Hugo set to without finesse.

'Do you want something to eat?' he said to her.

She shook her head.

He told her about the stuff in the washing machine. 'I think I'll have to wash it again.'

She didn't seem terribly interested.

'I might as well do that now.'

The old washing machine was in the kitchen, the hard plastic hook of the outflow pipe still secured on the edge of the sink. When he had started it, he went back to the bedroom. She was moving about, picking up her things from the floor, putting them on. 'Are you leaving?' he said.

'M-hm.'

'Why?'

'I want to go home.'

'Why don't you stay?' he said. 'For a while.'

'I want to have a bath,' she said. His tiny bathroom had only the mouldy shower stall.

'Stay for a while. It's pissing down out there.'

'I know,' she said, sorting her tights out. 'Have you got an umbrella?'

For a few seconds he said nothing.

'Have you got one?' she said, looking up.

'Yes.'

'Is it okay if I borrow it?'

'Of course.'

He fetched it from the living room, where the rain was thrumming noisily on the skylight.

'Why don't you stay?' he said, even though she was now dressed and looking for her shoes.

'I want to go home. I want a bath.'

They were standing in the hall. He switched on the overhead light and she put her shoes on. 'Is everything okay?'

Without hesitation, she shook her head and said, 'No.'

'I'm sorry,' he said. When he hugged her she just stood there. He handed her the umbrella. Then he opened the front door and she stepped out into the puddled area.

'I'll phone you later,' he said, as she shoved the umbrella open.

'Okay.'

'See you.'

Without turning as she started up the metal steps, she kissed her fingers and waggled them in the air.

*

In the early evening he took the Number 19 to Highbury and Islington. From his seat at the front of the top deck as it plied its way through the wet twilight, he tried Freddy again. He needed to pass on what Miller had said. Miller had said, first of all, that the mare had been assigned a mark of eighty by the handicapper, which he thought was a touch on the high side. 'Shouldn't stop her, though,' he said. (And James was worried by that *shouldn't* – he would very much have preferred *won't*. He was planning to wager every penny he had left on her, and was attached to the fantasy that it was impossible that she would lose.) And then Miller said, 'Listen, I don't think you should be at Huntingdon tomorrow. Not your mate either.'

'Oh?' James said. 'Why not?'

'Looks like you weren't expecting it to win that way.'

'I see,' James said. He wanted to be there when she won, however, so he said, 'Is that necessary?'

There was a stubborn silence.

Then Miller said, 'I think it is.'

'You're sure?' James said.

'I'm sure. So give Huntingdon a miss tomorrow. Okay?'

James needed to pass this on to Freddy. He also wanted to emphasise to him, not for the first time, the importance of putting the money on properly – meaning in small quantities throughout the London area. Not all in one place. And not on the Internet, that was very important. Freddy said he understood. When he had finished speaking to him, James pocketed his phone and stared at the blue perspective of Theobald's Road.

He was on his way to a dinner party in Highbury Fields. It was in a small first-floor flat that had been done up like a large house, so that it felt like a doll's house, a very expensive one, obsessive in its attention to detail. The hostess – an ex of his from long ago – was trying to live, and entertain, like her parents.

Thus the ten diners were squeezed into the little living room, in which there was also – somehow – a table set for ten. When they sat down to eat, it was extremely hot. Faces shone with sweat in the candlelight, and people kept apologising for elbowing each other. Shoehorned in next to a man who used to be in the army and was now in insurance, and a woman whose face was vaguely familiar from somewhere, he was not properly engaged with the situation. He talked a lot without any interest in what he was saying or in what was being said to him. While the main course was being served, he manoeuvred his way out of his place and withdrew to the minuscule loo. On his own, it struck him that he was quite drunk. He made some excuse and left straight after dessert, and it was like a liberation to walk out into the fresh night air and unurban quiet of Highbury Fields. The old street lamps made pools of pale light in the wide darkness. And now that the day was done, now that all the last preparations for the 'touch' were in place, his mind was empty except for one insistent thing –

Is everything okay?

No.

Everything is not okay. Standing in Highbury Fields – he has stopped walking and is just standing there, listening unsoberly to the wind in the trees – he feels a terrible need for things to be okay. From where he is, he would be able to walk to her flat in twenty minutes. Less.

'I'm in Highbury,' he says. 'I've just been to a dinner party. Is it okay if I come over?'

'Of course,' she says.

And now he is walking quickly towards Essex Road. The way she said Of course – that on its own has helped immensely. He is practically jogging towards Essex Road now, through the Islington streets and squares he used to know so well.

He finds her watching television with Summer. They watch television for an hour. Later, when they are in bed, he starts to talk about last night. She says, 'I was upset because you didn't *say* anything. That's why I was upset.'

He says, 'I didn't say anything because I felt so bad.'

'Well . . .' She seems exasperated. '*Say* something! Maybe if you said something you wouldn't feel so bad.' He just stares at her. She touches his face. 'I don't care about what happened. I don't care about *that*! If you don't talk to me, though, if you don't say anything, if you just go to sleep . . . How do you think that makes me feel?'

'I'm sorry,' he says.

'You've been feeling bad about it all day, haven't you?' He nods and she strokes his hair. 'I'm sorry I was mean with you this morning. That wasn't very nice of me.'

'It's okay. We had such a lovely time on Friday,' he says.

'Yes.'

'Why was that so lovely and yesterday such a fucking disaster?' She laughs. 'I don't know. Why?'

'I don't know either.'

'You see, I didn't even know that you thought that!'

'Thought what?'

'That yesterday was a fucking disaster.'

'Of course it was.'

She shoves him playfully. 'Well, how do I know you think that if you don't *say* anything? I thought you thought everything was okay.'

'No . . .'

'That was the worst thing for me.'

'I didn't think that . . .'

'*Say* something!' She sits up and has a drink of water. Then she says, 'Do you want some water?'

The way she says words like 'water'. The way she meticulously enunciates the Ts in the middle of those words – it makes him want to kiss her. *Why that?* he wonders, shaking his head – he does not want any water. *Why does* that *make me want to kiss her?* Why does it matter why? Whatever. It just does. He pulls her towards him and kisses her.

5

Four o'clock on Monday morning and Simon Miller is up in the washed-out light of the laptop monitor. His face looks puffier in that light – his eyes peer out from over a whole series of seamed, sleepless pouches. Two-fingeredly he types in a password, thinking of last Wednesday night in the horse transport, pulled over in a shuttered Sussex lane with the hazards flashing. *Then* he had little Kelly Nicholls out of them poncey jodhpurs at last, though it weren't easy, they were that tight . . . Logged in, he mouses his way towards the two o'clock at Huntingdon. And horses kept fartin of course. That's one problem, having it off in a horse transport . . . The market for the two o'clock is now on the screen and still sleepily savouring the memory of Wednesday – precious memories! – he scrolls down looking for his horse.

She is hardly a proper outsider at all. The top price on offer is less than twenty to one. He scratches his head and wonders who has been forcing the price in. Officially only five people know about the touch. Himself. The owners. Piers. And Tom. Word will be out though. Owners always talk, or take young Tom. He were shaggin that scrawny thing, the vet's assistant. He woulder told *her*. Probably fockin desperate to impress her, what with her being taller and intelligenter and posher than him. (None of which is that hard, mind.) He lights his second Marlboro of the day. He knows the markets. There is pressure on the price already. He'd be surprised if she was more than twelves with the firms in the morning.

As soon as it is light, leaving Piers to supervise the work session, he takes the Range Rover and drives to Trumpington. The sky is overcast except for in the east where it seems to have been torn open and a flame-blue pallor is sinking through like pigment into water, flooding the landscape with soft cold light. The wet meadows. The ploughed fields. He pulls up outside the Londis in Trumpington and switches off the engine. Kelly is not there yet, and he stands in the nippy morning air, smoking. There is no-one else in the street. Still, it is not quiet, exactly. The mumble of the M11 is faintly audible, and then a substantial plane passes quite low overhead, moaning, on its way in to land at Cambridge airport. Maybe a load of Sheikh Mo's horses, Simon thinks, watching it from his hunched shoulders, home from their winter in Dubai . . . Lucky for some. When Kelly turns up in her little Fiat – she only got her licence last year – he is back in the Range Rover with the heating on.

She sits on the toasty leather of the passenger seat and when he has finished feeling and kissing her – he has not shaved, his stubble is sharp – he produces an envelope. 'Thousand quid,' he says. His voice smells of smoke. 'I'm trusting you with it.' He tells her to drive to Northampton and then Milton Keynes and Luton and visit twenty betting shops putting some of the money on in each, not the same amount in all of them, and never more than £100 in one place. She takes the envelope and looks inside it. Then she zips it into the pocket of her fleece. He says, 'Our little secret, okay?' She nods. 'Okay,' he says. 'And one other thing. You're not to phone me or send me any messages today – not about this or anything else. Understood?'

'I understand,' she says, looking at herself in the wing mirror.

He stares at her with undisguised hunger. He was once handsome. Now his strong chin, halved like an arse, is submerged in a wall of wanton obesity. Years as an unusually tall jockey, starving himself to do the weight, the fingers down the throat, the tears, the fockin eating disorders – since all that ended (1990, a horrendous fall at Uttoxeter) he hasn't had the heart to deny himself much. His jawline went long ago.

His eyes are still fixed on her.

When he starts the deep-voiced engine, she says, 'Where are we going?'

And he says, 'Somewhere we'll not be seen.'

On the way home he meets another vehicle in the lane near the yard. The lane is only just wide enough for them to pass each other, and in fact they stop, and electric windows hum down. The driver of the other vehicle is Jeremy Nicholls, Simon's landlord. Nicholls sticks his blonde, wide-jawed head out the window and in his posh voice says, 'Morning, Simon. Not on the gallops this morning?'

'No, not this morning,' Simon says.

'Had other things to do, eh?'

'That's right.'

'How's Kelly doing?' Nicholls says. 'Pleasing you, I hope.'

'Very much so.'

'That's excellent. Excellent. So she knows what she's doing?'

'She does. And if there's anything she doesn't know, she picks it up soon enough. She's a quick learner.'

Nicholls is smiling proudly. 'She is,' he says. 'She is. Wonderful. I'll see you later, Simon.'

'See you, Jeremy.'

The windows have started to hum up when Nicholls shouts, 'Oh, Simon!'

'Yeh?'

He is still smiling. 'You don't have a tip for me, do you?'

'I'm afraid I don't, Jeremy.'

'You must have something at Huntingdon today?'

'None of em's got much of a chance.'

'No? Okay then. See you.'

Simon tilts his head for a moment in a sort of mock-salute, then powers his window up and drives on. He parks the Range Rover in the yard. There is nothing picturesque about the place. Even the old house is a morose-looking thing – small-windowed, white-washed, with its inevitable satellite-dish. Next to it is a warehouse-like structure with mossy fibreglass walls where the haylage and Vixen nuts are stored and the tractor and various other pieces of sourly oily machinery live.

He finds Mrs Miller in the overheated kitchen looking through a surgical enhancement prospectus. 'Where've you been?' she says. He puts two packs of Marlboro Reds on the table and pats her terrycloth haunch. 'Just fillin up the Range Rover.'

'Oh?' It hardly explains why he has been away for an hour and a half.

'Yeah,' he says, taking a seat with a tiny smirk on his face, 'just fillin her up . . .'

'Please don't pat me like I'm a horse, Simon.'

'Alright, alright . . .' he mutters, and starts to read the UKIP Members' Newsletter while she serves him his breakfast. He is quite involved politically.

He is still eating – trying to pick up a slick of yolk with a mushy triangle of fried bread – when his phone starts to sing 'You're Just To Good To Be True.'

You're just too good to be true
Can't take my eyes off of you
You'd be like heaven to touch
I wanna hold you so much . . .

Shoving his plate away, he answers it. It is Francis Moss, a well-known horseracing journalist, media personality, fellow UKIP member, and friend.

'Alright, Mossy,' Simon says. 'How are you? Alright?'

Mossy says something.

'Yeah alright,' Simon says.

Then he says, 'Oh, did you?' He frowns and using only his free hand unwraps one of the packs of Marlboro Reds. Then he says, 'Well as it happens, yes.'

Mossy speaks again.

'No, Huntingdon.'

And then – 'The two o'clock.'

And finally – 'That's just for you Mossy. Not for the service. I mean it.' As one of his many sidelines Mossy operates a tipping service, his familiar face smiling out of ads in the *Racing Post.* 'Nice one,' Simon says. 'Yeah, I'm going to be there. Okay, see you there. Oh, did you get the newsletter? Just got it in the post this morning.' For a few minutes they talk UKIP politics – who's in, who's out (of the EU). Mossy is a fairly senior tin-rattler for the party, on friendly terms with the national leadership.

Simon says, 'Listen, I've got to go, mate. Yeah, I'll see you at the track. Smashing. Yeah. Ta. See you there.'

Leaving his plate on the table, he lights a Marlboro, pulls on his Hunters and pushes his way through a fierce wet wind towards the stables, where Piers is supervising the loading of the horse transport.

*

In the first betting shop James enters, near Russell Square tube, the price is so short he thinks there's been some mistake. There had not. And then, as he watches, it shortens still further. With the price unstoppably shortening, he spends the morning lowering his estimate of how much he will win if the touch is landed, until at about noon, from somewhere next to a motorway in Neasden, he phones Freddy. 'Have you seen the fucking price?' he shouts.

'It's fucking short,' Freddy agrees.

'Do you think Miller's stiffing us? Do you think him and his mates got all the fancy prices?'

'There was some twelve to one first thing,' Freddy says. 'Didn't you have any of that?'

'No, I didn't . . .'

'Last night on Betfair,' Freddy says, 'there were some silly prices. I hoovered up everything down to twenty to one. There was even a few quid of hundred to one.'

'You didn't use your own account?'

'For some.'

'You used your own account?'

'For some of it. Why not? It's normal. I part-own the fucking horse . . .'

James says, 'If we get in shit for this I'm going to fucking kill you.'

'Stop worrying,' Freddy says. 'Everything's going to be okay. What's that noise? Where are you?'

'Neasden.'

'What the fuck are you doing there?'

'Trying to be subtle about it,' James says. 'I shouldn't have fucking bothered. I'll talk to you later.' There is little more than an hour to post time, and he still has nearly a thousand unwagered pounds in his pocket.

*

The scene of his triumph is a quiet William Hill's in Hendon.

Standing in the threadbare Hill's, his heart pumping, with two old men he watches his horse win easily on one of the screens. When she wins he experiences several seconds of pure satisfaction and pleasure. The pure stuff. Unmixed with anything else. Medical quality feelings. And then there is Miller on the screen, unmistakably flushed with triumph. From the way he is flushed, from the way he is windily speaking, it is obvious that he is euphoric. 'Wasn't expecting that!' he says with a laugh.

'Weren't you?' the interviewer asks him.

'No, not at all!'

'Well the market got it right.'

'Yeah. Wasn't my money though.'

'You didn't have a few quid on?'

'Not a penny. Unfortunately!'

While Miller is still speaking, James takes the first of his winnings from the teller and walks out into the traffic noise, the London light – sun smearing pigeon-hued pavements and striking the modest parade of shops of which the Hill's forms a part. In the end he won very much less than he hoped – not much more than £10,000 is his first estimate, which will last him only a few months, five at the most – and once the euphoria wears off a sort of disappointment sets in. He takes a taxi from Kilburn High Street in the late afternoon, and dusk is falling when he lets himself into the flat and hides his winnings, well wrapped in plastic, in the soil of a house-plant, a hibiscus, that he acquired especially for the purpose. If the stewards are suspicious, they or the police might look for the money, for *some* money – they were unlikely to find it there. Then he has a shower and dresses for an evening out.

*

When word got round that Simon had landed a nice little touch and was sharing the wealth in the usual way, the villagers packed the Plough like it were New Year's Eve. As for the karaoke it were like this – Simon sang a song, then somebody else sang a song, then Simon sang two songs, then somebody else sang a song, then Simon sang three songs . . . He did all his favourites. 'New York, New York'. *Start spreadinnn the noooze . . .* (Very flat on that last word.) *I'm leavinn terdaaay . . .* (Even flatter.) He did 'Let Me Entertain You'. And obviously 'You're Just Too Good To Be True' – soft-soaping the opening section with his eyes shut, and then absolutely yelling out *I LOVE YOU BAY-BEE!!* He was looking straight at Kelly Nicholls when he sang those words. That was unwise. Especially since her father is in. Jeremy is sitting as far as possible from the temporary little stage in its puddle of coloured light, smoking a Hamlet – the law on smoking in public places was not always observed in the Plough – and drinking a double Scotch. When Simon passes him on his way to the Gents, his face varnished with sweat and his voice hoarse, Jeremy says, with a smile, 'None of em's got much of a chance, eh, Simon?' It takes Simon a second to work out what he is talking about – their meeting in the lane. When he does, he just winks at him, without stopping, and proceeds to take his piss.

That double Scotch is not, of course, the only imbursement the Nicholls family has taken from the touch. Earlier in the evening – the karaoke hadn't started yet – he met with Kelly on the empty expanse of tarmac at the side of the pub. There he took from her the same envelope she had pocketed in the morning, only now it was very much fatter. It would hardly shut. He sat in the Range Rover with the vanity light on leafing through the immense wad and quickly worked out there was the thick end of £10,000 there. Moistening his index finger at his small mouth, he extracted £200 from the envelope, and then – experiencing a unexpected surge of feeling for his young mistress – supplemented it with a further hundred. She was still waiting on the wet tarmac when he lowered himself from the Range Rover and slammed the door. 'Here,' he said. Then he tenderly lifted her fleece, popped the button of her jeans and pushed the folded money down the front of her pants.

He had started his speech when she sat down in the pub. (He told her to wait outside for a few minutes, then follow him in.) He had a mic in his hand. The music had been turned off. There was a tolerant silence. The first words she heard were – '. . . but it wouldn't be nothing without you lot. I mean that. Every last one of you. Some might be more important than others, but every job matters. Even yours Piers.' Laughter. And in the short turbulence of the merriment did he wink at her? The moment passed so quickly. And then he was saying, 'I'm a sentimental old bugger . . .' When he said that, she smiled secretly at the floor, thinking of the extra £100 she had found when she transferred the money from her pants to her pocket.

The speech went on for some time – the thick end of half an hour. And it was hard to say when it happened, but at some point it seemed to metamorphose from a speech of thanks and welcome – thanks for the support and welcome to the party – into something else. The phrase 'European superstate' made the first of several appearances. He said something about 'as long as we live in an independent nation.' He said, 'I've nothing against foreigners, as most of you know last summer we had a French lad in the stables . . .' Towards the end there was some light-hearted heckling.

When it was finally over and the music was on again, Frank Moss, who had had a lift from Huntingdon in the front of the horse transport, took him aside. 'Top speech,' he said.

'Yeah, ta, Mossy . . .'

'We have *got* to introduce you to Nigel. Listen, there's a meeting in Eastbourne in a few weeks – how about then? And what about being on the platform? You'll have to say a few words. Alright?'

'What do you mean a few words?' Simon said, watching suspiciously as Dermot, one of the lads from the yard, went over to where Kelly was sitting and started to talk to her.

'If we're serious about this,' Mossy said, 'you need more profile. They love you here. That's obvious. You'd be a shoo-in here . . .'

'Well most of em work for me . . .'

'This is where you start from,' Mossy whispered excitedly. 'This is your heartland. Everyone in politics needs a heartland, Si. It's step by step. You start small, then you take the next step. Eastbourne, Sunday second of April. Put it in the diary.' Then he said quietly, 'Everything okay with the stewards?'

'Yeah I think so,' Simon muttered. 'I hope so.'

The Huntingdon stewards had had him in. They had had some questions for him about the mare. Standing there with young Tom, he had said that yes, she had shown striking improvement on previous form, he did not know why – perhaps it was the onset of spring? – and he wanted to be as helpful as possible with their inquiries. When the stewards said they wanted to speak to the owners, he said that since they weren't expecting her to win, unfortunately they weren't there. Then Francis Moss stepped in to testify that that very morning Mr Miller had told him he didn't think the horse had any hope of winning. The stewards said they would look into the matter. 'Okay,' Simon said. 'And if you have any questions just . . .' With his thumb and little finger he mimed a phone.

There is a lock-in, obviously. The Plough, with its horse-brasses and low beams, is still quite full at two.

*

In the early evening, with unprecedented promptness, Freddy had paid James the £5,000 he owed him for his share in the mare in the form of a novel-sized wad of £20 notes, which they proceeded to leave in a thick trail through the West End, finally picking up a flock of skimpily dressed Norwegian girls in a Mayfair nightclub. Two taxis whisked them all to Chelsea, where Freddy was their host.

The tall eighteenth century townhouse in which Freddy lives is not, of course, his own. Impressive from the outside – spilling out of the taxis onto Cheyne Walk the Norwegian ladies were palpably excited by its size and splendour – it is less promising once you step through the front door. Freddy's landlord Anselm inherited it in the Eighties in a leaky, mouldering state, and has since done absolutely nothing to it. The whole place smells mustily of dust and wet plaster. Inside, Freddy starts showing off at the piano, and while the others surround him or slip off to explore the house – naughty laughter in the unlit stairwells – James finds himself on the smaller of the sofas with twenty-two-year-old Maia, who had been taking a touchingly obvious interest in him from the start. (At one point she had placed his hands on her sparrowy diaphragm – what had that been about?) He is very drunk. Things have started sliding around, not least his voice, and she is sitting on his knee and kissing him. Her strong little tongue is moving in his mouth as they slide down onto the seat of the sofa. There, out of sight of the others, she whispers, 'I have a fiancé. *Hic!* In Norway. So we'll just have a one night stand. Okay?' In spite of the hiccups, she starts kissing him again, more forcefully, holding his head with her hands.

There is no shortage of empty rooms in the huge house. There are rooms overlooking the Thames. There are rooms overlooking the tops of mature trees. There are rooms full of antique furniture. There are rooms with four-poster beds . . .

'No,' he says, prising her off him. 'No, I'm sorry. I'm sorry.' He touches her nose and smiles. 'I'm sorry.' She says nothing, and for a few minutes they just lie there on the sofa. Then she stands up and joins the others at the piano. She seems sad, and watching her he wonders whether he should have taken her upstairs and fucked her in one of the four-poster beds. He wonders whether he *wants* to do that – does he *want* to do that?

He is still watching her and wondering when the door opens and Anselm is there in a satin duvet of a dressing-gown, his soft white hair askew, squinting in the light.

'Fréderic,' pronounced the French way, 'would you mind keeping it down?' he says petulantly from the threshold. 'Please.'

He seems overwhelmed and flustered by the sight of all those Nordic limbs, those laughing aquamarine eyes, those white-blonde heads. (Though Maia and one or two of the others are dark.) Immediately playing a kind of fanfare – *tan-tada-tan-tada-TA* – Freddy says, 'Ladies, this is my landlord. Won't you join us, Anselm?'

Though the massed ladies are making him shy, one thing Anselm does not seem is surprised. This is the sort of thing he expects from Fréderic; indeed it is the sort of thing that Fréderic encourages him to expect. Anselm is under the impression that his tenant is an international playboy of princely lineage, and though he would never admit it, he is flattered just to be involved in the life of such a person, and to be thought of as a friend by him. He loves telling his other friends about 'the prince.' To them, he patronises him. 'He's a drunken sod,' he says, showing off. 'On the other hand, he is quite a laugh to have around.' Except at times like this – perhaps twice a week. 'Just keep it down, please,' he mutters. 'It is four o'clock.'

*

Slumped over the wheel of the Range Rover, Simon has to shut one eye to see anything at all. He sang the last number – 'I did it myyyyyyyyyyyyyyyyyyyyyyyyyyyyyyyyyyyyyyyyyyyyyyyyyyyyyyy yyyyyyyyyyyyyyyyyyyyyyyyyyyyyyyyyyyyyyyyyyyyyyyyyyyyyyyy yyyyyyyyyyyyyyyyyyyyyyyyyyyyyyyyyyyyyyyyyyyyyyyyyyyyyyyy yyyyyyyyyyyyyyyyyyyyyyyyyyyyyyyyyaway' – to the empty pub. Then, still mumbling the words of 'My Way,' he stumbled out into oodles of moonlight. The moon was queasily full. In the kitchen he tries to work out how much money there is in the envelope. The problem is he has to hold each note at arm's length to see what it is and even then they are just fuzzy oblongs. It was his intention to watch the video of the two o'clock at Huntingdon a few times. When he has a winner he tends to watch the video a few times. There was . . . something very nice . . . about watching the video . . . when you knew . . . when you knew you were . . . If only, he sometimes thought . . . If only . . . If only . . .

*

James wakes up on a musty four-poster with early morning light pouring in through the windows. He is fully dressed. He looks at his watch – it is eight o'clock and he has not slept more than a few hours. For a minute or two he just sits on the edge of the bed, feeling like a Victorian ghost in the tall, thickly ivied house. The sound of trees swishing in the wind, otherwise total silence. He has things to do. He has to walk Hugo for one thing. It is turning into a habit, spending the night away from home and leaving poor Hugo to tough it out. He must stop doing that. In his jacket pocket he finds his wallet. Sitting on the edge of the four-poster, listening to the swishing trees, he opens it. There is less than £4,000 in there. Ergo yesterday he spent more than

£1,000 on a night out. Under the circumstances, that was perhaps unwise. Oh well. He pulls on his hard leather shoes.

On his way out, he looks into Freddy's room. It is as he thought. There are two people in the bed, two heads on the pillows – Freddy's half-bald head and a head of dark hair. He heard them. They were so uninhibitedly loud they woke him from his dead drunk sleep. He shuts the door and tiptoes down the stairs. It was a prurient thing for him to do, to look, and he wishes he hadn't. Somehow, though, it upsets him slightly that Freddy had the one night stand with Maia. He is not jealous. It is not that. (He is pleased that he did not sleep with her himself – he would have felt terrible, *terrible*, if he had.) No, it is a matter of piqued vanity. He had thought that she liked him. specifically him, when in fact she just wanted to get laid.

Piqued vanity. He walks out into the early morning light. The London light, flat and plain on London streets.

Vanity of vanities, all is vanity

* * *

She has just never been very moved by his love, that was the thing. It left her unmoved. On her way home on Monday night, she had thought of that weekend in February when they went to see his horse.

They left London late on Saturday morning and were at the stables by two. James seemed disappointed that the trainer himself wasn't there. They were met instead by a tall, lean, middle-aged, innocent-looking man – James introduced him as Piers – who emerged from a Portakabin and hailed them as they stood there under the snowladen sky. The stables were very miserable that Saturday afternoon. Some sort of liquid trickled along a spillway.

The smells were intense – the smells of horse-piss, of manure, of mouldy straw. The doors of the stalls were all shut; from some of them came a quiet whickering as they passed. They stopped at one of them and finally taking his hands out of his pockets – he was wearing a husky and fingerless gloves – Piers drew back the bolts. He had a tangle of old tack under his arm. He went in with it and emerged a minute later (the visitors stood shivering outside) with the horse on a halter. She had what looked like a filthy old duvet over her.

'See, she's looking super,' he said.

James patted the solid flank of the horse's neck and, smiling proudly, encouraged her to do the same.

'How old is she?' she asked.

'Five . . .?' James said. 'She's five isn't she?'

Piers just nodded, smoking.

'Five. Isn't she lovely?'

Lovely? Yes, okay. 'M-hm,' she said. She found it touching, his pride in this horse – and she seemed like a perfectly nice horse, if slightly odd looking. Thickly mottled, with a whiskery lower lip, the liquid hemisphere of her eye fixed on an ice-filmed puddle. The way she stood there so patiently, only her ears moving, made Katherine think of the horses in Tarkovsky's *Andrei Rublev* – those mute, unjudging witnesses of the human scene. Quietists. The perfection of some kind of monastic ideal. Leaving James to stroke the mare's nose, she looked into the stall. It was a musty, humid hole. She shuddered at the thought of spending a night in there.

The first isolated snowflakes were touching down in the mud and in the horse's tough mane. James was feeding her an apple. He had had it in his pocket all the way from King's Cross. He seemed delighted with the way her teeth and lips went at the fruit. They sheared off a whole half of it, sluicing juice everywhere. Then she lowered her huge head to pluck the second half from the unspeakable mud at their feet.

'Okay?' Piers said.

They turned down his offer of tea and went for a drink in the pub in the village. The Plough. Seven stars on the sign. The village was not much of a place, especially on a day like that. The pub was nice enough though. There was a fire, and they sat at the inglenook table.

Suddenly it was night-time, and the pub was quite full. James saw someone he seemed to know – a very slight man with skin of translucent whiteness, legs like tongs and some front teeth missing. He went over to speak to him. 'Jockey,' he explained. 'Tom.'

'Tom?'

'Piers's son.'

'Oh.'

He said impulsively, 'Why don't we spend the night somewhere near here?'

For a few seconds she said nothing. She was not sure whether she wanted to do that. With a faint smile, she examined his face, her eyes seeming to move from feature to feature. 'Like where?' she said.

An old-fashioned hotel in Cambridge.

And it was in that hotel, lying on a squidgy mattress, with a scalpel of moonlight dissecting the drapes, that he said, 'I think I'm in love with you.'

And what did she say? First she sighed. She sighed as if she wished he hadn't said it. Then, when several frozen seconds had elapsed, she said, 'I can't say the same, James. I can't say the same.' There was a long silence. She knew she had hurt him. It frightened her that he should say he was in love with her – or that he thought he was. It made her wonder worriedly what she was *doing* there, in that fusty hotel in Cambridge – which was probably why she then whispered, her voice making a plume of vapour in the moonlight . . .

He just doesn't understand her, she thought, standing on the mountainous up-escalator at Angel station, her face tiredly empty of expression. He doesn't understand her. No more than she understands him. She thought of those words of Saint Paul's, the ones you hear at weddings. They were heard at her own wedding. *Then will I know truly, even as I am truly known* . . . She thinks of those words, which unfailingly put a film of emotion on her eyes, as expressing a kind of ideal love. The idea of knowing, of being known. There is just no sense of that here. He does not *know* her. He does not understand her. He has no instinct for her. That was obvious, she pointed out to herself as she stepped off the escalator, from the start. On one of the first nights they spent together, she found herself lying there lightlessly. 'Are you awake?' she said. She had to say it several times, sitting over him. Finally he moved. 'Are you awake?' He mumbled something. He sounded as if he was under massive sedation. She sighed and made a sharp movement under the duvet. 'I don't feel we're together,' she said. 'I feel very separate from you.' And then, a few moments later, 'I feel lonely. Did you hear me?'

He said, 'I . . .'

There was a long silence.

'Please hug me,' she said.

With what seemed to be a huge effort, he turned over and took her heavy warmth in his arms. He kissed her somewhere on her head. 'Don't feel lonely,' he murmured. He squeezed her. 'You shouldn't feel lonely . . .'

'We're just not together,' she said then, sitting up. 'I don't feel I'm really *with* you. And you don't know how to make me feel okay.'

He did not seem to know what she was talking about. He said, 'What do you mean?' She threw her head onto the pillow. 'What do you mean?' he said, sounding more awake. She was staring into the darkness. 'What do you mean we're not together? I don't know what you mean when you say that . . .'

'That's the problem! You don't *understand*.'

Sometimes – usually when the sleepy sensation of skin touching skin seems of itself to hold some sort of mute insufficient promise – she still hopes that he might somehow start to understand her. The trouble is, she is unable to help feeling that it just doesn't *work* like that – that if he does not understand her instinctively then trying is pointless, even if it were possible. It just makes the whole situation seem so arbitrary – and if it seems arbitrary how is she to have faith in it? Why *him*, in other words? Why not someone else?

For instance, she had found herself looking at Jonathan tonight and wondering, his status as an ex notwithstanding, whether he might not suit her more than James. She enjoys him. She enjoys his wit, his warmth, his sophisticated friends. He was, and evidently still is, successful. Tonight was the launch party of some novel he is publishing and he treated her like a VIP, spent too much time talking to her, introduced her to some famous people . . . They were together for several years when she worked in publishing. It might easily have led to marriage, to white-stuccoed nook. She ended it – suddenly, shattering his heart – when she found that she was not *sure* that she was in love with him. She still sees the shy hope in his eyes, and when she saw it tonight she wondered whether she had been wrong to decline in him the sort of sociable life among the upper London intelligentsia that she had always imagined for herself. It was then, when she ended it with him, that she left publishing to pursue her idea of a small hotel somewhere near the sea. Would that make her happy?

That was what it was supposed to do. Letting herself into the flat, she thought of a story Jonathan had told her once. Madame De Gaulle is being interviewed by the BBC shortly after her husband's death. She is asked what she is looking forward to now, and says what sounds in her French accent unmistakably like, 'A penis.'

Summer was out. The stripped wood floor of the hall was littered with shoes. Tipsily searching the fridge, she wondered – Jonathan still vaguely in her mind – whether she had just expected too much. Was she just mistaken to have supposed that she had to be *sure*? That only *sure* would do? Had she thrown away a perfectly nice and happy life – white-stuccoed nook etc. – for that mistaken idea? And if so, how had she found herself possessed of such an idea? Well, that was obvious, she thought, eating a slice of Parma ham. It was everywhere. It was one of the most pervasive ideas of the society in which she lived, one of its main articles of faith, one of the most obsessively visited subjects of its art. We just wouldn't leave off it.

Putting on her pyjamas, she worried that she was too used to living on her own, too self-sufficient, too used to not sharing – not sharing her time, in particular. She wondered whether she should have spent the evening with James, whether she owed it to him to have done that. He wanted her to. His horse had won. She had said she had other plans, a 'prior engagement,' which was true. She washed her face. She tied up her hair. She made sure her phone was on the night-table. Then, instead of the poetry anthology, she took down from the shelf where it had stood untouched for years the New Testament and found 1 Corinthians 13.

6

On Friday lunchtime James is standing under a ledge, eating a damp, overpriced pasty with frozen hands. The small lumps of stringy steak in the pasty scald his throat on the way down. The pastry is soft and wet. He throws the floury nub into an overflowing bin, and joins the queue at a stall selling extortionate noggins of steaming whisky. He is at Cheltenham for the last day of the Festival – a long-planned excursion. Freddy is there too, visiting the malodorous piss-slick of the overwhelmed Gents.

Pretty much everyone on the eight o'clock National Express service from Victoria was holding a soggy *Racing Post*. The coach took its time leaving London, and then stood at Heathrow for half an hour in the faint stink of aviation fuel. When it finally set off again and started down the M4, it was in a miserable drizzle. Towards the middle of the morning, Swindon came and went, unseen in the flurrying Scotch mist. Not long thereafter, they left the motorway, and for a while the coach swung promisingly through hedgy lanes. Then, somewhere near Cirencester, it was suddenly snarled in traffic. An hour later, it was still stuck on the outskirts of Cheltenham, in a world of dowdy Wisteria Drives, and Freddy phoned to say they would be late. They were supposed to be meeting some friends of his there – or at least one of them is a friend of his – or at least he is a 'friend' of his. Freddy knows Forrest from the Phene Arms, his local in Chelsea, where he and the young American often drink together on those Sunday afternoons, perhaps half of them, when Forrest isn't in the office. Forrest and the other members of his party were having lunch in the Panoramic Restaurant when Freddy phoned a second time to say that he and James were there.

Since James and Freddy were not allowed anywhere near the Panoramic Restaurant, which was on the top floor of the newest segment of the stand, Forrest took the lift down and met them at the entrance. They looked pretty miserable, he thought. Weary and wet from the long walk to the track – taxis were not to be had for love nor money – Freddy was sporting a wilted fedora and sucking on a cigarette which he held with two fingers of a worryingly mauve hand.

'Hi,' Forrest said, lighting one of his own on the dripping threshold. He himself was stuffed into a green tweed three-piece purchased specially for the occasion. 'You get here okay?'

'Fine,' Freddy lied. 'You?'

'Well, you know.' Forrest seemed slightly embarrassed. 'We were airlifted in.' (And they were not the only ones – the air was full of the self-important mutter of helicopters, so many of them that they formed holding patterns over the lost summit of Cleeve Hill while they waited to land.) 'Tristan's idea,' Forrest said. 'He and Trevor paid for most of it. So . . . you know . . . it was kinda . . .' He seemed to search for the word. 'Neat, or something.'

'Sure,' Freddy said. He did not seem surprised. He did not seem impressed. Surprised and impressed were things that Freddy never seemed.

'We're just having lunch,' Forrest said. 'You had something to eat yet?'

'No, not yet.'

'Why don't you get something to eat,' Forrest suggested, 'and we'll meet you later?'

So while they headed for the enclave of steaming food vans near the main entrance, Forrest took the lift up to the fifth floor, where from the table in the warmth of the Panoramic Restaurant the track was a green jumble through the plate glass.

Looking out and down, Tristan watched the people putting up with the weather in front of the stands, and in the economy enclosures on the other side of the track. He was always struck by the social diversity of this event. There was nothing else quite like it. Drunken yobbos of all kinds – from the primordially working class to the most egregiously toffee-nosed, with large numbers from the swollen middle of society, from London and the south-east. There were soft-voiced older men and women from garden suburbs in sensible fleeces. There were farmers and their families. Peers. The Irish . . . In Tristan's view it was the horses themselves who made it this way. They were not part of the human situation – their appeal was universal. The waitress was serving the starter. Smoked salmon. What a yawn. *Typical of a place like this*, he thought. *Playing totally safe*. He smiled easily at the waitress as she served him. 'What do you like in the first, Trevor?' he said.

The Head of Structured Products and Securitisation was squeezing lemon onto the thick slice of salmon on his plate. He put it down and wiped his fingers on a napkin. 'Mister Hight,' he said, in his unhurried, thinking-man's Estuary English.

'Yeah?'

'Irish raider,' Trevor said. 'Should be too good for our lot.' He said something about a juvenile hurdle he had seen at Naas in January. Trevor's first visit to Prestbury Park was in 1973, when as an eighteen-year-old he hitch-hiked from London with a few quid in his pocket and won £100. One hundred pounds was a lot of money in 1973, for a tube driver's son, and the win inspired him to start out as a professional punter. However, he soon worked out that the sums of money to be made from horse racing – even by a hard-working pro – were minuscule next to what was on offer in the financial markets, while the essential principle was the same: not winners, *prices*. He made the switch from track to trading room in 1980, working first for old Etonians (Tristan's uncle was one of them), and then for a variety of foreigners.

'The best of ours is probably Hobbs's horse,' he is saying. 'Detroit City . . .' He puts the stress on the first syllable – *Dee*-troit.

'Detroit City?' interrupts Forrest.

Trevor ignores him.'. . . and he might win, but he'll be fav, and at the prices it's got to be the Mullins horse. For me anyway.'

'Detroit City?' Forrest says again.

Trevor just nods, has a sip of wine, pats his mouth with his napkin, and starts to eat.

'Well, you guys know I'm from Michigan?' Forrest says, smiling.

Without looking at him, Trevor says, 'You should back *Dee*-troit City then, shouldn't you.'

They finally meet – James and Freddy, and Forrest and his party – in the lead-up to the main event. They meet on the windswept apron in front of the stands, now a jostling sea of punters. Forrest makes the introductions – and stumbles embarrassingly when he finds he has forgotten James's name. There is a momentary pause, and then, with what seem for a second to be literally supernatural social skills, Tristan smoothly supplies it. 'James,' he says with a warm smile, putting out his white trowel of a hand. 'Tristan Elphinstone. Lovely to see you again.'

Of course! James thinks.

That tall man with the long pale face and the grey-blue eyes – not unlike James himself, in fact – had looked ominously familiar. He knew he had met him somewhere. The green tweed suit had thrown him. And Tristan was older now . . . It was suddenly all there. Tristan Elphinstone. He had worked for Lazard in those days, and Lazard was involved, with various others, in the floatation of Interspex. He and James had seen quite a lot of each other for a few months. Lunches, meetings in the offices near Moorgate, taxis. (In the taxis there was a strict etiquette, Tristan always sitting on James's left, facing the direction of travel, with their suited flunkies perched on the flip-seats opposite.) Lazard had invited him to Wimbledon that summer, the Men's Final – it was the last year that Sampras won. Tristan was host that day. They even went to New York together, had suites on the same floor of the Plaza. The next morning, the presentation on the umpteenth floor, with the snow swirling outside . . . Tristan Elphinstone. Wife an Italian aristocrat. Stunning, elegant, sexy. What was her name? Dorabella? Fiordiligi? James met her that Sunday in SW19 . . .

'Tristan,' he says. 'How *are* you, mate?'

Tristan laughs confidentially and leans closer to James (who is able to smell the Acqua di Parma emanating subtly from his tweed suit) to lower his voice and say, 'I'm not doing too well this afternoon, actually. What about you?'

'Me? I'm doing okay . . .'

'Had a winner?'

'Had the first two.'

'Fucking bastard,' Tristan says, still laughing quietly. 'Typical. What are you on in the next? I'll make sure I am too.'

'Forget The Past.'

'Nice one.'

Tristan is, of course, too tactful to ask James what he is 'up to now' or anything like that. He knows, obviously, that Interspex is no longer trading (not that it was ever exactly *trading*) – Lazard had filed a suit for several million pounds in unpaid fees. That was the liquidators' problem, though. James had nothing to do with that.

There is a lot of talk about who is on what in the main event, most of it about Trevor's £20,000 on War Of Attrition, a fifteen-to-two shot owned by Michael O'Leary, the Ryanair magnate. The prospect of a £150,000 win has made Trevor pensive, and he just loiters there in the tumultuous sea of people, with his hands in the pockets of his mac.

When War Of Attrition wins, he hurls the *Racing Post* he is holding into the sky and lets out a long wordless yell that makes the veins on his neck and temples leap out.

*

The apple blossom was out in Victoria Road. The tarmac shone in the unseasonable April sun. For the first time, he had the top down on the Aston. Pure pleasure, to slip through the streets of Knightsbridge and South Kensington with the top down and the washed air swirling and surging in his face, fresh and vigorous as springwater. His skin tingled. His heart tingled. Passing under the lofty young-leafed trees, he saw people on horseback in the park, trotting through the patchwork of the shade.

That morning he had met with Tristan Elphinstone at Lazard. Tristan had told him that everything was okay. He was a nice fellow, Tristan. And sharp too, very sharp. James had been passing through Moorgate anyway, so had suggested popping in for a quick meeting. 'Always happy to see you,' Tristan had said. James was passing through Moorgate because he had been out in

Mudchute inspecting the new servers. Five hundred thousand pounds' worth of servers had just been installed in the old warehouse there. Enough to cope with the next twelve to eighteen months of expansion. Then they would need more – the Mudchute installation was just a temporary measure. They were already looking for a much larger space, or rather the site for one. The idea was to build something the size of an airport hangar somewhere on the periphery of London. He was to look at one such site this afternoon. So he inspected the Mudchute servers – and even they were impressive, with their team of technicians and wall of loud ventilators, over which the head technician had had to shout to tell him that everything was okay – and when he had done that, he stopped off in Canary Wharf to have a word with Karl Meisner at Morgan Stanley. Everything was fine, Karl said. They were having no problems placing the shares. They had provisionally placed the first tranche already. They were ahead of schedule. Karl had wanted to take him to lunch but James said he didn't have time, which he didn't. In those days he never had time.

As he slipped through the lanes of Wapping, he phoned the office in Paddington to make sure everything was okay. He loved the office in Paddington. Everything was new there. The shining light-filled offices themselves were startlingly new, sprouting out of dereliction, out of a sad, forgotten, Victorian hinterland. He was proud to be in the vanguard of the new economy – and he *was* in the vanguard; there were even jungle drums suggesting that he might be invited to one of those parties at Number Ten, the ones where the Prime Minister mingled with envoys of the young and the new. They were the first tenants in the Paddington development, and the offices were still only half-furnished. Trucks full of stuff pulled up outside every day. His own office was still empty except for some essential furniture, a phone, and a specially made neon sign – in the style of Tracey Emin – saying 'Get Large Or Get Lost'. The lack of seats meant that meetings had to take place with everyone standing up. This worked so well, in terms of keeping everything quick and to the point, that he had decided to institutionalise it. Serendipitous. He was usually in by eight in jeans and open-necked shirt. They had taken two floors, though for the time being they only needed one. Not even one. Even so, within twelve to eighteen months they would probably have to take more. They were hiring people every day.

So he stopped in Moorgate to see Tristan, who ushered him into the plushest meeting room on the premises and told him that everything was fine. Yes, the markets had lurched lower in March, it was true. However, they were now heading strongly north again. Such things were to be expected . . . Sitting there in his charcoal suit – there was something otherworldly about the quality of the tailoring – Tristan had the softly unshakeable manner of a very expensive doctor, telling you that while he understood what was worrying you, and was pleased that you had mentioned it, you were in fact perfectly fine. The trip to New York in February had been a fantastic success; there was lots of interest from the American institutional investors who had been at the presentation. He said, with his usual winning smile, that he was now looking forward to their forthcoming trip to Frankfurt and Zurich to make similar presentations, and would look into organising something in Singapore. 'I wanted to see how New York went first,' he said. 'I'll get on to that straight away now.' He offered to take James to lunch. When James said he didn't have time, Tristan escorted him down to the lobby, and there, on the smoke-veined white marble, they parted. First, though, smiling mischievously, Tristan put a hand on his arm and said, 'Do you like tennis?'

'Tennis?' James said. 'Sure . . .'

'Fancy a day out in SW19 this summer?'

'SW19...?'

'Wimbledon.'

'Oh. Sure, why not...'

'Men's Final okay?'

James just laughed.

'I'll be in touch,' Tristan said. 'We'll speak soon. Lovely to see you.' He was still smiling. 'And don't worry! Everything's fine.'

James picked up a prawn sandwich from the Moorgate Pret, and then steered the Aston down Prince's Street. The Aston was still very new – he still enjoyed just sitting in it, especially in his slightly scruffy clothes and shades, soaking up the lustful looks it sucked in from men and women in equal measure. He passed the solemn ziggurat of the Bank of England, and spurred the sportscar towards the sun-touched dome of St Paul's. Everything was shining in the warm spring light. He parked in a side street near Ludgate Hill. He wanted to drop in on Chris at InfoWorks, one of the many technical teams they had on the payroll. James did not know exactly what they did. His own technical director, Magnus Petersson, a lugubrious Swede, handled that. Magnus – whose stock options that April had a paper value of £20,000,000 or so – was always meeting Chris, and the various other Chrises they had working for them, scattered contractors who never seemed to want to work with each other. Magnus sometimes said they should just take everything in-house, perhaps by simply acquiring them all – or sack them all and throw the whole thing to IBM or someone. If only it were that simple. Everything was half-made, half-done. No one knew exactly what was happening, or where, not even Magnus, though naturally he insisted that he did. To try and pick it apart at this stage would be impossible. You'd have to start from scratch, and there just wasn't time.

James liked to pay impromptu visits to the likes of Chris. He didn't want them to think he wasn't paying attention. Nor did he want Magnus to think that he never spoke to these people. InfoWorks was up a squeaking, twisting staircase on Ludgate Hill – more like the home of a small mid-twentieth-century publishing house than a hive of futurologists. Chris's own office was on the top floor, with small oriel windows overlooking the street. He was a short, hyperactive man – steel-rimmed spectacles, vainly shaved head – and he met James at the top of the stairs. He told him that everything was okay. Simon was hastily summoned – he was head nerd on the Interspex 'project' – and they had a meeting. James nodded, and improvised some questions. There were a lot of technical terms. They used them to fend him off. He was only in there for twenty minutes or so, and turned down Chris's offer to take him for lunch.

He was just starting the Aston when June phoned. June had been his PA when he was an estate agent in Islington too. She said that someone from the *Financial Times* had been on the phone, wondering if he would do an interview. James said he didn't think he had time. 'That's what I told them,' she said. 'I said you probably wouldn't have time.'

He parked in front of the house on Victoria Road. Though it still smelled pristinely of solvents, and faintly of sawmill, the upper part of the house was more or less finished. The expansive living room. The five en suite bedrooms. The study. The TV room. The first-floor terrace. Not all of these rooms were properly furnished. Two of the bedrooms had nothing except king-size mattresses in them, still in their plastic wrapping. The lack of stuff in the living room led to a vacant echo when you walked around on the newly laid oak parquet. The study held only a huge leather-topped desk and an early nineteenth-century admiral's swivel-chair. (Trophies of a sale at Sotheby's entitled

'The Age of Napoleon'.) The lower part of the house, however, was still in a much earlier stage of development, the spaces for the most part only sketched in in sharp-edged plaster. The drawing room, the dining room, the kitchen, the utility room, the maid's flat, the single-lane swimming pool . . . This last was still just a strange-looking concrete trench with various hoses in it. It was where James found Isabel and Thomasina.

The Italian tilers had started work, and the two women were standing on the edge of the future deep end, watching them mark things out with their spirit levels. James was surprised to see Isabel. She said she was there to talk to Thomasina about the wedding. Her wedding. Isabel's wedding. Isabel was wedding Steve that summer – finally, they had been together for more than twelve years – in the south of France. Specifically, she wanted to talk about the dress. Thomasina had some sort of fashion diploma from St Martin's, and still tinkered sporadically with her portfolio. They had been upstairs in the echoey living room, talking about it, when the tilers turned up.

That James and Thomasina now lived in a sort of palace was still something of a novelty. It still felt a bit strange to be standing there next to the single-lane swimming pool. To Isabel it just seemed slightly silly, preposterous. And what was even sillier – what was *much* sillier – what was almost too silly to think about or understand – was that when the floatation took place in the summer and James sold fifty per cent minus one share of Interspex (which had not even existed two years ago), he would 'net' – as the papers might put it – or 'pocket', or 'trouser', £125,000,000. Isabel had made it pretty plain, only half in jest – less than half in jest – not in jest at all, in fact – that when it came to the wedding present she was expecting something quite special. A house in Sardinia. Something like that. What Thomasina made of it, she did not know. She had been trying to work it out just now when they were upstairs drinking Nescafé out of mugs. Thomasina was quite inscrutable, in her way. On the surface, she seemed oblivious to the sheer strangeness of it all. She was probably still in shock. She floated around the huge house – smiling and laughing in her shy sweet vague way – one of the super-rich ... Oh insane! Fuck. It was *insane*!

For a few seconds some howling tool obliterated their small talk. The lower floors of the house were full of tattooed men in eye-shields operating howling power tools; and when the tools fell silent, there was the permanent tinny whiffle of paint-flecked radios – the same ten simple songs, the same ten news stories, ad nauseam. It was not a nice way to live, and James was starting to wish they had stayed in the flat in Islington until the place was totally finished.

They were standing on the edge of the swimming pool watching the Italian artisans at work. Isabel had a swig of Diet Coke to try and fend off the vertiginous feeling that had just wobbled her. Yes, she was jealous. Sure. That was normal. It would be weird if she wasn't. And she was pleased for him too. She was *proud* of him. When people at work pointed to something in the paper and said, 'Isn't that your brother?' she was proud of the fact that it was. It was just that this sudden surreal display of wealth seemed to be threatening to upstage the fucking wedding.

'What do I do with this?' she said, offering the empty Diet Coke can to no one in particular.

Thomasina took it.

'I have to go back to work.'

'And we have things to do as well,' James said – properly smugly, his sister thought – squeezing Thomasina's shoulders. 'Which way are you going? Do you want a lift?'

There was a sapphire-blue Aston Martin parked under the white apple blossom in front of the house. That was a bit vulgar.

And when she noticed the number plate she laughed out loud. 'Don't you think that's a bit . . .'

'Tacky?' James suggested.

'No? Isn't it?'

Thomasina evidently thought it was.

'Yeah, it probably is a bit,' James said, smiling. He didn't seem worried about it. Why would he be?

Isabel had to fold herself into the minuscule leather slot of the back seat. They dropped her at High Street Ken tube, and went on their way – looking, she thought meanly, like the fucking Beckhams. Except that James did not look much like David Beckham, except for those shades, and Thomasina looked absolutely nothing like Posh.

*   *   *

Forrest and his party had long since helicoptered back to London and were sitting down to one of those meals that's so expensive it becomes a minor news story when the eastbound National Express snorted out of Cheltenham in the dark. They almost missed it, James and Freddy, sprinting with their packages of hot starch. Later, the coach spent two unscheduled hours inching towards a pile-up on the M4 that had shut several lanes of the motorway, and when he phoned Katherine, about an hour into that experience, to tell her that he would be late into London, probably too late to see her that night, she informed him that he would not be seeing her tomorrow either – she was going to stay with a friend in Kent. He had just been weighing up the state of his life, with her and the weekend they were about to spend together on one side and more or less everything else on the other. Even so, he sounded no more than slightly petulant when he said, 'Well . . . I thought we were spending the weekend together . . .'

'Well, I'm just sitting at home now,' she said with a laugh. 'You're the one who isn't here.'

He said, 'What about Sunday then?'

'I won't be back in London till lunchtime. And I have to see someone in the afternoon anyway.'

'Who?'

A friend who was moving abroad, she said.

So when they did finally meet, in a pub near his flat, their weekend together had been pared down to the pathetic rind of Sunday evening. He was a few minutes late, and was withdrawing some money when she sent him a text asking what he wanted to drink.

Mysteriously, in the pub there was no sign of her. He did notice two untouched pints – a pint of lager and a pint of Guinness – on an empty table. It was the Guinness that threw him. He had never known her to drink Guinness.

She answered her phone in the Ladies and said that yes, those were their pints, and she would be with him in a minute.

Ten minutes later she sat down opposite him.

'What's that?' he said.

She had put a yellow Selfridges box, wrapped up with black ribbon, on the table. It was not for him, as for a moment he fondly imagined. It was a present from her friend, the one who was moving abroad – a pair of ivory silk pyjamas, neatly folded in tissue paper.

Later, in the forty-watt light of his bathroom, she would put them on. There was a lot that had to happen first, however.

They had to talk. Small talk. The house in Kent woodland where she had spent Saturday night. Her friend Venetia lived there with her fiancé and his eccentric father. She had quit her television job in London and now spent her time working in the woods – kerfing and piling and pollarding. She was not quite as happy there as she had hoped she would be. She had suggested to Katherine that she move into one of the old oast houses on the property – a suggestion that Katherine was apparently not dismissing out of hand. On Saturday there had been some sort of party. There had evidently been single men there, which made James short with jealousy for a minute or two. She wasn't talking about the men, though, she was talking about the woodland. She was full of praise for that old woodland, which she said was on the point of exploding verdantly in super-super-slow motion. She said he would have loved it there.

He offered to make some supper and they walked slowly home. They walked through Mecklenburgh Square, hooked snugly together at the shoulders, the waist. For a few moments, there, in Mecklenburgh Square, everything seemed okay.

She stepped out of her sopping shoes while he turned on the electric fire in the living room. It was an old-fashioned one, made to look like a hearth of coals. It was ticking and starting to pulse with orange light when she sat down on the sofa and pulled her legs up underneath her. The drizzle whispered on the skylight. The fire ticked. Hugo yawned. There was something nice about it. There was something so nice about it . . .

'Do you want a glass of wine?' he said.

'Okay.'

He went to the kitchen, and a minute later shouted, 'I'm going to put the water on for the pasta.'

He had just done so when he turned and saw her standing in the doorway. 'James,' she said.

'Yes?'

'I don't want to be your girlfriend.'

When he said nothing, she laughed nervously and said, 'You probably don't want to make supper for me now.'

When he *still* said nothing, she said, more seriously, 'Do you want me to leave?'

'No.'

'I'm sorry, James. I'm sorry I'm so shit at this . . .'

'Why?' he said.

She said, 'I . . . I'll tell you.' It was a struggle though. She stood there opening her mouth and shutting it. She laughed. 'I'll spit it out,' she said. Even then, it took another minute. She was looking off to the side when she finally said it. 'I . . . I want . . . to see . . . Fraser.'

She looked at him.

He looked at her.

She said, 'Should we have a glass of wine?'

The initial shock was subsiding. And it might have been worse. It was just Fraser. *Fraser*. There had been trouble with him before.

It was true that this did seem more serious. She was sitting there on the sofa saying things like, 'I know I shouldn't have started this in the first place. I wasn't emotionally available. It was selfish of me.' She looked very solemn. 'I haven't been honest with you, James. I've never been honest with you. I'm sorry.'

His most immediate concern was what would happen *that night* – the prospect of not spending the night with her *that night* was an utterly terrible one. He needed her more than ever that night, after what she had said. The prospect of spending the night *alone* . . . The prospect of her just *leaving* . . . He might eventually fall asleep, and then wake a few hours later, in the desolate misery of first light, with the whole day waiting there . . . He poured more wine.

Now she was talking about the oast houses. There were a few of them on the property in Kent, and she was saying that she wished they could all – he took 'they' to mean the two of them plus Fraser – live in their own oast house 'and just visit each other when we wanted to'. Though why he and Fraser would ever want to visit each other . . . And what would happen if he wanted to visit her and found Fraser already there, in her oast house? Or if one night together they should be interrupted by Fraser's heavy knock?

She was quite tipsy now. She stuck out her glass for more wine. 'I'm sorry, James,' she said. She smiled wistfully. Then she kissed him, properly and at length, on the mouth. 'I want to stay the night,' she whispered. 'Is that okay?'

'Of course,' he said. 'I want you to.'

'It would be just too sad otherwise.'

Once that was settled, they ate a piece of Parmesan and finished the wine. Then she went and put on her new silk pyjamas. Then he took them off. And what followed was ferociously heightened with the sense that it was now in some way illicit, with the furious, urgent sense that it might be the last time.

*

In the morning everything seemed evanescent. On the point of evaporating. Outside time. They lay there holding each other in the halflight.

She said, 'What do you think I should do?'

There was a whole minute of silence.

(A minute, he now thinks, in which everything stood still, and everything was still possible, waiting to hear what he would say . . .)

Finally he sighed with what seemed like frustration or impatience and said – 'I don't know, Katherine. I don't know.'

She squeezed him.

'Will you make some coffee?'

When he had made it he let in some more light, and they had it sitting side by side, propped on pillows.

'What time is it?' she said.

He picked up his watch. 'Eight fifteen.'

'I have to go.'

He watched her leave the warm sheets and tiptoe out. Heard her exchange a few words with Hugo. Listened to the shower's feeble sputter. To the quiet when it stopped.

Still wonderfully, luxuriously naked (her nakedness seemed like a wonderful luxury now) she sat down on the edge of the bed, in the soft shaft of London light that seeped down from the street. 'I might not see you for a while,' she said. He nodded. With his knuckles he stroked her sternum. She kissed him. Then she went to the living room to dress, and left.

In fact, they saw each other the very next day. Toby invited them for a drink – together, as if they were an item – near his Finsbury Square office. When Toby left, they stayed for another drink. In fact, they stayed until kicking-out time, by which point a tacit understanding seemed to have emerged that they would spend the night at her place.

They had to take two buses to get there. The first was totally empty as it leaped and jittered over the tarmac of the New North Road. They sat on the lower deck, near the door, kissing quietly in the harsh damp light. From Essex Road station they would have walked if it wasn't pouring so determinedly, if there weren't streams in the streets and waterfalls plunging into the drains – it was only two short stops on the 38 that emerged from the turbulent opacity of the night, and then a sprint down Packington Street which left them soaked. In the kitchen they stuffed their faces with a pack of *saucisson sec*. Once upstairs, they spent a lot of time, in various states of undress, looking through some photo albums she had produced from somewhere – earlier versions of Katherine Persson. He was still looking at them when she said (she was far from sober), 'What happens here?' and poked his hairy perineum.

'Nothing,' he murmured, still looking at the photos.

'No . . .' she mused, leaning over him, tickling it. 'I suppose not. With me it all happens there . . .'

'Mm . . .'

'It's funny to think that nothing happens there with you.'

'No . . .'

'With you I suppose it happens *here* . . .'

He left early the next morning – Hugo was in Mecklenburgh Street – with a perfunctory halitosis-laced kiss in the steady headache of first light. Still, so much for not seeing him for a while. The question was – what now?

On Friday he sent her a hopeful text – *See you this weekend?*

There was silence until Saturday morning, when this popped out of the ether – *No honey sorry doing things this weekend x*

He wondered what she was doing. It occurred to him, of course, that she might be with Fraser. In a strange way, he hoped she was. Fraser was somehow part of the furniture. He had probably been sharing her with Fraser, without knowing it, for weeks. He was used to that idea. It was the idea that she might be with someone else, someone *other* than Fraser – or even on her own – that was the heavier thought. And it did weigh on him, as that Saturday wasted away unused. Partly it was just a matter of knowledge. He was very keen to *know* what she was doing. To know whether she was with Fraser, or with someone else, or on her own. Not knowing was what was hard.

3

Friday morning the wind was screaming and yelling, screaming and yelling at him to shake a leg. He pressed out his Silk Cut and flung off the duvet. Today was the day. Today was the day he had been waiting for for more than a year. In the white nook of the kitchen, where the wind was fighting the unsnug window, he took the Tropicana from the fridgelet. The fact was, they were destined to be together, in spite of everything that had happened. It was pretty simple. He loved her, she loved him, and it had been like that from the very first moment. The moment when she looked up from the front desk, her manner as intimidatingly poised and together as always, and saw him there . . .

Pow!

A *coup de foudre*. (Or Cupid's twang.) Love at first sight. That never happened to some people. Some people never had that. Then last year he had nearly fucked it up – no, he *had* fucked it up – and now fate was offering him a second chance. *So do not fuck it up again, Fraser*, he instructed himself, pissing noisily in the wind-hammered suntrap of the bathroom.

He took a shower.

They were just so wonderfully easy, those long talks they had on the phone practically every night now. It was as if nothing had happened. Everything forgiven and forgotten. *Amor vincit omnia.* They still laughed at the same things. The same things made them happy. The same things made them sad. They understood each other. Soulmates. That was so obvious there was no fighting it. There was just no fighting it.

'Let's try again, Katie,' he had said last week, when they had just laughed at something together.

And then, 'Hello? You still there?'

'Yes, I'm still here.' Her lovely English voice.

'So,' he said, 'are we gonna try again?'

And she said. 'What exactly would that entail?'

'What would it entail?' . . . He said, 'Why don't we go away somewhere. Why don't we go away for a weekend somewhere. No pressure. Just see where things stand.'

He did not expect her to say yes straight away, and she didn't.

First she just laughed as if the whole thing was a joke.

Then she made him wait a few days.

She was stronger than he was. He knew that. Smarter and stronger. (Some men would find that hard to take – a smarter, stronger woman.) Strong as she was, though, she was suffering too. And she was doing all sorts of things to try and numb that suffering. That was her way. She wouldn't just suffer passively, like he sometimes did. She would never do that.

Towelling his furred solidity, his thoughts touched with a new twinge of shame on the incident that had provoked all this suffering. It was an incident that had preoccupied him much since last fall – sleepless nights and such – and specially the last few months. It was tough for a man like him to be married and do that sort of work. You know the sort of work. The model taking off one set of underwear and putting on another on the other side of the screen, talking merrily. Only the two of them in the windowless studio with the stainless-steel sink in the corner. And then she steps out from behind the screen and he tells her to lie down on the furskin and look sexy, or strike a Christine Keeler pose and look sexy, or use some prop and look sexy . . . Part of the trouble was he found women like that – women like Felicity, for instance – very easy to engage with. They *liked* him. They liked his energy; they liked his playfulness. It's fair to say there were typically a lot of warm feelings in that studio. And a lot of flirting – which was part of the job. The job was to make them look sexy, and to make them look sexy he had to make them *feel* sexy, so he had his professional patter. The thing is, when you say stuff like that, even if you don't mean it, even if you're just *saying* it, it has its effect. There is no such thing as a purely professional situation. That was something he had learned. He knew that all too well.

So they were alone in the warm studio, him and Felicity, a man and a woman, and it was late at night. And it was *her* idea to do the artistic shots. She was the one who said, as she stepped out of one set of transparent panties and into another, 'When we've finished these, I want to do a few arty ones for my portfolio. Is that okay?' And what was he gonna say? No, it's *not* okay? I don't think that's a very sensible idea? Listen, this was his *job*. He and Felicity were *working* together. A household name on the UK high street was paying him for those shots. Those shots were paying the mortgage. (Though they were just test shots. Felicity and the other models were just on try-out. Only one of them would feature in the pictures which would be on the side of every bus in the country next year. And it's possible that some of them, Felicity included, mistakenly thought that Fraser would have some say in deciding which of them it would be.)

They had just started the artistic shots – i.e. the nudes – i.e. he was in an isolated studio late at night with a naked underwear model – and she was making various pouts and swoony faces at the lens, and he was sort of squatting there over her, almost sitting on her legs, near enough to feel the warmth of her peachy skin, and telling her how sexy she looked, and how hot she was making him feel . . . No, there is no such thing as a purely professional situation.

When she started to undo his trousers he said, 'Oh no,' as if something terrible had happened. 'No,' he said, frowning tragically as she lowered the zip. 'No . . .' He was pleading with her, and she ignored him.

An hour later he drove her home.

And she invited him in.

And he sat at the wheel with a look of terrible pain on his face. Why did it have to happen when she was out of town? Why did this have to happen when she was in Madrid, for Chrissakes?

Well, he went in. And he has suffered for it ever since. Even when he was living with Felicity last summer, he was suffering. (And she threw him out as soon as she realised he wouldn't be useful to her professionally, that was the sort of person *she* was.) Yes, he has suffered for it, and he *needed* to suffer. That's the way he sees it now. To make himself worthy of her again, he needed to suffer. He needed to spend a year in purgatory. And now he had.

The VW Golf parked in the street out front was extremely old. It had the fully depreciated feel of its two hundred thousand miles, a semi-organic hothouse smell. Some sort of shy plant life seamed the window-seals. The top of the steering wheel and the head of the stick-shift looked like they had mange. He snapped his seatbelt on and started the engine – he had had some work done on it and it fired first time.

*

Fraser was late. From the living-room window, she saw him park a scrofulous Volkswagen Golf, silver, liver-spotted with rust, in front of the house. Instead of trying the doorbell, he took out his phone.

'Hello?' she said neutrally.

'Hi, it's me. I'm outside.'

'Okay,' she said. 'I'll be down in a minute.'

She was still watching him as he produced his pack of Silk Cut and lit one. And he still didn't look like a proper smoker; the cigarette still looked silly in his ursine hand. It had been his idea to spend a weekend together, somewhere out of London. 'Why don't we, uh . . . Why don't we see how things stand?' he had said. (Whatever that meant.) There was a long silence. Then she said she would think about it. She said it flippantly, without meaning it. It took her two days to see what some part of her had known all along – she *would* do it. It was the thing in the whole world that she most wanted to do. There was something hopeless about that. And also, she thought, staring sleeplessly out at the lobby the next morning, something uniquely hopeful.

She seemed tetchy as she slammed the front door and descended the four asphalted steps to the street with the handle of a shabby sports holdall in her fists. Smiling, he stepped forward and took it. 'New car?' she said.

'Newish.' He stowed the holdall. 'I've had it six months or so. I mean, it's not *new* new, of course.'

'You're smoking again.'

'Fraid so. Want one?'

She shook her head.

He took off his leather jacket and settled in at the wheel with enthusiasm. He seemed very pleased with himself as he turned the key.

The Golf was indeed not *new* new. He was talking about some work he had had done to the engine. (He knew about these things. She liked that about him. In Senegal, at Zebra Bar, he had been the unofficial onsite mechanic, spending most mornings hidden under the latest jalopy to limp into the stockade, helping hapless travellers, *homme de la situation* . . .)

The traffic was fairly light, and she did not say much as they negotiated their way out of London – Swiss Cottage, Finchley, signs for 'the North'. She just sat strapped into the tattered passenger seat, flicking looks his way every now and then. Sometimes she would ask a simple question, and he would answer at length. For instance, 'What sort of work are you doing at the moment?' (A question that had its own particular intensity.)

'Oh, this and that . . .' It was mostly parties these days, he said. He would show up in his old leather jacket and jeans and spend several underdressed hours wandering around with a Nikon D70 shelved on his paunch, looking faintly seedy as he snuck canapés into his mouth and asked trios and quartets of party-goers to smile . . .

She was experiencing his presence as something pungently strange. It was true that they had spoken several times on the phone. Long meandering talks, mostly late at night. He would phone at eleven, midnight – she liked that. She liked the intimacy of it. She liked lying in bed, listening to his voice.

'I miss you, Katie,' he had said one night.

To that, she said nothing for a long time. She stared at the wicker fan.

So they had spoken a lot on the phone. To be sitting there next to him as they zoomed north, however, was a very different proposition. (He was pushing the Golf hard up the M1, squinting out intently at the motorway.) His eyes, his long jutting jaw, his hands holding the mangy wheel, his substantial forearms, his jeans – it was a very different proposition from the telephonic spirit she had been tentatively engaging with for the past week. For one thing, the telephonic spirit had no smell. His smell. His own smell, and the smell of the Davidoff scent he always used.

She had spent the night with James on Tuesday, and she had worried that that might interfere with how she felt, that it might interfere with her *perception* of how she felt. (An interesting idea, when she thought about it – *her perception of how she felt*. What was the difference between her perception of how she felt, and how she *did* feel? In what sense did her feelings exist when she wasn't perceiving them – when she wasn't *feeling* them?) It was not something she had planned, that last night with James. Toby had invited them for a drink, and somehow they had ended up sleeping together, and she had worried that she would find it harder to know what she felt about Fraser – and that was why she was there, on the M1 near Luton, torpedoing through a heavy squall, to work out what she felt about Fraser – so soon after spending the night with someone else.

She need not have worried. James was not in her mind at all as they tore north, water scrambling to the edges of the windscreen and peeling from the windows in long, nervous trails. What *was* in her mind was something else. The trouble was, this entire escapade was predicated on the idea that she had *forgiven* Fraser for that. The nocturnal talks might have misled her here. Somehow they seemed to have taken place in a parallel world, a world in which it had simply not happened. A world in which she had never phoned him from Madrid.

'Where are you?' she says, as soon as he answers.

'I'm at home,' he says.

'Why haven't you been answering the phone?'

'What do you mean?'

'I've been phoning you all morning. You haven't been answering the phone.'

'I didn't hear it.'

'I've been phoning you *all morning*...'

'I was out.'

'Where?'

'The shops. Shopping...'

'When? What time?'

'Uh ... I'm not sure. Why? What is it?'

'Listen. You're at home, yeah?'

'Yeah ...'

'I'm going to call you on the landline. Okay?' Silence. 'Okay?'

'I'm not at home.'

She is in Madrid – a 'training week' – staying at her employer's Madrid hotel. It is supposed to be a sort of prize as well as training, and there is all sorts of free pampering on offer. Now she feels light-headed and shuts her eyes. 'You're not at home?' she says, without emotion.

'No.'

'Where are you?' Another simple, unemotional question.

'I'm at Nick's place.'

'Why are you at Nick's place?'

'We were out late,' he says. 'So I just slept on the sofa.'

'Why did you lie to me then?'

'I'm sorry. I don't know. I'm sorry. It was stupid.'

'Does Nick have a landline number?' she says.

'I guess.'

'What is it?'

'I don't know it.'

'Well ... will you ask him?'

He hesitates. 'Are you serious?' When she says nothing, he sighs. 'Okay.'

He is off the line for a minute, then he tells her the number, and she writes it down, hangs up on him, and dials it.

He picks up immediately. 'Hello?' he says. 'Is that you?'

'It's me.'

'Okay? Satisfied now?'

'Why did you lie to me?' she says, suddenly distraught. 'Why did you do that? Don't you understand that I *want* to trust you? Don't you see that if you lie to me that's just not going to be possible?'

'I'm sorry. It was stupid. I'm sorry.'

'*Don't lie to me! Just don't!*'

'It was stupid. I'm sorry.'

'Where are you?'

There is a momentary silence. 'I'm at Nick's.'

She thinks of asking to speak to Nick. Then she says, 'I'll be home tomorrow night.'

She had not asked for the number in order to prove, by phoning him on it from Madrid, that he was at Nick's. It proved no such thing, though he seemed to think she thought it did. He was quite stupid sometimes. (She had always worried – it was one of the things she worried about – that he just wasn't intelligent enough for her.) Perhaps he wasn't so stupid, though. Perhaps, in his instinctive way, he understood that she did not want to know the truth. That she probably wouldn't phone the number because she did not *want* to know that it was not Nick's number. Which she didn't. And since she didn't, why do it? Why phone it?

Hello?' A woman's voice. 'Hello?' the woman says again. 'Who is this?'

'Is Nick there? Please.'

'Nick?' It is obvious from the way she says it that there is no Nick there, ever. And then she says, 'I think you've got the wrong number.'

She wrote it all down. In writing, Fraser was obviously a shit.

And she, poor little thing, still loved him. What was so terrible was that she still loved him. She did not want to throw him out. It was something she had to force herself to do, in the knowledge that she should, like putting her fingers down her throat. And when she did, it was he who shed most of the tears.

What was so terrible was that she still loved him. She did not want to. She wanted to love someone else, and within a few weeks she tried. She was just about to tell him, this prospective lover, that she didn't fancy him at all, that she had no interest in him whatsoever, when he was kissing her. She slept with him that very night. He was sweet, intelligent, had a BMW. Within two weeks it was a sad failure – and then there was someone else fighting his little trickle of tears, his wobbly mouth, and only just losing. There was someone else earnestly wanting to know what everyone always wants to know.

Why?

*

They stopped to fill up and have something to eat at a service station somewhere near the heart of England. The sky was mild. The sky was neutral. Neutral like the system of slip roads and parking spaces, like the sharp white arrows stencilled on the tarmac, like the lines of stationary HGVs, the surrounding flat land, the inveterate soughing of the motorway. A place of horizontals. A non-place. Fraser was paying for the petrol.

While they ate – toasted paninis that looked like they had been flattened by a truck tyre – he talked about various people she half-knew, friends of his. Filling her in on what they were up to. There was something fairly lugubrious about this. Probably it was the thorough, systematic way he was working through them. He was talking about Ed O'Keefe, the veteran pap who was also well known in the soft-focus world of 'erotica', and some tax difficulties he was having with the Inland Revenue – or was it the VAT man? – when she interrupted him with what immediately seemed like obvious hostility. 'Should I drive for a while?' she said.

He stopped speaking. He looked hurt.

'Do you want me to drive for a while?' she said.

'If you want.'

They walked across the tarmac in silence and took their seats in the old Golf's muffling interior, and she drove them through Yorkshire, as neutral Midlands afternoon sloped into northern evening. Until they stopped, Fraser had done most of the talking, and now that he had shut up they travelled predominantly in silence. It was to be expected, she thought – noticeably more philosophical now that she was occupied with wheel and pedals – that it would be like this. It would have been naïve to expect anything else. Except that she did seem to have expected something else – she looked quickly over her shoulder as she moved out to overtake – which presumably made her naïve ... What had she expected? Just something ... Something less painful. It was painful, that was the thing. Though the pain was low-level, it had been there since the morning, and she just wasn't used to it any more. Since the end of last year, she seemed to have had the manage of it. She had filled up her time. She had left none of it vacant for pain to squat in, and in the process, she seemed to have forgotten the most obvious thing about pain – it was painful.

He was asleep now, in the passenger seat, with his head fallen and his hands in his lap. He had nodded off somewhere near Sheffield. He didn't say anything for ten minutes, then there was a single short snore. Though her first instinct was to wake him, she did not. With him asleep, she was able to imagine, staring out at the motorway's soothingly neutral space, that she was on her own, which had the effect of lessening the pain. When she did pick him up in her peripheral vision, though, it was stranger in a way to be there with him asleep than it was with him awake – with him just *sleeping* there, it was spookily as if the whole year of separation simply hadn't happened.

She flicked on the headlights.

The traffic streamed north in slate-blue twilight. On the other side, the traffic streamed south. That would be them, she thought, in forty-eight hours . . .

Since this morning, he had been trying very hard to be light. Unfortunately he wasn't light. He was heavy. It had been more and more obvious as the hours wore on. He just didn't have the energy to keep up the jolly-jolly act. When she thought about it, it was not surprising that he seemed depressed. The facts *were* quite depressing. He was forty-eight and lived on his own in a studio flat, scraping a living from menial photographic work. He saw his daughters once a fortnight or less. Physically, he seemed to be losing it swiftly now – his hair, his shape, his *je ne sais quoi* . . . He still smoked. He had no savings. No prospects. She took her eyes off the surging motorway for a second and, suddenly feeling sorry for him – the feeling pierced her shockingly, made tears spring into her eyes – she placed her hand for a moment on his sleeping thigh.

A little while later he woke up.

'Where are we?' he said.

'Nearly at Newcastle.'

'Do you want me to drive?'

'No,' she said, 'it's okay.' The driving was therapeutic, analgesic.

He moved in his seat. Yawned. Lit a Silk Cut. 'Maybe we should have picked somewhere nearer London,' he said, snapping open the ashtray.

'Yeah, or taken a plane.'

He yawned again.

'Anyway . . .' she said. 'It was your idea.'

*

The hotel was one of the most famous and expensive in Edinburgh. At about eight thirty – the last stretch, from Tyneside, had been surprisingly long – they strayed scruffily into the lobby with their sports holdalls. The lobby. A huge open fire. Stags' heads.

'I, uh . . . I got a reservation,' Fraser said.

'Okay sir,' said the man in the tartan tie. 'What's the nim?'

'It's uh . . . King.'

'How much are you *paying* for this?' she whispered frantically, while the tartan tie fussed with formalities.

Fraser shushed her with a hand on the shoulder. 'Don't worry about it. To tell you the truth, I got a special deal. So don't worry.'

A second tartan tie had been summoned and to this man – a Lithuanian – they handed their pitiful luggage.

'Should we eat first,' Fraser said, 'or do you want to have a shower first?'

She said she wanted to eat first, and they went upstairs for a few minutes to freshen up. The Lithuanian, having shown them how to turn on the TV, waited for twenty seconds then withdrew untipped. She was feeling strange – she stood there in the air of plush expectancy (Fraser was in the wetroom) wishing she was at home. Or at least that home was nearby, escapable to at any time. She felt trapped there, standing next to the troubling question of the tartan-festooned four-poster. This, she thought, was the inevitable bed. This was what the weekend was all about. It was what they had been speeding up the M1 towards – he had had his foot to the floor the whole way, while he was driving –

and what troubled her as she stood there was a sense that she might not want to sleep with him in it. She did not know whether she wanted to. Where once it was the most important, the most essential thing in her life, she felt, standing there, that she would need to think about it. She was just not sure what it would mean. What would it mean?

In a polo neck now, and extravagantly scented, Fraser emerged smiling from the wetroom. Something about her posture prevented him from putting his arms around her and taking it from there, as he had intended. 'So, should we eat?' he said. They took the lift downstairs – the hallways of the hotel were woollen in their windowless hush, with pools of halogen light on the floor – and were warmly welcomed into the dining room, where there was another spectacular open fire, another expanse of sombre tartan. They were shown to a table. She was suddenly feeling very depressed. She put down the menu and said, 'I think this whole thing might have been a mistake, Fraser.'

He looked up from his own menu with a notch of worry in his forehead.

'What are we *doing* here?' she said. 'This is just weird.'

'What are we doing here?' He put his hand over hers. 'I'll tell you what we're doing here . . .'

She pulled her hand away.

He had started to say something else – something about falling in love again – when she interrupted him. 'Should we order? I'm starving.'

He sighed. 'Sure,' he said. 'Sure, let's order.'

They sat in silence until the waiter had taken their order. Then they sat in silence some more. Fraser was looking at her. She was looking everywhere except at Fraser. The *Monarch of the Glen*-style paintings on the walls. The waiting staff in their long white aprons, their standard-issue tartan ties. The man in the tailcoat –

presumably the whisky sommelier – squeaking from table to table with his wheeled tantalus of single malts. The whole tree flaming in the fireplace . . .

'You're very angry with me,' Fraser said finally.

She looked at him.

Sitting opposite her, he looked somehow implausible in his auteur's polo neck. His shoulders were still powerful. His head – the dimpled imperial jaw – was still fairly splendid. So what was it? It was his eyes. His squinting eyes, with whose joyously sexual merriment she had once fallen thuddingly in love, were polluted with sadness. They were polluted with sadness and fear.

'Yes,' she said. 'I am.'

'Of course,' he said, shaking his head. 'I understand. This will take time. It won't be easy . . .'

'*What* will take time?' she said in a louder voice. 'What do you think is going on here?'

'I don't know. You tell me. What *is* going on here?'

'Fraser . . .' she said, sighing exasperatedly. 'Alright.' She seemed to marshal her thoughts. She seemed to focus herself. 'You made my life absolute fucking hell,' she said. Then, in a very much less matter-of-fact tone, 'Do you understand that? I sometimes wonder if you even *understand* that.'

'I do . . .'

'*Do* you? I'm not sure that you do . . .'

'Of course I do . . .'

'You made my life absolute fucking hell, and now you seem to think you can just take me to a posh hotel and everything will be fine. That we can just sit here and have a lovely time . . .'

'No,' he protested.

'There's something *insulting* about this. There's something insulting about the way I'm supposed to be swept off my feet by all this . . .'

'You're not –'

'It's a fucking luxury hotel! Wonderful! I spend all my time in a luxury hotel. Didn't it occur to you that I might not *want* to spend the weekend in a luxury hotel?'

'Katie . . .'

'No, of course it didn't . . .'

'Katie . . .'

'What is the point of this? What are we *doing* here? What do you think this is? A nice romantic weekend? Is that your understanding of emotions? Is that how you think emotions are?'

'I said it will take time . . .'

'Your understanding of emotions is just so fucking limited, Fraser. You trample on other people and then all you feel is self-pity. You're just so fucking selfish. I seriously sometimes wonder whether you've got some sort of problem. Otherwise how can you not see what you're doing? How can you not see how you're *hurting* people . . . ?'

She put her hand over her eyes to hide all the water that was suddenly there as the waiter solemnly put the starters on the table. Fraser looked on helplessly as he did. As soon as he had moved away, still hiding her face with her hand, she stood up and hurried out.

A few minutes later she sat down again.

'Okay. I'm fine now,' she said. 'Sorry.'

And she seemed fine in her new face. She started to eat.

'Katie,' Fraser said. 'I understand what I put you through . . .'

'Let's not talk about it,' she said. 'Not now.'

Looking shattered, he said, 'We *need* to talk about it.'

She nodded. 'M-hm. How's yours?'

'I, uh . . . I haven't tried it yet.' He looked down at the slice of venison terrine, the redcurrant sprig, the four perfect triangles of toast. He wasn't hungry.

She, on the other hand, seemed starving. She finished what was on her own plate and then ate most of what was on his.

He insisted, when they had finished the meal, on ordering two stupendously expensive whiskies from the tailcoated sommelier, and then – it was not even ten – they went for a short walk along Princes Street, as far as the floodlit Sir Walter Scott memorial.

When she stepped out of the wetroom in her silk pyjamas – and she had spent a long time in there – Fraser was lying nonchalantly propped on an elbow on the four-poster. He had taken off his shoes and socks.

'Hey, nice PJs,' he smiled.

'They were a present.'

His smile wavered. It went out altogether in his pale eyes. 'What – from . . .?'

'No,' she said. 'Not from him. From someone else.'

'So . . .' Fraser started tentatively. 'Who, uh . . . who was he?'

She was able to see him in the mirror, staring at his own heavy-duty toenails. And then, when she said nothing, lifting his eyes warily towards hers. 'Just . . . a person,' she said. 'Why? What difference does it make?'

'None.'

'I don't want to talk about it.'

'Okay.'

They had yet to touch each other in any significant way. It was one of the things that made the situation feel so strange. However, it felt no less strange – it felt stranger – when he stood up and perched his hands on the suave silk of her shoulders. 'Fraser . . .' He kissed her exposed neck. She shrugged him off. 'Nothing's going to happen tonight,' she said. 'Okay?'

'Okay,' he said, smiling at her in the mirror, trying to keep it light, his eyes all over the shining ivory silk.

'Now I'm going to sleep,' she said. 'I'm very tired.'

'Me too.'

She lay on the far side of the four-poster, on the luxurious solidity of the mattress, on the edge of its precipice, listening to him splashing and spitting in the wetroom. It went quiet for a while. Then he emerged and she felt him slide into the huge bed, sending a wave through the stiff linen. The lights went off. She was tense, expecting some sort of overture, an inquisitive hand . . .

'Goodnight, Katie,' he whispered, from quite far away.

Then stillness, silence.

Which made her feel that she had treated him unfairly, and she turned over and stretched out her own hand, stretched it out into the empty space of the sheets, until finally it found his flexed, naked knee. 'Night, night,' she said.

*

In the morning there was some smooching. He wanted more than that, of course. He was sharply desirous of more. There was something urgent about the way he started to unpick her pyjamas. He had undone half the iridescent little buttons of the silk jacket when she stopped him, seeing with sudden force as his eyes found the waxy scoop of her sternum how the situation would be transformed into something she did not want it to be if she let him undo them all, if she let him tug the silken trousers down. Fastening the jacket to her throat, she hurried into the wetroom and had a long shower.

When she emerged, wrapped in a towel, she squatted down next to her nylon holdall with her knees together and patiently extracted some things from it. She withdrew to the wetroom to put them on.

Fraser, when it was his turn, took a markedly different

approach. He left the four-poster in an unhurried state of flagrant nudity and had a shower with the door open. Still provocatively naked, he stood in front of the sink shaving.

'I'll see you downstairs,' she shouted from the far side of the room.

And he stood there full-frontally, his face foolishly white-foamed – in a way that tended to emphasise his otherwise total nakedness – and said, 'You're not going to wait for me?'

'I'm starving,' she said, looking him specifically in the face. His torso was flaccid and his stomach was pendulous. However, his penis, she had not failed to notice, had in full measure its old solidity and weight, its statesmanlike presence.

'You can't just wait a few minutes?' he said, his eyebrows frowning over the white mask.

'Okay,' she said. 'I'll wait a few minutes.'

'Thank you.'

She took off her shoes and sat on the bed.

When he finally put something on, they went down to the dining room, where he ate heartily of the terrific spread. Arbroath smokies and poached eggs, whisky marmalade on toasted muffins. The fire quietly informed the morning of its pinesmoke smell – the same tree as last night probably, now falling apart in a mass of white ash. Walking the length of tartan to the table, she felt underdressed in her jeans and zippered fleece. A sadness was stealing over her – worse, in its quiet way, than anything she had felt since they left London. And she had felt okay upstairs just now. She had even said to herself, as she sat there hugging her knees, 'It's okay. I feel *okay*.'

'So,' Fraser said. (What was *he* so jovial about?) 'What're we gonna do this morning?'

'What do you want to do?' she said plainly.

'I want to do,' he said, using a napkin to wipe his fingers individually, 'whatever you want to do.'

She shrugged. 'I dunno. What is there?'

'There's the whole fair city of Edinburgh to explore.' He smiled, tossing the napkin onto the table.

The joviality did not last long. The weather may have had something to do with that – a travelling mist of drizzle that hid the surrounding hills and filled the Nor' Loch with an obscurity pierced only by the weakly echoing voice of the Waverley tannoy. They spent the morning sightseeing. The streets of the old town, tangled like wet string. Holyrood House. The elegant, unexcitable probity of the headquarters of the Bank of Scotland. The National Gallery.

Towards lunchtime it did stop raining. The sky went white, with a soft luminance that suggested the sun was up there somewhere. They had a pizza. Pizza Express. It was profoundly uninspired – might as well have been in London – but then the whole morning had felt uninspired. Fraser just seemed sad, with nothing interesting to say. When he did speak, she found him tedious. She found him irritating. He had said things in the National Gallery that made her want to tell him to shut up. Once, as he struggled to say something impressive in front of Veronese's *Mars, Venus and Cupid* (in the past he would have made a joke; now he seemed to feel a simpering need to impress her), she laughed at him – she just laughed in his face, and then went on to the next painting. It had not been a nice thing to do, and she wondered shamefully why she had done it as she sliced up her pizza. He had said less after that. He had followed her in silence, in fact, only nodding when she tried, in a spirit of penitence, to solicit his views about this or that picture, about da Vinci's dog paws or Botticelli's Madonna.

*

After lunch she wanted a 'proper walk', a two-hour tramp up to Arthur's Seat or something like that. He did not, which was in keeping with his increasing listlessness, if not his willingness until then to do whatever she wanted. So they went for a walk in Princes Street Gardens instead, and it was there that he said it. The station tannoy started to quack, the sound floating through the treetops, and when it was finished she heard the rain – it was so quiet that you had to stop and listen for it. It sounded like soap suds subsiding. It was as quiet as that. 'You don't love me any more.' That was Fraser's sudden insight, and he said it as if it was a sudden insight, pulling up on the tarmac path. She herself said nothing. She was so struck that she just stood there as he started to sob, and once he had started there was no stopping him.

Some hours later she lay in the long tub listening to the same sound – the sound of soap suds subsiding. The wetroom was luxurious and well equipped. It was warmly lit and windowless. Except for the sound of the suds, and the womby hum of the extractor, and the occasional watery statement when she stirred, there was silence. There was silence in her heart as well.

She had just stood there on the path with her hands in the pockets of her fleece – it was not warm, there was a face-numbing, hand-hurting wind – and watched him sitting sideways on the bench, shaking like a diesel engine, with his fingers wrapped over his eyes. She was thinking, *How like him, how like everything that was unworthy about him to see the situation in those terms: You don't love me any more. How like him to be so surprised by that!* There was something almost solipsistic about it. The strange thing was, she was surprised by it too.

Finally she did sit down next to him and pat his shaking back. She did quietly suggest that they find somewhere warmer. It took a while to shift him. Eventually they stood up and walked out of the park. He had stopped sobbing, though he started again on the pavement of Princes Street, wandering among the shoppers. She did not know what to do with him. It was two o'clock on Saturday afternoon.

Lying in the tub two hours later – four o'clock on Saturday afternoon, time was passing slowly – she wished she was at home. It was one of those situations where the obvious thing to do – drive to London, immediately – had not occurred to her until it was too late; until they had had too much to drink, sitting in a pub in the New Town. Instead, while he lay in a foetal position on the four-poster (he had not even taken his jacket off), she locked herself in the otherworldly silence of the wetroom, and submerged her frigid extremities in the thickly steaming tub. She had not said that she didn't love him any more. That she had *not* said. She had said nothing. With languid hands she stirred the water in the vicinity of her sunken stomach. She had seen written somewhere – probably in some leaflet she had looked at while she was waiting for him that morning – that among the many other luxuries offered by the suite was the fact that it was equipped with 'anti-steam mirrors'. Now, with her head lolling on the edge of the tub, hair neatly piled on top, she saw through the warm fog that the mirrors were indeed mysteriously untouched by it, and wondered how it was done. Heated somehow, was the most obvious explanation. Or perhaps they used some sort of special substance . . .

She stood up, and stepped out, and towelled her flushed self while the tub slowly emptied. She stood in front of the unsullied mirror, kneading moisturiser into her face with her two middle fingers. She tidied up one of her eyebrows. She would have liked to stay there in the warmth of the halogen lights, in the humming silence, until it was time to leave for London the next morning. She felt safe there. Insulated from something. She lingered for a few unnecessary minutes, then she pulled on one of the white towelling robes that the hotel had so thoughtfully provided and stepped out in a whirl of steam.

The late daylight had the quality of wet slate. She sat down on one of the tartan tub chairs. Fraser was still lying there. He seemed to be in a less tight position, and in fact he must have moved – he had taken his jacket off. Nor was he asleep. His eyes were open. The tired light picked them out like marbles, staring at nothing.

There was one small mercy. On Sunday morning the clocks went forward, shortening the weekend by an hour.

2

He woke up with a strange feeling. Sunlight like a shivered mirror in the area, and his watch an hour slow.

In the afternoon he took Omar to the zoo. James has no memory of ever having been to London Zoo. Omar, however, seemed to know the place well. The first things they saw were some lizards. The lizards were in a darkened hall, walled up in waterless fishtanks full of rubber foliage. Omar stood on tiptoe to peer into the tanks or James lifted him. Mostly the lizards just lay there, looking sad. Probably they weren't actually sad, probably it was just something about the shape of their scaly mouths. Probably that's how they would look in the wild. Though in the wild, James thought, the ever-present fear, the need to fend for themselves, might make them less lethargic, might pep them up a bit. Nothing was about to happen to them in those fishtanks; they had probably worked that out by now. They were just waiting for their next meal – and they only ate once or twice a week. It was muggy in the lizard house. For a while Omar was enthusiastic, pointing and whispering as if they might overhear him. Then he lost interest – they had not even looked at the most impressive specimens, in a sort of shop-window of jungle – and wanted to leave.

They wandered around in the sunshine. The animals were strangely elusive. You had to seek them out down winding paths. They saw some medium-sized monkeys, making a stink like the inmates of a prison staging a no-wash protest. They were screeching, making a lot of noise – in spite of which they were just not that interesting. Omar seemed to find them shrugworthy. The silverbacks had more mystique. Sitting very still, they looked at the world through startlingly human eyes, scratched their necks with startlingly human fingernails. More or less extinct in the wild – a few score in their shrinking jungle, waiting for the end – they and their kind were now, James thought, in effect a species of high-maintenance pets. Wards of the state. There was something surreal about the sight of them, just sitting there surrounded by toys (a tyre, for instance) while twenty twittering children pressed their faces to the perspex.

They left the primates and found a neglected-looking structure that ponged very strongly of manure. It was not unlike the stink of Miller's stables. Ostentatiously holding his nose, Omar wanted to leave. He wasn't joking – the overripe stench of sweet manure was too much for him. There were tears in his eyes as James ushered him out.

It was quite a warm day – the warmest of the year so far – and Omar took off his parka. He was dressed exactly as Steve would be – Converse trainers, soft jeans, lambswool jumper, parka with polyester-furred hood. Essentially, James thought, taking the parka, the inmates of the zoo lived like the poorer human members of prosperous Western societies. Like them, they had to put up with miserable housing, monotonous food, persistent minor indignities. On the other hand, they wouldn't die of starvation, or exposure, or waterborne diseases. If they were ill, medical professionals would take a look at them. No, it wasn't perfect, but if you were eking out a terrifyingly insecure existence on a savannah somewhere, or in some jungle, you might take a second look at the zoo if offered a swap. The point was, he thought – perhaps trying to persuade himself – it was too simple just to pity the zoo animals. In many ways they were the lucky ones.

Omar was now talking about some fish he had once seen – they were odourless, perhaps that was their appeal – but James did not know where to find them. They passed the insect house, which neither of them wanted to investigate. They had an ice cream. They saw a serval cat with ears like radio telescopes, staring with psychotic intensity at a pigeon which had flown into its walled enclosure – there were portholes in the wall, through which the scene was visible.

Then Omar saw the merry-go-round.

As soon as he did, he lost all interest in the animals. James tried to explain that the world was full of merry-go-rounds; there would be time enough for them – the animals were what they were there . . .

Omar was now in tears. His puce face was like the sad mask of the theatre logo. The ends of his mouth were down by his chin. James had intended to tough it out, to at least make him look at one or two more animals before letting him loose on the merry-go-round. He felt that Omar *should* be more interested in animals than in merry-go-rounds, more interested in living things, our fellow tenants of time and space, than in tawdry machines. 'Let's just . . .' he said, squatting to Omar's level. 'Let's just have a look at one more . . .'

It just wasn't worth it.

Tears pursuing each other down his empurpled face, Omar was making a lot of noise. People were starting to stare.

'Okay,' James said, 'you can go on the merry-go-round.'

Instantly Omar's face was like the smiling mask of the theatre logo. He was living in the moment, there was no doubt about that. Holding the fibreglass neck of an undulating unicorn, he smiled at James as he went round. It was a smile which expressed an experiential purity quite elusive in later life – probably that was why it was so lovely to see, why it possessed such an immense vicarious pull. Helplessly smiling himself, James waved. He was worried about what Omar would do when the music stopped and he had to dismount. In the event, he was fine. To, 'Was that fun?' he answered with a mature nod. He said he wanted to eat. And when they had eaten, he seemed to tire and said he wanted to leave.

'But we've hardly seen any animals,' James said, smiling. It was true. They had hardly scratched the surface of the place, zoo-logically, and James felt they ought to stay longer. Omar had no such feelings of obligation. James managed to tempt him into finding the lions, or rather the lion – only one was visible, in her high-security enclosure – and then into a more immediate and much smellier encounter with the giraffes. The giraffes. Seeing them just standing there, being giraffes in the middle of London, James had an unprecedented sense of the strangeness of the world. As he and Omar left the giraffe house they were swept up in a stream of noisy, foul-mouthed French schoolchildren whose intention it obviously was to terrify the animals in any way they could. They were upsetting Omar too. And indeed he was now more and more intensely keen to leave. Even the energetically pointed-out okapi – a strangely neglected creature, it looked like a misunderstanding in a medieval manuscript – only held off the next wave of tears for ten seconds or so, and these tears were more despairing than the merry-go-round tantrum, with its all-too-obvious object, and emerged with long low-pitched wails and howls that it seemed nothing would staunch.

Except sleep.

He fell asleep on James's shoulders as they made their way out of one teeming zoo and headed towards the other, with its market and its lock, at the far end of Parkway.

Later, sitting in Isabel's orderly kitchen with a mug (Che Guevara) of Earl Grey while Omar told her what animals they had seen – and he seemed more enthusiastic then, talking about them, than he had when they were there, seeing them – James, for the first time, found himself envying his sister's life. The tidy, well-lit maisonette (lights on everywhere), Omar's kindergarten daubs magneted to the fridge, the Volvo in the parking space outside (the Volvo that went to the two-acre Sainsbury's in Finchley every Saturday), the quietly up-to-the-minute electronics everywhere, the sections of the *Observer* strewn on the sofa, where Steve had been lying after lunch, the Banksy prints in the hall – it was all just so safe and warm and middle class, and sitting there in the kitchen, he felt an envious tug towards something like that. Yes, even towards its intrinsic predictability. Even its faint smugness.

Omar was just telling Isabel about the merry-go-round when Steve appeared in the French windows, with frayed half-moons trodden out of the heels of his jeans and plump pale little Scheherazade in his arms. They had been out on the Heath – Scheherazade in her Bugaboo, Steve having a perambulatory script meeting with his friend Pete.

'Alright, mate,' he said.

'Hi, Steve.'

'How's things?'

James said things were fine.

He phoned Katherine as he walked down the steep street, under the sheared, leafing elms. Voicemail. He left a message.

*

Emerging from the tube half an hour later, his hope was that she had tried him while he was underground. She had not. The disappointment was so surprisingly potent that he wished he had not phoned her in the first place. He had felt okay leaving Isabel's house and now he didn't. He felt very alone.

3

Philippa Persson thought it would take two days. First thing on Tuesday morning, the house was totally empty. A freshly painted, four-bedroom void. They headed to Neasden in soiled, low sunlight. Katherine was driving. Philippa did not intend to tackle this on her own. She had enlisted her daughter to help.

Kate seemed surprisingly down. She was wearing sunglasses and torn jeans. On Sunday evening they had spoken on the phone for two hours – the Edinburgh post-mortem. Philippa had been pleased to hear that it had been a failure, and pleased that Kate, on the phone, had sounded okay. She had sounded no more than wistful, the persistent numbness of Saturday having thawed to a tranquil sadness. The eight-hour drive down to London, she said laconically, had not been much fun. The parting in Packington Street even less so. Fraser in tears. Philippa had permitted herself a quiet snort at that. She had never liked her son-in-law, had encouraged Kate to have nothing to do with him from the start, when he was still married to that other woman. Naturally she did not let on how pleased she was that the Scottish weekend had been a failure. She made sympathetic mooing noises while Kate said that in Edinburgh she had found Fraser tired, tedious, frightened, sad . . . Sad, she said, that was the worst thing. The way he was so *sad*. For her part, Philippa said things like, 'Well, maybe its for the best . . .' She said, 'You tried, Kate. Now I think it's probably time to move on . . .' *Time to move on . . .* She had been saying that for more than a year. And now, thankfully, the whole thing did seem to be over. As Kate herself put it, 'The love is dead.' She said it quite simply. 'The love is dead.' That was just how it felt. The sense she had was of silence, nullity, non-existence. On Sunday night she was just pleased to be home and she slept well.

On Monday morning she felt shockingly worse. There was a serious faltering of the idea that this was not something massively significant. She struggled through the day at work. In the evening she was supposed to meet some people, but the idea of pretending to be okay, of pretending to be interested in other things, was impossible. She went straight home.

Tuesday. Still on a frighteningly steep downward trajectory. A terrible sense of futility. What was the point? The love was dead. In a way she was thankful that she had something mindless to do. Drive to Neasden. Push the obese trolley through Ikea wearing shades. Smoke in the car park under the huge suburban sky, the massing chrome-fendered clouds. Whenever Philippa asked for her opinion, though – *These hand towels or those hand towels? Darling, which hand towels do you think . . . ?* – she just shrugged. She just muttered, 'I don't know.'

She snapped, 'Mum, I *don't know*.'

'Whatever,' she said.

She was thirty-two. She felt half that.

On Tuesday morning, they did Ikea. They *did* it. The long Peugeot estate was overloaded as it waddled onto the North Circular. And Philippa wasn't just taking the first thing she saw.

She would spend twenty minutes on the towels, ten on the toilet seats, half an hour on the light fittings. There were the soap dishes, the mirrors, the laundry hampers. The list of necessities seemed endless. Not everything was from Ikea. Over the next two days, many other shops were involved – mostly in their vast, out-of-town interpretations, skirted with acres of parking space. John Lewis weighed in heavily, for instance. It was there that Katherine's head started to throb as she was asked to look at forty different irons and make a decision. Two dozen toasters – which was it to be? Do we need a pizza slicer?

At two o'clock on Tuesday afternoon they unloaded the morning's shopping at the house, where Katherine's younger brother, Marc, an MBA student at the London Business School, was waiting for the various deliveries – the fridge-freezer, the washing machine, the sofas. The house was in West Kensington, past Olympia, the wrong side of the tracks. Nevertheless, Philippa was hoping for two thousand a week. That was why all the stuff had to be 'nice'. Even the hoover had to be 'nice'. (They found a nice one in John Lewis.) 'Have you been smoking pot in here?' she said to Marc, as she started down the stairs to the kitchen.

'No . . .'

'What's been delivered?'

'Nothing yet.'

'*Nothing?* I'd better phone them.'

While she made some sharp enquiries into the whereabouts of her things – 'Yes, you said between eight and two. It's now twenty past and there's no sign of them . . .' – Marc had found the Waitrose bag and was eating a lobster sandwich. Katherine was out on the patio smoking a Marlboro Light.

That afternoon they spent mainly in John Lewis (an hour among the lamps, two among the linens), and it was dark – in spite of Sunday's shift to summer time – when Philippa dropped her in Packington Street. 'See you nice and early tomorrow,' she said. 'We haven't even started on the living room yet.' Kate waved at the parting Peugeot and unlocked the door. *We haven't even started on the living room yet* . . . There was something depressing about those words. How much stuff *was* there in a house? And in *every* house. To imagine the same mass of stuff they had just spent the day so expensively and systematically marshalling in every house in London, in England, in Europe, in the world . . . It made her feel queasy and depressed.

On Wednesday morning it was suddenly all too much. She had just parked the Peugeot in the John Lewis lot – they were there again, with much to do – when she found herself in tears.

'Darling?' Philippa said. 'What is it?' Philippa was not at her most assured in these situations. She put out a hand. 'What is it?'

Katherine shook her head.

She had shed a few tears the previous night when, having let herself into the flat, she opened her mail. Among various other mailshots were two appeals for money. (Her small portfolio of monthly direct debits – a sponsored orphan in Sri Lanka, the RSPB, Shelter – meant that she was flooded with further appeals. The hungry, the persecuted, the terminally ill – every day she hurried them into the plastic tub on the kitchen floor.) One was something to do with polar bears, whose unique and pathetic plight was well known. The other, orang-utans. They were shamelessly sentimental. The polar-bear one featured a picture of a sad-looking mother and her young. The other was about an orang-utan orphaned at only a few months old – and thus presumably doomed – in some sort of logging incident. They tried to make the point, those well-meaning flyers, that while things were terrible, they were not yet hopeless. Weren't they though? They seemed hopeless to her as she stood next to the table in the living room, shedding her few surprising tears. What was the point of even pretending? The straight line that led from how she had just spent the day to what was happening in the Arctic, in the Indonesian jungle – what was left of it – was too obvious to overlook, whether she wanted to or not. And it was equally obvious which was the stronger force, the stronger by many orders of magnitude – those sentimental leaflets or the force they were up against. Her. Katherine Persson. She was the stronger force, and there was simply no way it was going to be stopped.

She filled in the forms and set up two new direct debits – a total of £10 a month. And just that day she and her mother had added a thousand times that to the strong force. (And what was *that*, if not a mammalian mother single-mindedly providing for her young? The house in West Kensington, with its hundred and ten per cent mortgage, its wealthy tenants, was intended as a sort of trust fund for Katherine and Marc.) Yes, it was hopeless. Nevertheless, she went to the pillar box on Essex Road and posted the forms. She did not do it thinking it would make a difference. It was just her way of saying that she knew what she was doing, she understood, she felt terrible. But she wouldn't stop doing it. She just didn't want to enough.

Setting off the very next morning to add another £10,000 to the strong force was, however, too much. As she switched off the engine, she lowered her head. Tears fell onto the steering wheel.

'Darling?' Philippa said. 'What is it?'

And of course it wasn't just the poor, puzzled species being steadily shunted into oblivion, being shunted out of existence without ever understanding what was happening or why. (And they would do the same to us. We were just doing what any animal would.) It wasn't just the hopelessness of *that* situation. That was there all the time. It was a much more personal hopelessness, of which that was nothing more than an echo. The love was dead. It was dead. She did not love him any more. The terrible thing was she did not love him any more.

*

It was still those memories. The hotel that week in October. The tambour of her heart. The flat in Battersea that first night. The lift in the morning – 'I'm in love with you.' The experience had acquired a definitive quality. It had turned into a definition of what love was. She had thought, that October – *Yes, this is what people mean when they talk about love.* She had previously been in love once or twice. Fraser was not the first. And those experiences were not nothing. They were still important to her. In some significant way, though, they were lesser. With them, she had not felt with the same heart-walloping surety that *this* was what people meant when they talked about love. There were moments there which seemed qualitatively different from everything else in her life. They would be the moments she thought of at the end. They would be the things she thought of at the end of her life. In a sense, they *were* her life. Specific moments, mostly from that first week, or the first few weeks, or the first few months. When she tried to write them down, however, they had none of their force. Writing them down, trying to transcribe them, made them seem mundane, normal. Nothing special. She stopped trying. What was the point anyway? Only that she wrote down everything else, so it seemed strange that the most important, the most significant things were not there.

It was still those memories. It seemed impossible that any other man would ever be able to lessen their importance. Even if she were to have a similar experience with someone else in the future, which was not impossible, what it would lack would be the feeling that it was unique, that it was the final word. It would be hard to have that kind of faith in any feeling in the future. When she said, 'The love is dead,' she had a terrible sense that what she was in fact saying was, 'For me, love is dead.' She wondered whether her experience of this was unusual, or whether it had just happened to her unusually late in life. (She had started sleeping with men unusually late in life, after all, not until she was twenty.) Did most people have an experience like this, she wondered, when they were much younger – in their early twenties, even in their teens?

Those memories.

She was unable to escape the sense that the most intense love of her life was now in the past. The love was in the past. The love *itself* was in the past – she no longer felt it, not even in a lesser, hugely watered-down form. She no longer felt it. It no longer existed. In Edinburgh she had wondered *why* she had once loved Fraser. It didn't even seem to make sense any more.

The love is dead . . .

For me, love is dead . . .

She had perhaps known, the whole time she thought she wanted to stop loving Fraser, that this was the situation she would find herself in if she ever did. It seemed she had staked everything on him, and now she had nothing left for anyone else. Perhaps that was why she never truly *did* want to stop loving Fraser. And it had been easy – it had been easy *not* to stop loving him – when he wasn't there. She thought of the words of that poem –

> In the mind ever burning;
> Never sick, never old, never dead,
> From itself never turning . . .

Yes, something like that. Except it does have to turn from itself when its object finally *is* sitting there with sad eyes in a silly polo neck that misguidedly flaunts his paunch . . .

Thoughts like that tended to make her question everything. Tended to undermine the very idea of things. That was indeed the whole problem perhaps.

More words, more poetry – *Never such innocence again* . . .

And still more – *After such knowledge, what forgiveness?*

4

Freddy at school was an out-and-out weirdo. An insolently effortless top-setter, a heavy smoker, a purveyor of particularly extreme pornography – those tattered scraps of flesh-toned images – he was, with his halo of frizzy hair and plump putto's face, a frightening outsider to many of the others. To many of the teachers too. A hand up in the middle of the French lesson. Mr Ellis is the terrified herbivore at the front near the whiteboard. 'Sir?' 'Yes, Munt?' (With a weak smile.) 'Does wanking make you weak, sir?' Little explosions of laughter from all over the room. Ellis obviously mortified, lady-faced, fully unable to deal with the situation. *Does wanking make you weak, sir?* Ostensibly – and this was very much the tone in which it was asked – it was an innocent appeal for information from an older, more experienced man. That, however, would be to miss the merciless overtone, enormously present that morning in the language school – *You,* Mr Ellis, does wanking make *you* weak? Is it wanking that makes you so *weak,* sir? Are you so weak, *sir,* because of all the wanking you do?

James was there for that incident, quietly reading a newspaper at a sunny desk near the windows. He was in the top set in

French, and only in French. His father lived in France and he spent four months of the year there.

Mr Ellis might have stammered something.

More probably he just froze for a few seconds, and then with unseeing eyes kept murmuring the prepared text of the lesson as if nothing had happened.

Freddy was neither popular nor unpopular. For one thing, he didn't do sport, which in itself placed him so far out of the mainstream as to be practically invisible. (James did do sport. He was in the second XV, which had a certain slackerish cachet, and was one of the stars of the hockey first XI, and on the tennis team too.) As for Freddy, he had once fannied about with the other anaemic four-eyed specimens on their twig-like legs, milky white thighs signally failing to fill shorts – and there was absolutely nothing to be said, in terms of social status, for the fourth XI, the fifth XV. They were for malcos and flids. They were for spastics. The slackerish cachet, such as it was, ended with the second team.

Freddy's liberation from sport was the piano. While this was not particularly helpful for his image either, it was infinitely preferable to stumbling around in the mud on that polder of playing fields west of Hammersmith with someone like Mr Ellis timidly peeping the whistle on Tuesday, Thursday and Saturday afternoons. (The staff room had its own sports hierarchy, which, while it exerted itself more subtly in social terms, more or less exactly mirrored that of the pupils.) So, the piano. The long, polished Steinway in the main hall of the music school. Mr Harris, the head of music, said Freddy was a 'wunderkind', and finally he persuaded the other Mr Harris – this one was head of sport, a far more exalted figure, a figure of papal mystique – to let Freddy off sport totally and permanently, so long as he instead spent the time practising the piano. This indulgence – which was unprecedented – massively enhanced Freddy's status

as a louchely unusual outsider. Indeed, with no further involve-
ment in sport, he no longer seemed to be fully or properly part
of the school. He spent most of his time in the music school –
it looked like a small rococo theatre in an isolated part of the
grounds – playing the piano and smoking. Mr Harris let him
smoke in the music school; it was his own little kingdom, where
all sorts of strange practices obtained. For instance, Freddy was
on first-name terms with him – 'Morning, Mike' – as he was with
most of the other tweed jackets and bluestockings of the music
staff. At the age of fourteen, he took Grade Eight, and started
to work his way through the semi-professional qualifications that
followed it. The life of a professional musician – even some sort
of star – seemed there for the taking.

The September of his final year. Mid-morning in the music
school. Miserable autumn weather. (There is a pail out in the
middle of the parquet, slowly filling from a weeping fissure in
the moulding overhead.) The multicoloured application forms
for the Royal College of Music are there on the table, waiting to
be filled in – and in Mike's opinion the application is no more
than a formality. Freddy is of a much higher standard than is
necessary to win a place most years . . .

When Freddy interrupts to say that he has no intention of
applying to the Royal College, Mike looks as if he has just been
told his Yorkshire terrier, Lulu, has died in a lawnmowing
accident.

'Why?' he says finally.

Freddy says that as a professional pianist – and he seems to
have no doubt that that is what he would be if he persevered
with the piano – he would simply be performing the work of
other men. *They* were the artists. The musicians were mere
performers. Monkeys . . .

Anticipating Mike's next point with a lifted finger, he says that it just isn't possible to *write* music now. Not serious music. Serious music was fucked. (He did use the word 'fucked'.) No serious music of any value was being written. As a medium it was quite possibly finished. He did not intend to waste his time on it. (Thus, incidentally, he flushed Mike's life's work – numerous suites and sonatas, one of which, the 'West London Sonata', had had an outing at the Norwich Music Festival – down the toilet of history.) No, what Freddy intended to do, he told the now misty-eyed Mike, was write. He would be a novelist, and he would start by taking an English degree at Oxford.

When he had said his piece, he lit a Gauloise filterless. He waved out the match and placed it neatly on the unused application forms. He looked up at the ornate plafond.

Though he would never admit it, he has, in the years since, spent much time pondering that miserable morning in the music school.

He went to Oxford, but there was no degree. He was sent down in his second year for doing no – *no* – work.

Through an intricate mechanism of interlocking nepotisms, he eventually found himself working first as a stringer and then as a staffer on a Fleet Street newspaper. These were the John Major years. He managed to spin out a decade or so of journalism – he was supremely plausible when he wanted to be – all the time incubating his masterpiece; wallowing in the tired sleaze of the times, and always planning to start it soon. In truth he started it on numerous occasions. Secretly, cigarette in mouth, he would type a few pages of a Sunday morning, and then, with a sneer on his face, scrumple them up and throw them away. They were never good enough to justify that morning in the music school. They were never anywhere near good enough. The futile, putrid soap opera of Tory politics circa 1995 was what he was in fact writing about. Malicious diary stuff mostly. For a while in the mid-Nineties he was a well-known quidnunc schmoozing the Commons bars.

Towards the end of the decade things started to go wrong. He was drinking too much. Of course, he had always been drinking too much from a medical standpoint; now he was drinking too much even to hold down his job as a political hack and diarist, with its semi-nocturnal hours and intense professional interest in watering holes. Stories went unfiled. He missed important things. (Was not answering his phone, for instance, on the afternoon of 11 September, 2001 – he was passed out on the sofa.) There was an AIDS scare. In the office for a while, the story was, erroneously as it turned out, that Freddy was HIV positive. Still, his hair and teeth were starting to fall out, and he couldn't afford a proper dentist. (Someone said that ended his dreams of television-pundit stardom. Freddy said, 'What about John fucking Sergeant?') And his old school-friend James, for a year or so, looked likely to find himself quite high up the *Sunday Times* Rich List. That didn't help Freddy's mood in the late Nineties. He had always looked down on James slightly – an unusually subtle jock perhaps, but fundamentally a philistine – and he found it hard to stomach the fact that, in the eyes of the world, he might ultimately prove more successful than him. Much more successful. Freddy was freelancing now, living hand to mouth – or mouth to hand – off his ability to winkle information out of people in pubs. The first New Labour landslide hadn't helped. The immense shuffling of seats it entailed – the sudden and violent swings of status – were mirrored in the world of journalism. And to the extent that he was in with anybody, Freddy was mostly in with Tories. He had of course tried, too late – his self-interest was by then painfully transparent – to start making friends with some Labour people, but his main sources were still Tories, and no one was very interested in what they said or thought any more. Loose ends from schooldays – he hadn't even tried to start his magnum opus for several years. Nor, for several years, did he see James. He was just unable to stomach the success of Interspex. When he saw in the papers that it had failed, he was pleased.

In many ways they were unlikely friends. Though they were in the same French lessons, they were in different houses and did not speak to each other until they shared a taxi to Heathrow at the end of their first term. They both had parents living over-seas. Freddy's parents – he was the sort of person it was hard to imagine having parents – lived in Dar es Salaam, where his father was a diplomat. There was a fellowship among the expat students. They were like orphans on the last day of term. Sometimes they had to spend an extra night in the empty school. Even if they didn't, they were usually the last to leave. They seemed more worldly than the others, which in itself made them to some extent outsiders at the school. If Freddy's mode of outsiderdom was obvious, however, James's was more subtle. A tall, manly teenager – the infrequent spots looked out of place on his face and neck – a sportsman and in terms of schoolwork middling at most, he was in many ways a model lad. Perhaps he lacked some of the jocular oomph of the mainstream lad, and though he sat at the lads' table in the dining hall – the loudest table, a mass of egregiously fashionable haircuts (flat-tops) and shoes (Doc Martens) – though his place there was entirely secure, the others might have felt at times that there was something semi-detached about him. Sometimes he seemed, in a mysterious way, to be several years – i.e. significantly – older than they were. There was that sense of worldliness. There was a lurking seriousness. To the younger pupils, he seemed like a proper man among them, someone their parents might know. That was one thing.

His friendship with Munt was another. (And it was a measure of James's status that he was able to be friends with Munt at all without significantly impairing his own standing.) Most of James's other friends thought Freddy was a fucking weirdo. A fucking sicko. Most of his other friends were the sort of people who soberly tried to ignite their own farts. They were locker-room types. They were pack animals par excellence. The self-selecting school elite. A loner like Freddy made no sense to them. And most of Freddy's other friends ... Well, Freddy had no other friends.

In 1984, he spent the ten-day Michaelmas half-term with James in Paris. They stayed out very late every night, loitering hopefully in Pigalle, and drinking Pernod (the advert in the cinema with the naked woman under water), and walking into the skanks of Maghrebi drug dealers in the vicinity of the Gare du Nord. The following summer the same station was their jumping-off point for a month's inter-railing – the zenith of their early friendship.

When they left school two years later, in spite of widely divergent paths, they still saw each other sometimes. James has unpleasant memories, for instance, of the time he visited Freddy up at Oxford. He was not in his element there. The students, even Freddy, did not seem to speak the same language as him; he literally did not understand quite a lot of what they said. He himself was just starting out as an estate agent at Windlesham Fielding – something he instinctively hushed up – and had moved into a place in Islington with Miriam. The pizza franchise, the film – such things filled the last few years for him. In one way or another, he spent much of his time thinking about money. The squalor of the house in which Freddy lived with various other people shocked him – he had been prepared for something squalid and it still managed to shock him. It had been the plan for him to stay there on the sofa. When he saw the sofa – dank in the spliffsmoke – he opted for a hotel. Which didn't make him any more popular. Freddy's squeeze, Isolde, who was something in the student union, subjected him to an irritating interrogation – she kept insisting that he tell them what he thought of 'Thatcher' – as he tried to feel at home sitting on the ashy floor with a can of Carlsberg in his hand. The extraordinary thing was, these people were his own age – twenty, twenty-one. The places where they went out at night were just depressing. Hitting London in the Audi on Sunday evening, looking forward to dinner with Miriam, he promised himself he would never visit that freezing, foggy shithole again. And he didn't. Freddy was sent down a month later anyway.

The latest phase of their friendship – following the hibernal period around the turn of the millennium – started in 2003. The post-Interspex phase. *Plush* magazine. The magazine was Freddy's idea. Not having spoken to him for years, he phoned James to suggest he might like to invest in a magazine he was planning to set up. It seemed at the time that any idiot could set up a 'lifestyle' magazine – sex and shopping – and make a fortune. James no longer had any money to invest, though he knew how to find some, and he liked the idea. It was a potent formula – his own entrepreneurial know-how and experience, Freddy's journalistic flair, and other people's money. Unfortunately several dozen similar magazines were launched at about the same time, and two years later the few outstanding assets were still being digested in the intestine of the legal system, dissolved in the enzymes of the law. In the end there were just two issues, January and February 2005. The March issue had in fact been written and laid out – it was little more than a load of naked ladies; under financial pressure, the whole project was quickly simplifying into straightforward soft porn. It was never printed on account of the printers insisting on payment in advance.

One of the wiped-out investors was Freddy's landlord, Anselm. His £50,000 was the only money Freddy himself had managed to raise. It helped that Anselm was under the impression that Freddy was the last surviving heir of Tsar Nicholas II, and that he was involved in a legal struggle over a vast fortune held in Switzerland since the First World War. (Freddy's Dostoyevskian appearance helped with this – his low brow and sunken eyes, and the way that on hungover days, when he wore a long winter coat, his skin had a mortal yellow tinge.) He insisted that the Russian trove in Zurich was legally his, and Anselm had lent him significant sums to pay 'legal fees' and other expenses – fact-finding missions to Switzerland during the skiing season, for instance – in the expectation of a share of the spoils. (Freddy had promised him, in writing, first ten and then twenty per cent.) Nor, while living in Anselm's house for the past few years, had he ever paid him a penny of rent – the idea was that that too would come out of the Swiss money in time.

The investment in *Plush* would not. That was an investment, not a loan, and Anselm demonstrated his faith in the existence of the Tsarina's diamonds by making the distinction. The loss made him dyspeptic and unhappy. He hated losing money. Still, when the end was nigh, Freddy did ask him for another £50,000, to put towards the printing costs of the pornographic March issue. Which was perhaps to push him too far. Sitting in front of the terminals on which for more than twenty years he had tried, with a startling lack of success, to play the stockmarket, Anselm turned on his swivel-seat and looked at Freddy strictly over the top of his spectacles. He said, 'Fréderic. Do you think I'm a fool?'

Freddy laughed as if the idea was ludicrous.

In fact there was, in Freddy's opinion, something medieval about Anselm's foolishness – it was scarcely believable, off the scale, like something out of Chaucer or Boccaccio. So naturally he had slept with his wife, Alison, a former airline stewardess with a sort of saucy appeal. He had been sleeping with her since the first week he lived there. Sometimes he told her that he was passionately in love with her, that he wanted to take her away from that miserable house, where the viscid leaves of the overgrown trees in the garden shut out the light and the hot water trickled from a tubercular Ascot. He told her that he wanted to take her to Zanzibar – *Zanzibaaah* – where he had spent his sun-kissed youth.

*

Why he did it, he still doesn't know. It was madness. Its only possible end was disaster. Maybe, he thinks now, on the tube with his haversack, that was what he wanted – to push Anselm to the point of disaster; maybe he was just no longer able to take the foolishness, which had acquired a kind of ear-splitting dissonance. Maybe it wasn't even that. Maybe it was just the hangover.

Whatever it was, two Saturdays ago he woke up and found Alison – she was watching TV and having her first G & T of the day – and told her to pack a suitcase. They were finally going to do it. They were going to leave, and start new lives. She downed her drink and hurried upstairs to pack. And even then, waiting for her in the hall, leaning tiredly on the paint-thickened, time-stained anaglypta, with the keys of Anselm's Rolls-Royce in his hand, Freddy knew that this was likely to end in disaster. And he did not even particularly want to do it. That was the strange thing. He knew it was likely to end in disaster, and he didn't even particularly want to do it, and he still did it. There was a self-destructive element, no question. There was a self-destructive ennui at work. He watched her tiptoe downstairs – Anselm was snoring up there somewhere under his *Times* – in what she may have thought was some sort of old-school elopement scenario. Except she was already married. She stumbled and fell down the last two steps – perhaps it wasn't her first G & T of the day after all. He took her suitcase and they slipped quietly out onto Cheyne Walk. It was one of those old Seventies Rolls-Royces, its paintwork – chocolate with a cupreous gleam – sticky with substances that had fallen from the tree under which it was parked.

Two hours later they were still in London, stuck in traffic not far from Shooter's Hill.

'Where we going?' Alison said – she had expected Heathrow and Zanzibar.

'Dover.'

She laughed. 'We going to *drive* to Zanzibar then?'

To drive to Zanzibar in an old brown Rolls – as an idea, it was not without style. However, Freddy said, 'I thought we'd . . . spend a few days in Paris first.'

'Oh. Alright.'

She lit her tenth cigarette of the journey with the car's chunky cigar lighter. They were both smoking. Smoke poured from the lowered windows. Inasmuch as he had had any sort of plan, it had probably been to spend a few days somewhere – a hotel somewhere. Yes, perhaps Paris. As they finally merged onto the motorway and picked up speed, however, he found that spending a few days with Alison was the last thing he wanted to do. He was already sick of her. She was talking quite a lot now and he wished she would just shut the fuck up. When he put on Radio 3 and found, to his joy – it was *exactly* what he wanted – Richard Strauss's *Metamorphosen*, she listened with a frown for a minute or two. Then she said, 'Do we need to listen to this? It's really depressing.'

'Yes, he said. 'We do.'

In his peripheral vision he could see her fat knees, her stomach straining in her short skirt . . . She was wearing a short skirt, sheer tights, tall leather boots. Proper mutton-dressed-as-lamb stuff. Freddy was never embarrassed. Nevertheless, he wasn't particularly looking forward to stepping out with her.

Dover ferry port on an overcast Saturday afternoon in March. As someone once said – *Sad like work.* The indifferent sea. The stony embrace of the breakwater.

Jouncing on its sluttish suspension the old Rolls freewheeled down the slope, and squeaked to a stop in front of the P & O ticket office. It was while he was in there that Freddy settled on what to do.

With seagull outriders the ugly ship moved slowly away from the pieces of off-white cliff. They spent the two-hour voyage entirely in the on-board pub, the screwed-to-the-floor table pitching and tossing. Somewhere a huge engine was thrumming. It elicited a steady tinkling from the bar. Outside the salt-blurred windows drizzle slicked the green iron decks. The question of who was going to drive when they made landfall in France, since they were now both totally pissed, was not asked. For Freddy it was not pertinent. As the ship entered Calais harbour, he said he had to visit the Gents. And he did visit the Gents – the doors of the stalls swinging and slamming – then he made his way quietly to the foot passengers' disembarkation point, disembarked, walked to the station and took a train to Paris. He hadn't had any luggage anyway. He had nothing except his passport and a scrumpled, folded envelope with £10,000 in it – the proceeds of the 'touch'. He spent the last of it a week or so later on a first-class Eurostar ticket, and a taxi from Waterloo to Cheyne Walk.

He knew that Alison would be there. He knew that she would have had to account for her absence that Saturday. He expected her to have done so without involving him in the story. He expected, essentially, everything to be okay. What he did not know – though he should probably have thought of this – was that the ferrymen had not allowed Alison, who was hardly able to stand up, who was tearful and incoherent, to drive the Rolls off the ship. One of them had parked it on the quayside tarmac for her, warned her in pidgin English not to try to drive anywhere that day herself, and left her there in the whipping salt-spray. She would have phoned Anselm straight away, except for one thing. This Freddy did not know about, and had no way of knowing about. Sentimentally, unsoberly, she had left a note for her husband saying that she and Freddy were going to start a new life in another part of the world, and that she was sorry, and that she would always think of him with love, and that she thanked him for everything he had done for her, and that she was sorry, and . . . *Please please forgive me, Alison.*

She spent most of Saturday night sobbing in a hotel in Calais, and very early the next morning took a ferry to Dover and thence, at the wheel of the unwieldy Rolls, made her mascara-smudged way to London. There she had a tearful, hour-long negotiation through the intercom before Anselm finally let her into the house. Once inside, she threw herself on his mercy. Speaking through steady tears, she said that yes, something had indeed once passed between Freddy and herself. (Anselm lowered his face.) She said that Freddy was obsessed with her, that he had forced her to write that terrible note and more or less kidnapped her. How he had forced her to write the note she did not say, nor did Anselm ask. He had no interest in picking holes in her story. He sighed, very tight-throated. Then, sensing that he wanted more, she told him that Freddy was not a Russian prince or princeling or anything like that. He was just an out-of-work journalist. This Freddy had told her only a few weeks before – and he wished he hadn't as soon as the words were out of his mouth. He had told her out of vanity, of course. Vanity. As he well knew, it was his worst weakness.

When he turned up at the house that dreary Wednesday afternoon and found the locks changed, he immediately feared the worst.

'Yes?' crackled Anselm's voice, suspicious over the intercom.

'Hi. Anselm. It's me.'

A long, fizzing silence. 'What do you want?'

'What do I want?' Freddy said with a laugh. 'I live here, don't I?'

'No. You don't.'

Something was obviously very wrong.

Finally he managed to persuade Anselm to let him into the house – he had his own hour-long negotiation through the intercom – saying that he would be able to 'explain everything'. Though it was far from obvious to him how he would do this as, warily saying, 'Anselm?' he mounted the spongy stairs.

He found him in the first-floor drawing room. No lights on. A deathly atmosphere. And worryingly, he was holding an iron poker.

'You lied to me, Fréderic,' Anselm said.

Freddy's intention was of course to deny everything, and the first thing he said was – 'What are you talking about?'

'You aren't Russian.' The only sound was a trickle of plaster dust falling from the ceiling. 'Your father's a British diplomat. And his father was a policeman in Swansea.'

That was a shock. Freddy had not expected Anselm ever to find *that* out. There were two obvious options – deny that his father was Oliver Munt of the FO or . . .

'Yes, but my mother –'

'Your mother's from St Albans,' Anselm said, in a strange voice, somehow monotone and sing-song at the same time. He had evidently done his homework – there might even have been a private detective involved, for all Freddy knew – and faced with this he suddenly felt very tired, too tired to pretend. Too tired even to explain. And what was there to explain? It was all fairly obvious. 'Who told you?' he said. 'Alison?' Perhaps it was a mistake to have left her in Calais. In *Calais* of all places . . . Hell hath no fury like a woman scorned *in Calais*. Though she didn't know any of the details about his parents – just that he wasn't a Russian prince.

And then there was another shock.

'I know that you . . . you once slept with her,' Anselm said, hanging his head and looking at the floor. He made a strange little expectorant noise. 'She told me.'

Now this was very strange. Why on earth had she done *that*? It just didn't make sense.

'I thought you were my friend, Fréderic.'

For a long time Freddy just stood there. Then he shrugged. 'I don't know what to say,' he said.

'Please just leave.'

'Anselm . . .'

The poker twitched.

'My things?'

Still staring at the floor, Anselm nodded.

Freddy went upstairs and put his things into the khaki haversack. They fitted quite easily – he had few possessions. He wondered whether to try to speak to Alison on his way out;

he was puzzled as to why she had told Anselm everything. There must be something he didn't know about. Some factor he wasn't taking into account.

He descended the stairs, with their steep mahogany handrail; the series of landings whose scurfy sash windows were filled with mature trees.

On his way out, he looked into the first-floor drawing room. Anselm was nowhere to be seen. The whole house, in fact, was eerily silent.

Outside in the twilight he shifted the haversack onto his shoulder and walked to the tube station. He had just enough money for the ticket to Russell Square.

*

While Freddy, haversack on shoulder, was taking his place in the ululating lift at Russell Square station, James was sprawled unsuspectingly on the sofa in Mecklenburgh Street wondering whether to nip out to the Four Vintners on Gray's Inn Road for a half-litre of Jack Daniel's or dark rum. Sitting forward, he stared for a few more seconds at the TV. All-weather racing from Wolverhampton, seedily floodlit. Encased in puffa jackets, the pundits held their microphones in numb hands, exhaling mist into the frore Midlands night. Without switching them off – merely silencing them – he jacketed and scarfed himself, leashed Hugo and went out into the street upstairs.

In spite of the many messages he had left since Sunday, he had still heard nothing from Katherine – a silence that seemed increasingly meaningful – and he was miserable. He had spent the day drifting through London like a wind-blown plastic bag. He had a solitary lunch at one of the Bangladeshi places on Brick Lane – one of the unpretentious ones up near the Bethnal Green Road end. Plastic cups, Formica table-tops. The sound of traffic from the door. When he had eaten, he wandered up to Victoria Park – vacant in the spring sunshine – and from there walked along the towpath. He passed the flat where he had once lived, on the other side of the black, sun-struck water. It was strange to see it now, someone else's home. There was some unfamiliar outdoor furniture on the terrace – and how strong, as he stood there, was the sense of being shut out of the past! The sense of the evanescence of things, experience, time – no solider than the jellying light on the under-sides of the bridges. The sense of time slipping very slowly away.

From the start, it seemed to him now, he had not *felt* enough. At the important moments, there was just an insufficiency of feeling. When she told him that Fraser had been in touch with her. When she told him, two weeks later, that she wanted to see Fraser. And when she said to him, in the half-light the next morning, 'What do you think I should do?' It was not that he thought he had failed, on those occasions and others, to express what he felt. He had just not seemed to feel enough when feeling was most needed. It troubled him, this sense that it was a failure of feeling, and not a failure of expression. A man unable to *express* his feelings. That was magazine normality, nothing to worry about. A man unable to *feel* his feelings. Well, that did sound worse.

He thought of the night they spent in that hotel in Cambridge, of how he had said, as they lay there next to each other, 'I think I'm in love with you.' She sighed as if she wished he hadn't said it, and several seconds elapsed, each worse than the last. It was a moment when he wished she was more able to pretend, when he wished she was not so painfully honest, so subject to the tyranny of the truth. She said straight out that she was not in love with him, and suddenly he felt very unsure of everything. What had he *meant* when he said, 'I think I'm in love with you'? He did not seem to know. Had it been somehow speculative then? Had he just been seeing how it sounded? And then, while he was still wondering what he had meant, she said, 'This isn't what I expected.' *This* presumably being the fact that he was in love with her. Or thought he was. Or said he was. Or said he thought he was.

In the morning they went to see her alma mater; she persuaded the porter to let them into the wide quad. When they had done that, they went for a walk. Something had stirred up the weather overnight. The tall trees were swaying. They walked up into a small wood, still in the browns and greys of its winter-wear, loudly inhaling the wind on its hill.

There are memories that make his heart yurr-yurr like an engine struggling to start. Their setting is uniformly wintry. A few London afternoons of wintry exiguity. Thinking of them, he wondered why they had not been enough, why they had taken him only as far as that hedged, faint-hearted statement in the old-fashioned hotel in Cambridge, with its squeaky floorboards and its tired dried flowers. Something had failed. That was how he felt. Something had failed in him. (It was quite frightening.) The engine of his heart.

He used to eye the men fishing from the towpath with scepticism when he jogged past them. He never saw them enjoy so much as a twitch on their lines. They just perched on stools, and inspected their seething maggot jars. *Were* there any fish in that oily water? That was what he had always wondered, as he pounded the path with sweat-fogged eyes.

He took the tube home and tried to interest himself in the televised horse racing. There was a meeting at Taunton, and the last there was quickly followed by the first at Wolverhampton. He had by then been sprawled on the sofa for several hours winning and losing pennies, and was wondering whether to nip out to the Four Vintners – a dusty cage of booze on a bald corner – for a half-litre of Jack Daniel's or dark rum.

He was starting down the metal steps with the blue plastic off-licence bag when he noticed there was someone in the unlit area. It was not Katherine, as for a fraction of a second he wildly hoped. It was Freddy. And ominously, he seemed to have luggage with him.

'Freddy,' James said, unleashing Hugo and following him down the steps. 'What's up?' Freddy was looking suspiciously at the inquisitive St Bernard. 'Um,' he said. 'I've got a bit of a problem.'

'What?'

'I need to stay for a day or two.'

James stopped on the penultimate step. 'Why?'

'Anselm kicked me out.'

'Why?'

'I don't know.'

'Well . . .' James sighed helplessly. 'Haven't you got anywhere else to stay?'

'No.'

'What about your parents' flat?' James knew that Freddy's parents had a small flat in Bayswater.

'Tenants in it.'

Freddy's father was in the final posting of his career – Her Majesty's ambassador to Surinam. The previous year a sympathetic superior had taken pity on him and, knowing how important it was to him – as it was to all of them – had looked around the world to see if there was a suitable ambassadorship opening up. Thus he was sent to Paramaribo for twenty months, and would sign off as an His Excellency, which was the only thing, in professional terms, that he had ever wanted. That and the K. Sir Oliver and Lady Munt.

Still standing in the freezing area, their son was now explaining to James that he couldn't stay in a hotel because he didn't have any money.

'What about the money from the touch?' James said sternly.

Freddy was disinclined to say that he had spent the money from the touch on world-renowned hotels and Michelin-starred meals and €1,000-a-night escorts in Paris. Which was what he had spent it on. And yes, it had been foolish to spend it all. He had not intended to. The fact was, there was one particular €1,000-a-night escort, an American – her work name was Lauren – and he had become . . . possibly slightly obsessed with her? She had had €4,000 of his money anyway. She was tall and sandy-haired, with freckles on her nose. Twentyish. After the second night he had wondered whether she would see him . . . He forgets how he put it exactly. Essentially he was asking for a freebie. He had made what he knew very well was the innocent's mistake of thinking she liked him just because she seemed to when he was paying her €1,000 a night. She handled the situation with typical tact. She said she would love to, but she had a fiancé. 'A fiancé?' Freddy said, with mild incredulity. 'M-hm.' 'Does he live in Paris?' 'M-hm.' 'Is he French?' 'He's French.' 'Does he know what you do?' She fudged on that. However, in her mind it seemed quite simple – if she had sex with someone else without being paid for it (even if she took less than her usual fee), she was being unfaithful to him. Though Freddy tried to shift her from this position, she was sweetly immovable. So finally he paid her another €1,000 and they went to eat. Later, in his splendid suite at the Georges Cinq, he said, 'So you're not

239

being unfaithful now?' The question was slightly unfair, in that she was unable to speak – her mouth was full – but she shook her head.

She was there when he fell asleep, never when he woke. She always managed to slip out without waking him, and he never saw her in the frailer morning light.

Of course, it had been his intention to save *something*, to leave himself a small emergency fund. Then on his final night in Paris he had found himself scraping together his last €1,000 and dialling her familiar number. Yes, he was possibly slightly obsessed with her. He was still thinking about her now.

He told James he had paid the money to Anselm.

'And he still threw you out?'

'I owed him much more than that.'

'So he took ten grand from you, and then threw you out?'

'Yes.'

James sighed, for about the tenth time, and shook his head.

Freddy laughed and said, 'Look, can I at least come inside? I'm fucking freezing.'

So they went in.

It was warmish in the living-room, where the electric fire was on. 'What have you got there?' Freddy said, unwinding his scarf. 'Jack Daniel's?' He had dumped the haversack in the hall. 'Yes, please.'

He sat down on the sofa wiping the freezing moisture from his pate. 'Fuck me it's cold,' he said. 'How are you?'

'Okay.' James handed him a Jack Daniel's and Coke.

'Thanks very much. Mind if I smoke?' He lit a Gauloise filterless – he did have eight hundred or so Gauloises filterless squashed into the haversack somewhere. 'I find it very nostalgic,' he said, 'smoking these.' There were then some phlegmy noises, which went on for quite a while. 'Fuck me . . .'

James stood there watching him, swinging his glass slightly, making the ice tinkle. Freddy did look out of sorts – with a suspicious, unfriendly eye on Hugo, he was sucking saliva thoughtfully through his teeth, which made a quiet squeaking sound. For a minute that and the ticking of the fire, and the tinkling of the ice, and Hugo's quiet panting, were the only sounds. The television was muted, pictures only.

'What the fuck are you going to do?' James said, not unsympathetically.

Freddy had enormous faith in his own powers of sorting something out. He had been able to sort something out in the most unlikely situations in the past. His present situation had seemed pretty tricky, however – it had seemed frankly intractable – until, waiting for a Piccadilly-line train at South Kensington, he had thought of something.

'Looking forward to Sunday?' he said.

James shrugged. 'I s'pose.'

Sunday was Plumpton, and Absent Oelemberg's next outing. (Her final outing under their ownership – they needed to sell her just to pay Miller what they owed him in training fees.) Ten days ago she had won at Towcester under a penalty. The plan had been to turn her out quickly under a double, but she had emerged sore from the Towcester win, so Miller had let her have a fortnight off. On Sunday she would run from her new mark, which was eighteen pounds higher than her old one. Miller said he still thought she would win.

'Planning to lump on?' Freddy said, matter-of-factly.

'I don't know,' James said. 'I haven't decided yet.'

'Mm.' Freddy nodded.

'Shame you missed her last time.'

'Yeah.'

'Where were you?' Freddy had never properly explained why

he couldn't make it to Towcester that day. (He was in Paris.) He just waved a hand in the air and said, 'I had some things to do. I was wondering,' he went on. Then he stopped.

'What?'

'If you could lend me some money.'

When they spoke, some seconds later, it was simultaneously. James said, 'How much?' And Freddy said, 'I mean, to bet with.'

'To *bet* with?'

'Yes.'

'How much?'

'Five thousand?'

James laughed. 'Are you out of your mind?'

'Why do you say that?' Freddy said, impressively straight-faced.

'I'm not going to lend you five thousand pounds *to bet with*.'

'Why not? I'll be able to pay you back on Sunday . . .'

'You will if she *wins*. What if she loses? Then what? Then I'll never see the money again, will I? Why would I do that? Don't be a fucking idiot, Freddy.'

Freddy looked away. He was sucking his teeth again – it was a habit he had had since school.

*   *   *

Later he finally spoke to Katherine. She finally answered her phone. He was standing in the living room, in the Gauloise smoke, slightly drunk. Freddy was out procuring more Jack Daniel's.

'Hello,' he said, surprised. He had lost count of how many times he had phoned her since Sunday – he had stopped even hoping that she would answer. 'How are you?'

'I'm okay.' She didn't sound okay. 'How are you?'

'Fine.'

They talked for while. This and that. He did most of the talking. Then he said, in an offhand way, 'What were you doing last weekend?'

'I saw Fraser.'

'Did you?' There was a silence which started to stretch out. 'And?'

'And it's over,' she said simply. 'The love is dead.'

His instinct, since she was obviously in some sense in mourning, was to say, 'I'm sorry.' That seemed just too dishonest, though. He was not sorry. He was not sorry at all. The way she put it was so wonderfully absolute. It was *dead*. Her love for Fraser King was *dead*. He tried to keep his voice sombre when he said, 'Well . . . how are you feeling?'

'Very sad.'

'Mm,' he murmured as sympathetically as he could. 'What did . . . ? Where did you . . . ?'

'We went to Scotland.'

'Oh. Well . . .' And then finding himself with nothing else to say, he said, 'I'm sorry.'

She said nothing, so he went on. 'And what have you been doing? For the last few days. I've been trying to call you . . .' He was irritated to hear the querulous note in his own voice.

'I know you have. I'm sorry.'

'So what have you been doing?' he said.

She said she had been shopping with her mother – furnishing the house in West Kensington.

'And what are you doing for the rest of the week? At the weekend?'

'I don't know.'

He heard Freddy unlocking the front door. 'Will I see you?'

'I don't know,' she said, as if it was something she simply didn't know.

'Well,' he said slightly exasperatedly. 'Do you *want* to see me?'

She sighed. 'I don't know. Maybe.'

'Maybe?'

'Do I want to see you?' she said, as if putting the question to herself out loud would help. 'I just don't know. Maybe. Maybe if you think of something fun to do . . .'

Freddy was there, taking off his overcoat. James waved him away.

'Do you want to come to Plumpton on Sunday?'

'No,' she said without hesitation.

'That isn't fun?'

She laughed – a weak laugh, like someone ill. 'No.'

If he had not managed to feel very sorry when he heard of her sad weekend, he did feel something like joy when he heard her laugh. 'No,' he said, smiling. 'Okay. I'll try and think of something fun to do. I'll be in touch. Okay?'

'Who was that?' Freddy said, unwinding his long schoolboy's scarf.

'Um.' James seemed to be somewhere else. 'It was Katherine.'

5

Simon were well aware that he were sweating. He wishes it weren't so hot in the hall. Staring out at the local membership with an impassive expression on his face, percolating in his tweed three-piece, he slides a hand through his hair. He had it done specially this morning, at the place in Trumpington. While he outstared himself from under the smock, the lass laboured over it for an hour with all the tools of her trade, and now it is a magnificently perfect peruke in silvered sable. The upper part looks like silky racoon fur. It is short at the sides – with flashes of wisdom at the temples, like the president in an American film – and neatly squared off on the pink neck. He knits his fingers in his humid tweed lap and tilts his head thoughtfully. They are on a makeshift stage, himself and the other VIPs, sitting in a line under the important lights, facing the party faithful. Politics.

On his feet at the podium, Nigel has been speaking for some time. Simon long ago lost the thread of what he was saying. From the stuff they send him in the post, he is familiar with Nigel's positions on more or less everything. On Europe anyway. They are the same as his own positions. That was the point. (Mechanically, he joins in an episode of applause, without having heard the line that set it off.) What's more, he is nervous about his own speech. He is up next.

For a long time, from his oblique angle of view slightly behind and to the left of him, he had kept his eyes loyally fixed on Nigel. He had noticed, staring at him for minutes on end from only a few yards away, how his dark hair, dense as fungus, tapered into two prongs on his thin neck. He had noticed the organic debris on the shoulders of his suit. The long fleshiness of his inelegant ears. He had noticed the way he kept flexing and straightening his left leg. After a while, however, it was a strain keeping his neckless head turned to two o'clock like that and, hoping that no one would notice and overinterpret the movement, he had let it find a more natural position facing the audience. They're an elderly lot. ('Half of this lot'll be dead at the next election,' he had whispered out of the side of his mouth to Mossy as the VIPs made their way through the hall and onto the platform, to pleasing applause. Mossy laughed at the impiety. 'The ones that aren't will definitely vote, though.' When Mossy said 'vote' it sounded like 'volt'.) What Simon would have liked to see is a few more people of his own vintage – serious men in their prime, mature and experienced, and deeply worried about the future of their nation. *They* all seem to be up on the platform, while what he sees in front of him puts him in mind of an old folks' home. They are not of the present, these blue-veined people. They very obviously have nothing to offer the future. And the future is what is at stake here – the future of this island as an independent nation, and what the fock was more important than that?

An hour ago, out in the foyer, they talked through what would happen. When Nigel was finished, Simon would be introduced by Nick LaRue, the local party secretary, and would then speak for fifteen to twenty minutes. Fifteen to twenty minutes ... He feels himself start to sweat more urgently. Even now, just sitting there, he feels exposed on the stage. When they talked last week about what he should say, Mossy told him to keep it light. Keep it personal. 'Tell some jokes about mad European directives that have affected you personally.' 'Like what?' Simon said, pen in hand. 'I dunno,' Mossy said. 'Maybe something like, "They'll be telling us we can't use miles and furlongs next . . ." Doesn't matter. You can't go wrong with that sort of stuff. Just imagine you're in your local. I've seen you in action there. You'll be fine.' Simon wishes he *was* in his local, in the Plough. His face twinkling with sweat, he is staring at the illuminated green exit sign at the far end of the hall. The first speaker of the evening was the party's local MEP, Pierre Papworth. Still in his twenties and unsettlingly intense, Pierre is on the extreme wing of the party. He some-times gets into trouble with things he says in the press – they are never 'meant seriously' – and the members love him. When Pierre had finished, Nigel took a more statesmanlike tone.

He is still speaking. On the platform in the hot sports-hall – Simon notices various lines on the dull green floor – no longer even trying to look interested, he suddenly feels very sleepy. He had a few wines in the foyer to settle his nerves, and it has been a long day. His feet feel sore and smelly in his shiny leather shoes. That morning he'd had to teach young Dermot a lesson. Dermot was one of the lads in the yard – over from Ireland – and he fancied little Kelly. In fact they had some history, those two. They'd had a fling, last summer. Trouble was she weren't inter-ested now, and when she told him, Dermot started to pick on her. He'd slag her off in front of the other lads and lasses. He'd hide her boots or fill them with warm manure. He'd throw her posh velvet helmet into the pissy mud of the yard. That sort of thing were typical, of course. Went on all the time. Lads will be lads. Whenever a new lad joined there were the usual pranks. Dermot himself had been stripped naked and left tied up in the tackroom overnight, his privates smeared with stinging hoof oil. Piers found him there in the morning. Luckily it were a mild night or he might have died of hypothermia! He shouldn't have picked on Kelly, though.

Yesterday at evening stables, when she was just finished doing Mistress Of Arts, plaiting her mane and everything, Dermot told her she was wanted in the office and, when she went, he smeared the shining mare with manure and dumped Kelly's kit all over the floor. When Piers saw that, Kelly got a tongue-lashing. She had to stay on late and do the mare again – Piers weren't interested in excuses.

That night she told Simon about Dermot and everything that had happened, and this morning Simon was waiting in the stables with a heavy steel spade.

They told the ambulance men that Dermot had fallen off a horse in the outdoor school. That was always happening. The ambulance was there several times a week, its blue lights flashing in silence. Still, it was a stressful start to the day.

And then there was the last meeting of the season at Plumpton, the long drive down to Sussex. No winners unfortunately. He'd hoped for one or two. The little ex-French mare – he thought she'd win. Maybe her new mark was a touch too high. Maybe she wasn't quite as useful as he'd thought. Maybe she was just tired . . . And the owner, the tall one – fockin hell, the look on *his* face. He must have lumped on with everything he had, he looked that sick. 'You were on then?' Simon said as they stood on the terrace afterwards. The tall fella just nodded. 'Well. You win some, you lose some,' Simon said philosophically. 'Went to the well once too often, I suppose. Put her away for the summer now, and have another try in the autumn. Okay?'

'Actually, I'm looking to sell my share.'

Simon took that in. He said, 'Your mate too?'

'Yes.'

He lit a Marlboro watchfully. 'Well, I'll have a look, see if I can find someone to take it.'

'How much, do you think?'

Simon let the question hang there for a while in the faintly faecal-smelling spring air. It was a fine spring day. 'Well,' he said, enjoyably smoothing the silkiness of his salon-fragrant hair where it met the hard paunch of his neck. 'She's done her winning. Or most of it. That's the thing. That's the problem. She's exposed now.'

'So how much . . .?'

He sighed. 'Might be able to get you four or five grand,' he said. 'No promises, though.'

'The thing is, it's quite urgent.'

'Well . . . That doesn't help.'

'I know. Of course not. Would you pay five thousand for our share?'

'Me?'

'Yes.'

'Me personally?'

'Yes.'

'No, I wouldn't.'

'How much would you pay?'

Simon thought for a minute. How much *would* he pay? He would be able to sell a half-share in the mare for £5,000 tomorrow . . . 'Two and a half?' he suggested, thinking vaguely that this would pay for his two weeks in Barbados with the missus, his end-of-season treat, same as every spring.

'You just said a half-share was worth . . .'

'It's worth what someone'll pay for it,' Simon said, with a laugh. 'And I don't want it. I'd need to sell it on. What I'm saying is,' he went on, 'if you need to sell urgently, that's what

I'm willing to pay. She doesn't owe you anything, does she.' He wasn't in the mood to haggle. He had more important things on his mind. His speech. Politics. The future of the fockin nation.

He notices that the audience is applauding and feels an icy finger trace the full length of his spine. Nigel has finished his speech. There is some awkward shuffling on the stage as he makes his way back to his seat and Nick LaRue takes the podium. They do that thing where, heading straight towards each other, they simultaneously swerve one way, then the other, then the first way again. The audience laughs. Nigel makes some joke that nobody hears. He sits down, smiling inanely. Towering over the lectern, Nick LaRue is also making a joke about the incident. Then he starts the preamble to introducing Simon. Despite his insanely loud pinstripe – he is wearing a stripy suit, it is as simple as that – he is emceeing the evening with enviable style. Simon's mouth is suddenly very dry. He hears Nick LaRue say something about 'one of the leading National Hunt trainers in the country'. At the sound of his own name he feels a hard prickle of adrenalin in his armpits and leaves his moulded plastic seat – prematurely as it turns out. He has to wait there, standing next to the podium and sweating under the lights – he is able to smell himself, his own smells – while LaRue finishes his introduction.

The applause stops sharply. It seems very quiet when he takes his place at the lectern. *You could have heard a pin drop*. Those words tumble woozily through his mind. There is nothing else there. His mouth is now unprecedentedly dry, and he picks up the jug and pours himself some water. His hand is shaking so much the jug audibly ding-a-ling-a-lings on the lip of the tumbler. He has a tiny sip of water. He puts down the tumbler. He takes the sweat-soft printed sheet from the tweed pocket of his suit.

It immediately starts flapping in his hand. He looks up – sees nothing. He starts to make his speech.

*

It is still light when James gets back from Plumpton, when he walks through Mecklenburgh Square and lets himself into the familiar smell of the flat. Still light at seven o'clock. These sudden light evenings. It is spring now. It was spring in Sussex. Petals shook in the sharp wind. In the parade ring, there were speckles of sunlight on the shivering narcissi. Trees were unfurling leaves from blood-red branch tips in suburban gardens the train passed. It was spring.

The mare had lost, though for much of the way she had looked okay. Hard on the steel, she had taken it up half a mile from home. Then she flattened out on the turn, found nothing. Faded up the hill to finish a tired fourth. James only had a few quid on. There was a time when he might have staked everything on her. Now he just wanted to hold on to what he had. He had understood that on the train down to Sussex at lunchtime, when he was still wondering whether to lump on. When he decided not to – silently, staring out at flooded fields – he immediately experienced a flat feeling of peace.

He just stood there on the terrace for a while in the uncertain sunshine. 'You were on then?' Miller said. He seemed to misunderstand what James was feeling, to misinterpret the expression on his face. James nodded, and Miller started to produce various platitudes. Then he said, 'Put her away for the summer now, and have another try in the autumn. Okay?' James told him he was looking to sell, and made his way to the sleepy station at the far end of the track.

He phones Katherine as he walks through Mecklenburgh

Square. When she does not answer, he feels a sharp pinch on his heart. They have not spoken since Wednesday. He tried her from the platform of Plumpton station – a tiny thing, lost in the Sussex landscape – while he waited for the London train. Now, when she still does not answer under the leafed planes of the square, the light-filled sadness of the spring evening pierces him – it is just so fucking sad, the way everything is moving on, starting something new.

To his surprise she phones him later. They talk for a long time. He tells her about the last meeting of the season at Plumpton, about how they have to sell the mare. He is lying on the sofa. The vent is open in the skylight.

'What are you doing tonight?' he says eventually.

'Staying in, I think.'

'You don't want to meet up?'

'No,' she says.

'How about tomorrow?'

'I can't tomorrow.'

'Why not?'

'I'm seeing someone else.'

'Maybe in the week then, or next weekend?'

'Maybe,' she says.

6

She is in the National Gallery when he phones. She has looked at Piero della Francesca's half-finished *Nativity* and tried, as usual, to put her finger on what it is about the picture that fascinates her. It seems to tease her. There is something wrong with it – the elements do not seem properly integrated – and yet it still fascinates her, still maintains the hold on her imagination that it has had since she was at school and there was a small, pale reproduction of it on the wall. Its modesty was what used to trouble her then, studying it while some teacher spoke – even the singing angels, such a modest little quintet. The whole scene one of hardscrabble poverty. Franciscan. It had disturbed her teenage sense of propriety.

Now she is standing, with a few other people, in front of the equally familiar image of *The Arnolfini Portrait*. It exerts a similar fascination to the *Nativity*. It too seems to have something wrong with it. The figures of the fifteenth-century financier and his wife medievally large, the space flat – except for the profound shadows of the mirror – and yet the plain light so true. The light from the window specifying the texture of their few small luxuries. The light was the same then . . . She answers her phone.

'Hello?'

'I'm okay,' she says.

'I'm not sure,' she says a few moments later.

One of the blue-uniformed museum attendants, having left his seat and tiptoed up to her, whispers something.

'Look,' she says. 'I have to go. I'm in the National Gallery and they're telling me I can't use my phone in here. I'll call you back. Okay.'

She spends another minute looking at *The Arnolfini Portrait*. Strange, she thinks, this practice of looking at pictures, standing there ogling and hoping for some sort of effect – waiting for something like Auden's 'Musée des Beaux Arts' perhaps to pop fully formed into your head. 'About suffering they were never wrong, the Old Masters ...' Slowly she makes her way down the wide stairs and out of the museum into the sunlight of Trafalgar Square. Traffic, tourists, fountains, statues, sky. Four o'clock faintly audible – a fine wind pushing the fountains' spray. She puts on her sunglasses. She was here last night, or not far from here. She and her mother saw *The Marriage of Figaro*, at the ENO. It is the sort of thing they do once a month – spend the afternoon shopping, then an early supper and the opera or the theatre or some hirsute intense Slav playing the piano in the Festival Hall. They parted on St Martin's Lane at twenty to eleven.

Standing on the pavement in front of the Sainsbury Wing, she phones James. They had a tentative plan to see each other today. She is not sure she wants to. She would not have phoned him if he hadn't phoned her first. In fact he says he has a hangover and suggests they meet tomorrow instead.

'No,' she says. 'I have things to do tomorrow.' And then, 'I'm going to Greece on Monday.'

'Greece?'

'Yes,' she says.

She has written a letter to her employer. She has not sent it yet – first she has taken the two weeks' holiday they owe her, and she will spend those weeks in Greece, looking for somewhere, some idyllic shore, where she might open a small hotel. Then she will work her month's notice while the people from Windlesham Fielding find tenants for Packington Street. There is plenty of equity in the property, and the loan forms are waiting on the table in the living room. Her father has promised to invest too, if she finds somewhere with potential. This she explains to James.

'So . . .' she says.

'Well . . .' He sounds shocked. 'Let's meet tonight then.'

For a second she says nothing. She wishes that he had not phoned her, that he had not put her, just when things were starting to seem simple, in this infuriating position of not knowing what she wants.

*

Last night, drunk, Freddy fessed up. He told James about his ten days in Paris – about that young American, that fantasy of freckled, milk-fed wholesomeness, with her spangled exiguous dresses and eight-inch heels, her thousand-watt smile in the plutocratic settings. The money from the touch all spent. Wondering whether the story furnished an example of utter foolishness or sublime wisdom – he was simultaneously envious and extremely pleased that he was not in Freddy's position – James said, 'What the fuck are you going to do now?'

And Freddy said – surprisingly – that he intended to go into posh primary schools and take photos of the pupils in their ties and haircuts and milk teeth, and then send watermarked samples to their parents, offering proper prints for a substantial fee. All he would have to do, he seemed to think, was persuade the school authorities that he was not a paedophile and he would be able to take thousands of pounds per school. 'The point is,' he said, smiling, 'it's a test of *love*, isn't it. For the parents. They won't want Toby to be the only kid in the playground whose parents don't love him enough to get a photo of him. That's why they *have* to be fucking expensive – if they're not expensive enough it won't work, it won't be a proper test of love.'

Later, somewhere noisy and subterranean in Notting Hill, they found 'Alan-friend'.

Fey and palely Oriental, Alan-friend stood on his own, occasionally snapping his fingers and shuffling his feet to the music. In the old days, he was there every night, and every night he was on his own, a strange figure of metropolitan loneliness. James and Freddy used to wonder who he was. The insane offspring of a Hong Kong trillionaire was a favoured explanation; the insanity having less to do with the senior naval officer's uniform he was always wearing – though that was not particularly sane – and more to do with the fact that he spent every night in that one Notting Hill venue and never spoke to a single person there – and if you did speak to him he turned out to be a total fantasist, explaining with quiet seriousness that he was involved in the development of various spaceships and futuristic weapons systems and other top-secret science-fiction nonsense. So last night, for old time's sake, they talked spaceships with Alan-friend for a while, and Freddy asked him if he wanted to invest in his new business, and Alan – in his vice-admiral's uniform – said without hesitation, without even knowing what the business was, that he would be happy to, that he was always looking for 'opportunities'. They agreed to meet and talk about it 'seriously' at some point in the near future.

Leaving Alan to his liqueur – he tippled weird liqueurs, though he never seemed even slightly drunk – James and Freddy ended up in some place in South Kensington where Freddy knew the eponymous proprietress, a middle-aged American woman who had had some famous lovers in the past. The photos of these lantern-jawed men – half-familiar faces from the Eighties, politicians, newspaper editors, presidential emissaries – were on the walls.

In the morning James had a stinking hangover, which worsened until he switched off the TV and just lay there on the sofa. Later he took Hugo for a walk. He stared into the empty fridge. He had a shower. He phoned Katherine.

They went to the Old Queen's Head. She was in a surprisingly talkative mood. She was frolicsome. She was tipsy. He insisted on paying for the food and drink, and produced a huge wad of money from inside his jacket – a market trader's wad that made her laugh out loud. He was just like the men she saw in Chapel Market, she thought, those sharp-eyed men, forever permutating over their stalls of tat. She smiled and let him hold her hands over the tabletop. He was nicer than that, of course. He had been telling her about starting a business, the things she needed to think about – he himself had been starting businesses since he was seventeen. She liked the way he had done it, without patronising her, or not much. Now he was talking about his friend Freddy, how he had spent thousands of pounds – the money he won on their horse – on a single week in Paris, and about some prostitute he seemed to have fallen in love with . . . It was a funny story. It made her laugh. Perhaps that was why, looking at her watch, she said, 'Do you want to watch a film or something?'

Walking down Packington Street in the hook of his arm,

however, she started to wish she had not invited him home. She even wondered, unlocking the front door, whether to say to him, *Look, I'm sorry, I've changed my mind. I don't want to watch a film. I want to be on my own.* Instead, she preceded him into the downstairs hall, pressed on the timed light, and started up the thin stairs. She said, 'What do you feel like watching?'

'I don't know. I don't mind.'

He made himself at home. Took off his shoes. Flopped down on the sofa, feet on the pouf.

'I don't have anything to drink,' she said.

'That's okay.'

She turned on the TV. There was some film on TV, and they just started to watch that. Obviously feeling encouraged, he tried to kiss her at various points, tried tentatively to start undressing her. Each time, she went along with it for a minute, then fended him off, and there was another stretch of staring at the television, until he tried again. In fact she was no more interested in the film than he was and in the end she let him undress her. Sometimes she had to augment her lover with her own finger to make herself have an orgasm, and that was obviously easier if he found his way into her from behind, and easier still if he forewent her sex altogether. This she encouraged him to do, awkwardly using her unseeing hand to alter his angle until he understood what she wanted. 'Please,' she said. For a while she felt the floor's nap under her face. Then, starting to hyperventilate, she did not feel it. She felt nothing. There was only light, and pleasure.

Finding her suddenly limp and heavy, he finished with a few hurried movements, immediately toppling over and experiencing a soft occipital tingle as the blood flowed once more into the parts of his head that think.

They were lying on the floor.

The film was just ending. Worried now about stains, she sat

up and looked at him, lying there naked, his hairless thorax still heaving.

*

In the morning the light was white. The light was tender, like something unhealed. She woke with the first twinges of period pain and Fraser in her formless thoughts. She lay there, encircled by James's arms, thinking for a few moments, as the sleepworld faded, of Fraser. He kissed her neck. He said quietly that he had to leave, and finally unsqueezing her, he left the bed and started to dress. There seemed to have been so many mornings like this. Him leaving early, perforce, to walk poor Hugo. It was later than it usually was when he left. It was eight. 'Do you want some coffee?' she said. He did and while he was dressing she went to make it.

There was a Sunday-morning quiet. The espresso maker mumbled on the hob and she looked out the window. Packington Street. The weather still making up its mind what to do.

They drank their coffee in the white kitchen. They did so in silence.

When he had finished his coffee he put his arms around her and she put her head on his shoulder.

She said, 'Don't you want to know what happened with me and Fraser?'

He shrugged. 'Okay. If you want to tell me . . .'

'It's not that I want to tell you!' she said impatiently, almost pushing him away. 'Do you not want to know? Are you just not interested?'

'No, tell me,' he said, holding her. 'Of course I'm interested. Tell me.'

'We went to Edinburgh,' she said, putting her head on his shoulder again. 'If it makes you feel any better, I didn't let him have sex with me. I know it's ... important to men.' He said nothing. 'Isn't it? Fraser was jealous when he heard about *you*.'

'Was he?'

He felt her head nod on his shoulder.

'So you went to Edinburgh ...'

'It was depressing,' she said.

'Why was it depressing?'

'I don't know. Fraser was depressed.'

She put her feet on his – her naked feet on his larger socked feet. He was looking down at them. For a long time he looked down at them.

'And now?' he said finally.

'Now?'

'M-hm.'

'I don't know. I'm going to Greece.'

He sighed. Tired and sad and slightly exasperated. Still looking down at their feet, he said, 'I just wish it was ...'

'Simpler?' she suggested.

'Yeah.'

She nodded.

'Will I see you later today?'

'No,' she said. 'I have loads of things to do.'

'What time's your flight tomorrow?'

'Nine o'clockish. From Stansted.'

'I wish I could spend the whole day with you ...'

'No.'

He squeezed her firmly for a second or two, then went into the hall to put on his shoes. 'I'll phone you when you get back from Greece,' he said, stooping.

'Okay.'

'When is that?'

'I'm not sure.'

'What do you mean – you've only got a one-way ticket?'

She nodded.

His shoes were on. He straightened up and put on his jacket, which was there on an overloaded peg. 'Okay . . .' he said. 'Well . . . have fun.'

'Okay.'

What to do now? They were standing in the hall. There seemed to be no natural way for him to leave, nothing that would do justice to the situation as he saw it, nothing that would not seem hopelessly peremptory. Finally – it *was* hopelessly peremptory – he just kissed her passionlessly on the mouth and said, 'Bye.'

'Bye,' she said, and opened the door for him.

He was halfway down the stairs, halfway to the narrow hall, where the ownerless sideboard was swamped with letters for people who no longer lived there, when she shouted his name. In the shadowy space halfway down the stairs they kissed properly, for a whole minute perhaps, while the wind fiddled impatiently with the street door.

'Okay,' she whispered unentangling herself. 'See you.' She scampered up the stairs and went into the flat, leaving him to take the final steps, to pause in the familiar stillness of the hall, and then to pull open the door – even the way it stuck for a moment as he pulled it was familiar, seemed like something he had once loved – and step out into the light.

While he walked to the tube station, she was upstairs leaning over the pummelling tap. With her hair tied up, she stirred the water with her hand. She was thinking of tomorrow morning, of the taxi to Liverpool Street. Of the train through east London and the flat landscape of Essex. Of the light-filled airport.

Acknowledgements

As always, I would like to thank Dan Franklin, Alex Bowler and everyone at Jonathan Cape, and my agent, Anna Webber.

www.vintage-books.co.uk